PENGUIN BOOKS

Two Sides to Every Murder

Two Sides to Every Murder

DANIELLE VALENTINE

PENGUIN BOOKS

PENGUIN BOOKS

UK | USA | Canada | Ireland | Australia
India | New Zealand | South Africa

Penguin Books is part of the Penguin Random House group of companies
whose addresses can be found at global.penguinrandomhouse.com

www.penguin.co.uk
www.puffin.co.uk
www.ladybird.co.uk

First published in the USA by G. P. Putnam's Sons, an imprint of
Penguin Random House LLC, and in Great Britain by Penguin Books 2024

001

Design by Rebecca Aidlin
Set in Arno Pro
Printed and bound in Great Britain by Clays Ltd, Elcograf S.p.A.

The authorized representative in the EEA is Penguin Random House Ireland,
Morrison Chambers, 32 Nassau Street, Dublin D02 YH68

A CIP catalogue record for this book is available from the British Library

ISBN: 978–0–241–72204–6

All correspondence to:
Penguin Books
Penguin Random House Children's
One Embassy Gardens, 8 Viaduct Gardens, London SW11 7BW

To Sawyer Rollins

— D. V.

7:17 p.m.

Gia North's lungs ached as she tore through the trees. The woods pushed in around her, hiding the cabins and Camp Lost Lake lodge from view. It felt like she was in the middle of nowhere.

It's not too late, it can't be too late, she thought, willing her short legs to move faster. The muscles in her calves screamed.

She leapt from the grass to the hard, packed earth of the trail—

Her foot slipped out from beneath her. She felt a sharp crack through her chin and tasted dirt in her mouth before she even realized she'd fallen.

It was the worst possible time to trip.

She pushed herself off the ground, catching sight of her hands as she did. They were splayed in the dirt, and her fingers, her knuckles, her wrists—every inch of visible skin was covered in blood.

"Get up," she told herself, her voice ragged. "Get *up*, Gia."

She was tired and panicked and terrified, but lives depended on whether or not she found help.

She stood.

Gia, breathing hard, noticed her camera on the ground; it had fallen out of her pocket and skidded across the path. That camera was probably the most important possession she had right now. The police would want to see the footage she'd just taken. She needed to put it back in its hiding place, where she could get to it later. She glanced over her shoulder, into the woods she'd just run through. Did she have time for that?

Making a quick decision, Gia snatched her camera off the ground and stuffed it back into her pocket, hurrying to her hiding place, past the trees and up the stairs to the camp director's office, stopping at the window. Hands shaking, she removed the faulty piece of trim no one but her knew about, pulled the camera out of her pocket and stowed it in the little hole in the siding, then slid the trim back in place.

She exhaled, relief flooding through her. *There.* At least that was done.

She had started to turn back toward the stairs when she noticed something lying at her feet. It was the camp key card she'd been carrying around for the last two days. It must've also fallen out of her pocket when she pulled the camera out again. She leaned over to pick it up—

And froze. From where she was standing, she could see all the way across to the archery range.

It was starting to get dark, but she could just make out the shapes of two figures standing in the field. She was about to lift her arms, to call out to them for help, but something stopped her. Were they arguing? Gia squinted, trying to see who they were. That was the blond hair and tall, broad-shouldered build of Jacob Knight, the camp's archery instructor, but she couldn't tell who the other person was. They were slender and shorter than Jacob—

probably a woman, Gia thought. But there was something wrong with her face. It looked misshapen, old, haggard, with green-tinted skin and long, stringy gray hair, and her eyes were black, sunken, surrounded by deeply lined, rubbery skin, her nose long, hooked, covered in warts—

A mask, Gia realized. The woman's face looked so messed up because she was wearing a mask.

As Gia watched from her perch outside the office, the woman in the mask plucked an arrow out of the nearest target and lunged for Jacob, stabbing him through the throat.

Jacob grabbed at the arrow protruding from his neck, blood spurting through his fingers. A spasm jerked through him. He fell to his knees in the dirt. A moment later, his body crumpled to the ground.

Gia released a choked scream. She pressed her hands over her mouth to muffle the sound, but she was a beat too late. Her voice was already echoing through the woods.

And now the woman was lifting her head. She was looking right at Gia.

No, Gia thought. She turned, grabbing for the office door. Her hands were shaking badly, still slick with blood, and it took her two tries to get the knob to turn.

Before she could throw the door open, Gia glanced over her shoulder. The woman had picked up a bow from the ground and loaded an arrow. She aimed—

The air whistled as the arrow flew, with perfect aim, at Gia's face.

1

Olivia

I was ten years old when I first heard the story of the Witch of Lost Lake.

It was at Maeve Lewis's slumber party, of all places. That was the year Maeve decided she didn't like me—for reasons I never understood, despite putting a considerable amount of research into the subject—and I could tell something was up within minutes of getting to her house with my overnight bag. She kept shooting me sideways glances, smiling like we were good friends, which, by the way, we *weren't*. Even now I feel a chill straight down my spine whenever I think about it.

Maeve waited until we'd all gotten into our pajamas, a dozen tween girls in *Frozen* sleeping bags, then she'd loaded up this fake crackling fire clip on her iPad and told the story of the Camp Lost Lake murders.

"The woods around here have been used as campgrounds for, like, a hundred years," she'd said, looking right at me as she added, "owned by the same family the whole time."

She was talking about my family, of course. Everyone knew the D'Angelis owned Camp Lost Lake. This used to be a badge of honor, or so I'm told. Years ago, the camp was beloved in our small town. Every local business had the words HOME OF CAMP LOST LAKE proudly printed on its signs, usually along with a WELCOME, CAMP LOST LAKERS! banner that hung in its windows or doorway every summer. Once upon a time, the camp was a big moneymaker. Half the residents of Lost Lake, New York, worked there and nearly everyone attended for at least a year. It was most people's first job, their first night away from home, the place where they had their first crush.

At least, that's what my older sister, Andie, told me. Andie's a lot older than me, so she actually got to go, but the camp's been closed since that night back in 2008. Now, most of us only know anything about it because of stories like Maeve's.

"Get to the story already," my best friend, Hazel Katz, told her, and I shot her a small smile of thanks. Hazel's been my ride or die since we were in kindergarten. Even at ten, she didn't tolerate bullies.

"Fine," Maeve said, rolling her eyes. "So there's this story that a witch lives out in the woods. The witch sleeps all day and only comes out at night, and if you happen to be in the woods after dark, she'll kidnap you to use in her *spells*."

At ten, we loved stuff like this. The other girls all squealed and covered their eyes, but I just swallowed. So far, this wasn't too bad. "So, the witch is sort of like the boogeyman?" I asked.

"Totally," Maeve said. "Just like the boogeyman. People think the camp counselors made her up to keep the little kids from sneaking out at night. But then, ten years ago . . ." Here, Maeve lowered her voice. "Those . . . *murders* happened. And people say the woman who did it, Lori Knight, was wearing a witch's mask when she stabbed her husband through the neck."

No squeals this time. The group was dead silent. We were young, but most of us had already heard bits and pieces of the story from older siblings or friends. We knew all about how Lori Knight lost it and took on the Witch of Lost Lake persona, donning a cheap witch's mask and killing her cheating husband, Jacob, with his own bow and arrow. And when she saw that some nosy camp counselor, a teenager named Gia North, had been watching her, she killed her, too.

At first, people thought those were the only two people she'd killed. Until they realized that Lori's son, seventeen-year-old Matthew Knight, was missing, too. Blood and signs of a struggle at the top of the lighthouse made most people assume he was pushed out the window and drowned in the lake below, but they never did find his body.

Three murders in just one night. This town hadn't seen anything like it before or since.

"People say Lori *became* the Witch of Lost Lake that night," Maeve continued. "They think she killed Gia because Gia was misbehaving. She was out in the woods at night when she wasn't supposed to be, so Lori punished her, just like the witch did to the kids in the story. The cops never caught Lori; she could still be out in the woods today, waiting for another kid to wander back into her camp to kill them, too. But there's another part of the story, a part not many people know . . ."

"Stop it," Hazel said, glancing at me. She must've already figured out where Maeve was going with the story. I thought I knew, too.

I'd heard the story before. I thought I knew every detail. My mother, Miranda D'Angeli, had been the director of Camp Lost

Lake back in 2008. Lori was her assistant. I already knew my mom was at camp that night, that she'd told the cops she'd seen Lori running from the scene of the crime covered in Gia's blood. I figured that's what Maeve was going to tell everyone.

But Maeve shocked me by adding the part of the story I didn't already know, the part my own mother had neglected to tell me for ten years:

"The trauma of witnessing a *murder* caused Mrs. D'Angeli to go into early labor," Maeve said, smiling right at me. "She had her baby right there, in the Camp Lost Lake parking lot, just seconds after the most gruesome crime this town has ever seen."

A dozen sets of eyes turned to stare at me. Because, of course, *I* was the baby Maeve was talking about.

Maeve was probably hoping I'd cry. I cried pretty easily back then, whenever I got a bad grade on an assignment or saw a sad movie, or when someone said something mean to me or anyone else, really.

I managed not to cry that night. I waited until all the other girls got distracted braiding each other's hair and discussing which boys did and did not have cooties, and then I did what I do best: my homework.

I slipped Maeve's iPad off her sleeping bag, and I read all about the Camp Lost Lake murders.

Maeve hadn't been exaggerating. My mother had given birth to me in the parking lot right outside her office while Lori Knight ran through the woods to escape the cops.

After the sleepover, I made Mom tell me everything about the night I was born. I know how far along she was—thirty-seven weeks—and how long she was in labor—two hours. I know the camp groundskeeper, Henry Roberts, helped deliver me before my dad arrived, and that they couldn't even call an ambulance because Lori had cut the cord to the landline. The only place at camp with any cell service was the top of the lighthouse, and no one wanted to leave Mom alone. I know I was born at 7:37 p.m., after just ten minutes of pushing.

I know everything, every last detail of my birth story.

Or I thought I did.

And yet here I sit, sixteen years after the night I was born, staring down at my phone and grappling with a pretty big gap in my knowledge. I hold my breath as I reread the latest email from the genetic company for the twelve-thousandth time. Particularly the part that reads *probability of paternity*.

I keep expecting it to change, but it doesn't.

It started with my history class final. The assignment was to "trace your family's ancestry as far back as you can and make a prediction about what their lives would've been like a hundred years ago." I sent my DNA sample to one of those online ancestry places; I planned to pick a region in Italy to focus on once I got the results back. My dad's entire family is Italian, and I was sure I'd find some ancestors from the Tuscan Valley, or maybe Naples or Rome. It was going to be perfect. My schoolwork was always perfect.

Only I couldn't complete the assignment, because my ancestry results came back, and it turns out I have zero Italian in my blood. Not a single drop.

I didn't understand. My name is *Olivia D'Angeli*. We have the actual trunk one of Dad's great-great-great-grandmothers brought to Ellis Island when she immigrated from Sicily two hundred years ago. Every weekend Dad makes a Sunday gravy and meatballs using my nonna Mia's recipe. Two summers ago, we visited his cousins outside of Genoa. I *know* we're Italian.

I'd written back to the company and calmly explained there'd been an error. The list of regions on my profile were clearly only from my mom's side of the family: England, Sweden, Norway, Wales, etc. It was like they'd left my dad off entirely. They'd invited me to submit again. Which I did. *Three* times.

I only did the paternity test to prove to them that they were still getting it wrong, that there was a mistake.

The results of the test came in this morning.

Probability of Paternity: 0%

The DNA place hadn't made a mistake. *I* had. The man who'd spent hours helping me research my first computer and taught me how to choose a ripe tomato; the man who shares my love of travel documentaries and ethnic food; the man who makes me spin the little globe in his office every year on my birthday, close my eyes, and point to some new, distant place I'm going to travel to once I graduate, *that* man isn't really my dad.

Tears blur my eyes. I want to print out the results so I have something to rip into a million pieces. I want to throw things. I want to scream.

"Olivia?"

I flinch. My dad's voice. No, not my dad's—*Johnny D'Angeli's* voice. I blink a few times to get the tears out of my eyes before I turn.

"You coming down for lunch?" Dad (I'll never be able to think of him as Johnny) asks, leaning in through my bedroom door.

A lump forms in my throat. Does he know he's not my real

9

father? If he doesn't, the truth will kill him. And as angry as I am, as betrayed as I feel, I refuse to be the one to do that. Not if I don't have to.

I click out of my email account, forcing a smile. "Yeah," I tell him. "Be down in a minute."

Downstairs in the kitchen, I notice an old Polaroid of my mom and dad taped to the door of the refrigerator. In it, Mom's waving her hand at the camera, a tiny purple gemstone sparkling from her ring finger, and Dad's got his arm around her, beaming. They're standing behind the counter of Dad's restaurant, the Lost Lake Diner. He proposed by dropping her engagement ring into her morning matcha latte—which they didn't even have on the menu, but he learned to make just for her. Mom said she was so surprised she spilled the whole cup down her shirt. If you squint, you can see the green stain.

The picture has been on the fridge since I was born, but I find myself studying it as though seeing it for the first time, noticing all these little details about my mom that I never thought about before. Like the PTA T-shirt she got when she ran the bake sale at Andie's school; the fancy, solar-charging hiking watch she bought herself for her thirtieth birthday; the heart-shaped locket she wore, which contained a picture of Andie as a baby—she added a picture of me, too, after I was born. Even the engagement ring is a little clue about who she is. It's not a diamond but an amethyst, which is her birthstone, because diamonds are too expensive and not always ethically sourced.

I feel my chest tighten. I thought I knew who my mom was, a responsible woman who loved the outdoors and her family, who cared about the environment, who thought of Dad's diner as a second home. Now, those details feel like a costume, like she's trying to convince me and the rest of the world that she's this good person. But how much of it is really true? Is *any* of it true?

"Olivia, honey, is that what you're wearing?" Mom asks. I hadn't heard her come into the kitchen behind me, but the word *LIAR* flashes bright neon in my brain at the sound of her voice. I pull my eyes away from the photo and turn to face her.

I look like my mom. My older sister, Andie, and I both do, which makes sense since Johnny isn't Andie's dad, either; my mom had her right after high school. The three of us are bird-boned, with big, heart-shaped faces. We look like the people in the restaurant who are going to ask you if you could please turn the heat up, it's getting cold in here.

Mom has the same blond hair as me and Andie, but she wears hers in a blunt bob that falls just under her chin. She's short and trim and close enough to my size that we could share clothes if I suddenly developed a taste for Eileen Fisher and artsy clogs. We never had one of those angry, shouty relationships like you see on TV. I always trusted her. She was the person I called to bring me a fresh pair of jeans when I got my period during junior high study hall, and she was the only one I told about my crush on Simon Collins my freshman year or when I accidentally walked out of the general store without paying for my dark chocolate sea salt KIND bar. When she realized I was more into books than the outdoors, she made a point of mapping out the nearest bookstore whenever we took the camper out for the weekend and, in return,

I made a point of taking a break from reading to go on a hike with her every once in a while.

Does Mom know Dad's not my real dad? I wonder. *She has to, right?* I run through the most likely explanations for what happened. Maybe they couldn't get pregnant the old-fashioned way? Maybe they used a donor?

Or maybe she cheated.

The thought turns my stomach. The image I have of my PTA-shirt-wearing, environmentally conscious, outdoors-loving mother breaks apart in my head.

Maybe I don't know her at all.

"Olivia," Mom says my name slowly and a touch louder than usual, like she sometimes does when she's asked me a question a couple of times but I'm too in my own head to hear her.

"Uh . . . you said something about my outfit?" I glance down at what I'm wearing: basic V-neck T-shirt, jean shorts, cardigan tied around my waist, work boots. My hair's pulled back in the same no-nonsense ponytail I wear daily, except on special occasions. I don't usually give my clothes a ton of thought, and today the only thing I worried about was putting on something I could work in. "What's wrong with it?"

"Andie wants everyone in their Antlers polos, in case of press." Mom's already wearing hers, I notice. I instantly recognize the logo my sister designed for her new coworking space: a pair of deer's antlers curving out of a wreath of twigs and flowers, the word ANTLERS weaving through them in elaborate script. It's cool and classy, like everything Andie does. On the back of the polo are the words: WORK. WELLNESS. PLAY.

"Are you coming with us to the campgrounds?" I ask, frowning. Antlers is taking over the old Camp Lost Lake grounds, the first time that place has been open to the public since the murders.

Mom smiles. "Just wearing the shirt in solidarity so your sister knows how much we all support her."

I give her a thin smile, though I can't imagine a world in which Andie doesn't realize how much our family supports her.

Mom's checking out my boots now. "Maybe think about changing the boots, too," she adds. It's the voice she uses when she doesn't like something but won't actually come out and *say* she doesn't like it. Heaven forbid she express a negative opinion.

"They're *work* boots," I say, the annoyance obvious in my own voice. "You know, for *working*? You're the one who's always telling me how important it is to wear the right gear."

To be fair, I'm pretty sure she was talking about being sure to wear hiking boots that fit correctly and appropriate helmets and protective equipment when playing sports. But I feel like starting a fight.

Mom folds her arms over her chest, seeming confused by my tone. I don't usually argue with her. I'm a pretty typical people-pleasing perfectionist. I'd do anything for a metaphorical gold star.

"Honey, is something wrong?" she asks. "Are you feeling okay?"

I'm about to continue our argument when a crunch of tires in our gravel drive cuts me off. Mom's eyes light up. "Andie's here," she says, clearly relieved for a natural end to the great work boot argument of 2024. "Hurry, go change."

I dig around in my closet for a few minutes, not even looking for my polo, just pulling clothes off racks, letting jackets fall to the ground, throwing shoes. I need to work my frustration out.

I should go right back downstairs, confront my mom, and make her tell me the truth. But she's already lied to me my whole life. She lied on my *birth certificate,* which . . . I don't even know if that's legal. And she probably lied to my dad, to Andie. Why would she tell the truth now?

No, if I ask my mom who my real dad is, she's just going to lie some more. She'll do it with a smile on her face while pretending to examine her trim, neatly manicured nails. I need proof. I can already hear how she might explain the DNA test away, telling me I used the wrong strand of hair—which is impossible. I got the hair from my dad's mustache comb, which no one else uses. I want the whole truth. No matter how painful it is.

I'm still in my head, running through the possibilities, when I walk in on my sister and mother in the dining room. They're hugging and . . .

I frown. Wait . . . are they *crying*?

Holding my breath, I duck behind the wall that separates the front hall from the dining room so I can observe without being super obvious about it. Andie's thin shoulders are shaking, her dark under-eyes stark against her pale skin, like she hasn't been sleeping much. She isn't making any noise at all, which is how she cries when she's really upset, big silent sobs like she's keeping all the pain locked up inside. Mom has her arms wrapped tight around her shoulders, a single tear rolling down her cheek, carving an unseemly line through her normally flawless, understated makeup. Andie's dog, Pickle Rick, is sniffing around their heels, whining a little, clearly stressed by their distress.

I feel a chill on my skin, watching them. We're not a family that cries. When I was in the middle of one of my preteen crying bouts, I distinctly remember my mom pulling me aside and telling me I needed to calm down, that tears made people uncomfortable. She even let me use her handkerchief to dry my eyes. It was so beautiful, silk and floral and gossamer thin. I remember thinking it looked like it had never been used.

Something's up. I'm starting to wonder if I should back away quietly, pretend I never even saw them, but Pickle Rick catches my scent and turns, yipping as he trots up to me.

My mom pulls away from Andie, swiping the mascara from her cheeks. "Olivia," she says, laughing like I've just told a joke. "I'm sorry, baby, I didn't see you there."

Pickle Rick has his front two paws on my legs now, asking to be picked up and snuggled. I scoop him off the floor and give him a scratch behind the ears.

"Is everything okay?" I ask. I direct the question to my mother, but I'm staring at the back of Andie's head. Andie keeps her hair shoulder-length, like mine, but she flat irons it so it's pin-straight, the bottom edges cutting a sharp line across her shoulder blades.

"It's nothing," Mom says, touching Andie's cheek. "I'm just so happy to see my baby again, that's all."

"Oh," I say, frowning. It's not just tears that our family doesn't do. We all love each other and we're pretty close, but this outburst of emotion is unusual. Mom's way more likely to make a joke than sob when she's overcome. She didn't even cry when Dad proposed; she broke into laughter.

This is weird.

I keep staring at the back of Andie's head, willing her to look at me. When she finally does, her eyes are bone-dry, and there's not a hint of red on her cheeks. There wouldn't be. Andie's an expert at appearing cool and collected, no matter how she feels below the surface. My whole life, she's been the model for how a "good girl" acts: effortlessly perfect.

"You ready?" she asks.

"Uh, yeah," I say. "Just let me grab a granola bar. I forgot to eat lunch."

"Okay! I'll be out in the car."

Back in the kitchen, my boot slips on something on the floor and I lurch forward, steadying myself against the wall. I glance down to see what I stepped on.

It's the photograph of my parents that had been taped to the fridge. I must've knocked it off the door when I stormed out of the room. I go to pick it up—

And then I pause, noticing something I never registered before.

There's another man in the frame with my parents. He's a little blurry, but I recognize him anyway.

Of course I recognize him. He's famous around here. Or notorious, I guess. The most notorious cheater in all of Lost Lake.

Jacob Knight, the husband Lori Knight murdered for cheating on her sixteen years ago, is sitting at the end of the counter where my newly engaged parents are standing. His tiny, blurry eyes seem to be fixed on my mother, and he looks . . .

Angry. He's staring at my mother with his jaw clenched.

Something cold fills my stomach.

There aren't a lot of reasons I would accept my mother lying to me about who my real dad is. But they never did figure out who

Jacob had been cheating on his wife with. Come to think of it, I don't even know how people knew he was cheating on his wife. But, if it was my mom, if she'd been pregnant with *his* baby the night Lori Knight turned into a witch . . .

Well. Maybe the lie was justified.

2

Reagan

I press down on the gas—hard. I don't even want to go faster, I just want to feel the surge of adrenaline in my blood as I speed right through a stop sign, barreling out of the trees and onto the dusty, one-lane highway leading south.

South. I love going south. South means the city, civilization, *people.* I miss people.

I haven't been driving for long when I see a guy standing by the side of the road, thumb out. He's tall, Asian, with ear-length black hair that's parted down the middle, nineties-teen-heartthrob style. He wears a flannel shirt, red buffalo plaid hanging open over a gray tee and loose-fitting jeans.

I pull to the side of the road and ease down on the brake. "Hey," I shout. "Where you headed?"

The hitchhiker looks at me without a word. "That depends," he says, voice low. "Where you going?"

"Camp Lost Lake."

"Don't you know? That place is cursed. Anyone who steps foot in those woods comes face-to-face with the Witch of Lost Lake. You should turn around and go home, little girl."

It's the "little girl" comment that does it. I throw my door open and jump out of the car. The hitchhiker's eyes go wide, and he puts his hands up—maybe he expects me to hit him. Instead, I wrap him in a big hug.

"Whoa," he says, his voice muffled by my jacket sleeve. "Do you hug now?"

"Just this once." I squeeze a little tighter. "Deal with it."

"I think you got taller."

"Or you got shorter. You definitely feel shorter."

"You know, I woke up feeling short today, so that must be it."

He curls his arms around me, and suddenly I'm wrapped up in the softest flannel and the kind of firm muscles you only get from doing manual labor.

I jerk away seconds before the hug changes from a *friend* hug to a *something more* hug. And then, just to prove that I haven't lost my edge, I slug him on the arm as hard as I can.

He rubs his arm, pretending to wince. "*Ow*. Damn, Reagan, for someone so tiny, you really know how to *hit*."

"Thanks for fitting me in," I tell Jack, genuine gratitude in my voice. He and his family are headed to Beijing in a few days to visit family. Today was the only day we could both be here. "I don't think I could've gone alone."

"Of course," he says. His smile shows all of his teeth. "I've always wanted to solve a murder."

"Three murders," I correct him. "Technically, we're solving three."

My cell phone—an ancient Nokia brick that I found at the Salvation Army last year—is already rattling in the cupholder when we climb back into my truck. I glance at the screen: *Mom*.

My stomach drops. She was taking a nap when I left, but I guess it was too much to hope I'd have another hour before she noticed I was missing.

"You have to answer it," Jack says. He and his mom are close, despite having nothing in common. She's this political artist and he's much more like his dad, into sports and the outdoors. But he tells her everything. It wouldn't even occur to him not to answer when she called.

I feel a pang. My mom and I used to be like that, too.

"What's she gonna do?" he asks, holding the phone out to me. "You don't have another car, right? And it's not like she's going to call the cops. Just tell her the truth."

I shoot him a look. He has a thing about the truth. It's one of the reasons he agreed to come with me. He actually gets my need to get to the bottom of what happened.

Feeling braver, I wedge the phone between my ear and shoulder, steering one-handed for a second. "Hi, Mom. What's up?"

Despite being an alleged murderer and legendary fugitive, my mom, Lori Knight, the Witch of Lost Lake, doesn't really get angry. In fact, she rarely raises her voice. But I must've really pissed her off because the second I answer the phone she starts yelling so loudly that I cringe and hold it away from my ear.

"Reagan Eleanor, did you take the truck? What were you *thinking*? Turn around right now—"

"You know I'm not going to do that," I tell her. "I tried talking to you about this, but—"

She cuts me off. "I told you, this isn't a discussion. I'm the mom and you're the kid. *I* make the decisions."

"And look where that's landed us!" I shout back. I never raise my voice at my mom, and I can tell, immediately, that I've gone too far. There's a pointed silence on her end of the line that's a million times worse than the yelling. Next to me, Jack makes an *oh shit* face.

I exhale and blurt, "I only need it for a few hours and then I'll come right back, I swear."

"There's a bus leaving for Lost Lake, New York, in twenty minutes." She has, of course, guessed exactly where I'm headed. "If you don't turn around right now, I'm getting on it and coming after you myself."

Crap. I hadn't thought she'd take a bus. In the last few years, she's developed pretty bad arthritis in her hands, and it can make it hard for her to do easy things, like take her backpack on and off and tie her shoes.

It kills me a little, but I hang up the phone. This doesn't change anything. All it means is I have to hurry. I left my mom in a pop-up tent about two hours north of where I am now. If she catches that bus, she could make it to Camp Lost Lake in six hours. Less, if it's an express.

I don't think I've ever hung up on my mom before. We have one of those obnoxiously close relationships you usually only see on heartwarming sitcoms. Except for the fact that the moms in those shows aren't wanted murderers.

I've spent a lot of the last year asking myself how it's possible that I didn't have a clue that my mom was wanted for the murders of three people. In my defense, for most of my life, the Camp Lost

Lake murders weren't very well-known. Not until this amateur podcast, *How to Be a Final Girl*, did a season on them. I didn't listen to the podcast when it first came out—I wasn't into true crime—and then I refused to listen to it on principle. But that didn't matter. Within a year of its release, it seemed like everyone knew the story.

Before the podcast aired, I was a normal fifteen-year-old. I liked fried chicken and bad sci-fi movies. I was good at drawing, good enough that I was thinking about applying to Pratt's graphic design and illustration program for college. I was on my school's swim team, and yeah, okay, maybe I wasn't going to the Olympics, but I was good. Good enough that my coach thought I could've made varsity as a junior, which almost no one did. I had a bike, a bed, and the same three best friends since kindergarten: Hallie, Liza, and Sam. The four of us were practically a family. Or so I thought.

If someone had told me back then that my mom—the woman who nursed the stray cat who'd lived in our yard back to health, who sang that Beatles song "Blackbird" to me before bed every night, who made elaborate cakes shaped like cartoon characters for my birthday—if you told me *that* woman was secretly on the run for murdering her family, I never would've believed you.

But then the podcast went viral and everything went straight to hell. Suddenly everyone we knew was talking about the Camp Lost Lake murders. And not just talking about them, but reading about them, studying them, looking up Lori Knight's picture online, joking that she sort of looked like my mom, who was living under the name Lauren Karl at that time, and ha-ha wasn't that so weird?

I can't pinpoint exactly when our neighbors began to watch us just that much more closely; when Sam, Liza, and Hallie stopped putting me in the group chat. But I'll always remember the night my mom shook me awake in the dark and told me in a whisper to get in the car, that there was some stuff she had to tell me.

Looking back, there were signs. Like how my mom refused to talk about my dad or any other member of our family. How her entire life seemed to start the year I was born, the same year we moved to the small town of Pittsburg—not Pittsburgh, Pennsylvania, but Pittsburg, New Hampshire. She always said her life before I was born wasn't important, that being my mother was the only thing that mattered, that I was her "fresh start." And yeah, okay, I got a little suspicious that something was up when she flat-out refused to get me a passport, or when I went looking for my birth certificate and she claimed I didn't have one. But I never would have suspected the truth.

She didn't do it. I *know* she didn't do it. The night we went on the run she told me the bullet points: she'd been framed, the local cops zeroed in on her from the beginning, there was no way she would've gotten a fair trial. And she gave me a choice. *She* had to go on the run, but I didn't. She said she understood if I wanted to stay behind, if I wanted to keep my normal life. She has and always will do anything to give me the life she thinks I deserve. But if I left, I'd never see her again.

I chose her. I will *always* choose her. But I don't have to be happy about it.

We've been living out of a beat-up old pickup—the only car my mom could afford to buy in cash—for twelve months now, bouncing from one under-the-radar mountain town to another, staying in cheap rental houses when we have the cash, moving on before anyone looks too closely or asks too many questions. I can't remember the last time I ate fried chicken or wore nail polish or swam. I can still draw, of course, and I've been taking high school classes online whenever we have access to computers and free Wi-Fi at a library, but I'm assuming Pratt expects their incoming freshmen to have actually graduated from high school, so there goes that dream.

That's what today is all about: the stolen truck, the trip south. I've been trying to get Mom to come up with a way to clear her name for months now, but she won't even *talk* to me about it, no matter how many times I bring up the topic, no matter how many defense lawyers I look up online. She acts like it's over, like we just have to accept that this is our life. But I can't do that. I want my real life back. And I want my mom in it.

We're still a few blocks from Camp Lost Lake when I spot the blue-and-white cruiser sitting at the side of the road. My chest feels suddenly tight. Cops in general are not good. But cops here? Now?

Jack, oblivious to my terror, lifts a hand and *waves*.

"What are you doing?" I snap at him. "You can't wave at a cop!"

He looks genuinely confused by my reaction. "That's not a cop. I mean, it is, but it's just Karly. She comes out to fish on our land sometimes. She's cool."

A shiver moves through me, and I have to grit my teeth to suppress it. It seems to take us forever to drive past Karly's cruiser, and it might just be my imagination, but I feel like she studies my face extra closely. My mom and I don't look much alike. We're both fair-skinned, but I'm freckly and blond, and she's much paler, with gray hair that she's dyed brown ever since we went on the run. Even so, my cheeks flare. I'm sure that, any second now, this cop will realize I stole this car from my mom, that I'm on the run, that I'm notorious fugitive Lori Knight's daughter.

I hold my breath, waiting to get busted.

But Karly just smiles like we're friends and waves a little harder. Weird.

"Turn here," Jack says suddenly, pointing out a narrow dirt road I'm about to drive past. I jerk my steering wheel to the side, taking the turn too sharply. Jack braces his hand against the top of the car and shoots me a look. "I thought you didn't want to get pulled over?"

"Sorry," I murmur. But I feel better now that we're off the main road. Less exposed. I've seen pictures of Camp Lost Lake online before, tons of times, but I'm still not prepared for how beautiful it is here. Green, tree-covered hills rise to either side of a low valley, like we're tucked in a massive, leafy pocket. Small wooden cabins pop up here and there between the trees. Ahead, there's a lodge with a pitched roof and circular windows, and to the left is the old camp director's office, a lighthouse towering over it. Just beyond there's the lake, deep and so clear that I can see the whole sky reflected on its surface.

"Damn," Jack mutters, but he doesn't sound awed—he sounds annoyed. I follow his gaze to the dirt parking lot tucked to the side of the office. It's filled with dusty cars and, now that I'm paying closer attention, I can hear people in the distance, talking, laughing.

Oh no. This was not part of the plan.

"Park over there so they won't see the truck," Jack murmurs, nodding at a dirt road twisting off into the trees.

I take his advice and follow the road around to the other side of the director's office. From here I can see that the patio behind the camp office is filled with teenagers rummaging through boxes and old camp equipment. A cleaning crew, maybe?

I scowl through the windshield. "I thought the grounds were supposed to be abandoned."

"Yeah, I heard some woman from town is turning it into a bougie hipster retreat or something." Jack glances at me. "You want to leave?"

I chew my lip. I *can't* leave. If I go running back to my mom with my tail between my legs, she's going to do everything in her power to make sure I'm never alone with her car—or any car—ever again.

This is my one shot. If I don't take it, goodbye normal life. I would hate myself forever if I let a chance like this get away.

"No," I say, shaking my head. "I came all this way; we'll have to try to . . . avoid them. I guess."

"Okay." Jack sighs through his teeth. "What's the plan? Are you still looking for this M. Edwards person?"

The name hangs in the air between us, ominous.

I ignored the *How to Be a Final Girl* podcast for as long as I could, but after everything that went down with my mom, I realized I needed to work up the nerve to listen. I wanted to know the whole story of what happened that night, not just the parts my mom felt like telling me.

After I did, I became something of a Camp Lost Lake obsessive. There isn't a single thing about the case that I don't know. And in all my research, the thing that truly surprised me is that I'm not alone in thinking the details don't add up. There aren't many people out there who don't believe it was my mom, but once I started combing through true crime forums, I found a few other armchair detectives who doubted the official version of events. But none of their theories seemed quite right to me. Most of them were focused on figuring out what happened to Gia North's video camera. Gia had been notorious around town for filming gossipy videos, and the theory goes that she caught something about the witch on video and that's why she was murdered. But the killer would have destroyed the camera after she killed Gia, right? It seems silly to spend so much energy on it.

For the last year I've studied the case the way most high school juniors study for the SATs. I've read through every witness statement and police report and DNA analysis I could get my hands on. And I think I found the one clue that doesn't make any sense, something no one else seems remotely curious about, maybe because the only mention of it was a single note at the very bottom of a photocopied, impossibly hard-to-read evidence list:

A camp key card with the name M. EDWARDS written on it.

Camp key cards were given out to campers on their first day of camp. Campers used them to get into the lodge and the cafeteria and their cabins, and they allowed the camp director, Miranda D'Angeli, to keep track of which campers went where and when. The murders happened two weeks before camp officially opened, so there weren't any campers on the grounds. An old record of key card usage I found online showed only Mrs. D'Angeli, my mom, and a few other counselors using their key cards throughout the day.

The M. Edwards key card was only ever mentioned once, in that badly photocopied list of evidence collected the night of the massacre. It had been collected from the deck outside Mrs. D'Angeli's office, but the key card usage record doesn't show it being used at all that night. So what was it doing there?

The key card never seemed to be considered particularly important by either the detectives who investigated the case or the many podcasters, filmmakers, and true crime experts who've delved into the facts in the years since. So far, the only other person who even mentioned it was a cohost from the original *How to Be a Final Girl* podcast, and they just assumed some past counselor left their card on the deck and didn't give it a second thought, especially since the evidence against my mother was so strong.

But here's the thing: there's no record of anyone named M. Edwards working at the camp in 2008. I know; I checked.

My theory is that M. Edwards is an old Camp Lost Lake counselor who dropped their key card when they were sneaking around camp the night of the final murders. I think this might be the person who stole a bow and arrows from the archery shed, killed Gia and Matthew, and framed my mom. Gia's body was found near the key card. Maybe she took it on purpose, maybe she even meant for it to be a clue for the cops.

Archery is a niche skill, even at a camp like this. One of the reasons people were so willing to point the finger at my mom was because she used to be a really great archer, and the bow used had belonged to her late husband, Jacob Knight. Jacob was the archery instructor at Lost Lake, and his initials, JK, were carved into the side. He was the first victim the night of the murders. I'm also pretty sure he was my dad.

Before the podcast, whenever I asked about my dad, Mom would get this really sad look in her eye and say something like "I don't like to think about that time in my life. You're my family now. You're my second chance." And any follow-up questions I asked about her *first* chance made her go all quiet and distant.

But then the podcast came out, and it made it impossible for her to keep her past a secret. She would've been married to this Jacob Knight guy when she got pregnant with me, and about a year ago I found a picture of him. We have the same nose.

But anyone could've stolen that bow. And I have to believe someone else had the archery skills to pull these murders off. I think it's this M. Edwards person. But I can't prove that until I figure out exactly who M. Edwards is.

That's why we came here. The murders happened a few years before everything in the world was digitized. If I can sneak into the old camp director's office, there's a good chance I can find hard copies of their files. Getting M. Edwards's full name won't entirely prove my mother is innocent, but it could point me in the right direction.

After a moment, Jack inhales like he's gearing up to say something big, and asks, "Are you sure you want to do this?"

I glance at him. He's always understood my need to know what happened that night. It's weird of him to pull back now that we're so close. "I *have* to do this, you know that. I have to know the truth. It's the only way I can get my life back."

"Yeah, I know, it's just . . ." He shrugs and glances out the window.

"It's just *what*?"

"You only get your life back if you prove your mom didn't do it, right? What happens if . . ."

He doesn't finish his sentence. Probably because he doesn't have a death wish.

"My mom didn't kill anybody." I'm so angry, I force the words through my clenched teeth.

"I don't think that, I swear," Jack says. "All I'm saying is . . . C'mon, Reagan, the evidence against her is bad. If she didn't do it—"

"She *didn't* do it," I interrupt, glaring at him. "This M. Edwards person did."

Jack lifts a hand, placating me. "Okay."

For a moment, we're both quiet. There's a distant, muffled rumble of thunder, a reminder that, even though it's sunny now, there are storm clouds waiting on the horizon, threatening rain. Despite myself, I shiver.

Finally, Jack sighs and says, like he can't help himself, "It's just . . . if you're so sure M. Edwards is the real killer, why not call the cops? They still have an anonymous tip line for the murders, I looked it up. All you'd have to do is call the number and leave a message telling them what—"

"I already did that. Months ago."

"Then shouldn't we wait for them to investigate? That's the *right* thing to do."

The word *right* hums through me. It's such a Jack thing to say. As though doing the right thing should protect me somehow. My hands tighten around the steering wheel until I'm gripping the vinyl so hard I feel my knuckles go numb.

Doing the *right* thing hasn't exactly done me any favors. Before the podcast went live I got the right grades and I hung out with the right people, and where did it get me?

Woken up in the middle of the night, dragged away from my nice home, my good friends, and my whole respectable, upstanding life.

I can taste the tears in the back of my throat. This is the part that still gets to me, even now, a year later: I'd really thought that being good and doing the right thing would be enough. Maybe it sounds naive, but back then I didn't know any better. I really thought if I did what I was supposed to do, then everything would turn out okay. It makes me angry, now, that I was ever so stupid.

"I'm not really interested in what's right," I say, swallowing my anger. "I just want to get my mom off the hook and get my life back."

"Okay, I hear you." Jack levels me with a heavy look. "But this M. Edwards person, whoever they are, could still be out there. They could have a whole life, and I'm willing to bet they'd do anything to keep from being found out."

The Day Before the Murders

Officer Karly Knight was perched on her regular barstool at the far end of the counter in the Lost Lake Diner, looking through her Key West brochure. She'd thumbed through it so many times that the corners were all dog-eared and soft, but she couldn't help it. Every time she saw the pictures, she smiled.

In just a few weeks, *she* was going to be sitting on one of those white beaches, looking out over the impossibly blue waters, the Florida sun beating hot on her shoulders. She'd snorkel through reefs and take a kayak tour of the mangroves and wake up at dawn to go deep-sea fishing. She couldn't wait.

"Did you know that forty-one degrees is the record low temperature in Key West?" she asked as Johnny D'Angeli, the guy who owned the Lost Lake Diner, leaned over the counter to pour fresh coffee into her cup.

"Is that right?" he said, good-naturedly. Karly had been filling his head with Key West facts almost every morning when she came in to grab coffee before her shift.

"And it's only ever gotten that cold *twice*, once in 1981 and once in 1886," Karly read from the brochure. "It says here that most days are in the seventies and eighties, no matter what time of year it is."

"Sounds boring," chirped a voice from below the counter. A moment later, Johnny's pregnant wife, Miranda, appeared, holding her baby bump with one hand and a fresh sleeve of Styrofoam coffee cups with the other. "I think I'd miss having seasons."

Karly's smile tightened. She couldn't figure out what Johnny saw in Miranda. Johnny was down-to-earth and no-nonsense, the kind of guy who always said what he meant. Karly appreciated a guy like that. Miranda might like hiking and camping and stuff, but she was also almost aggressively cheerful. She'd dated Karly's older brother, Jacob, back in high school, and Karly never liked her much. Everything she said sounded like it ended in an exclamation point.

"Well, *I* think it sounds like paradise," Karly said, turning back to her brochure. She hated how cold it got up here. Last January it dipped below zero degrees every day for a week. She'd wanted to move away from New York since she was seven years old, but, of course, she could never do that before, not with her mother's condition.

Early-onset Alzheimer's. Barbara Knight was diagnosed when Karly was seventeen years old. With her dad out of the picture and her older brother already away at college, she'd been the only one to take over her mother's care. Instead of applying for colleges and researching majors, Karly had been talking to doctors, taking notes on treatment, researching drug trials.

But, a few months ago, she and Jacob finally sat down and had a little talk, and they both agreed it was his turn to take care of their mother, that it was only fair. In just a few short weeks, Barbara would move in with Jacob and his family, and Karly would retire on the beach.

Miranda said something about a missing sleeve of to-go lids and had disappeared below the counter again when a jingle announced the diner door opening, bringing in a flurry of chilly spring air. Karly shivered. It was already June and the temp still hovered around sixty degrees, a full twelve degrees lower than Key West's average of seventy-two. She cupped her coffee with both hands, thinking of sand and sun and miles of blue water.

Her seventeen-year-old nephew, Matthew, slid his elbows onto the sticky counter beside her. "Hey, Auntie Karly," he said, flashing a smile that she was well aware all the teen girls around here thought was impossibly charming. Matthew was a bit of a town golden boy, just like Karly's brother had been back when they were in high school. Track-and-field star, top of his class, and something about his face made all the girls think that everything he said sounded deep. Maybe it was the eyelashes? As far as the rest of the town was concerned, Matthew could do no wrong. Jacob had been exactly the same way. Matthew even looked remarkably like his dad. At a distance, Karly sometimes mistook one for the other.

Karly took another sip of coffee to hide her grimace. She had also been a track-and-field star and at the top of her class, but when you were a girl, you had to work a little harder to impress people. At least, she always did.

"Hey there, Matty," she said, swallowing.

Matthew's smile faltered. "You know Mom's the only one I let call me Matty."

Karly knew. But she thought it was good for Matthew that at least one person in town hadn't completely succumbed to his charms. "I used to change your poopy diapers, Matty, I'll call you whatever I like."

An annoyed expression crossed Matthew's face, looking all wrong with his tousled blond hair and little-boy dimples. But then Johnny snickered, and Matthew shook the look away.

"Fair enough," he said easily. Turning to Johnny, he added, "Hey, Mr. D'Angeli. Can I get a coffee and a banana muffin to go?"

Johnny went to pull a muffin out, but Matthew stopped him. "No, the one on the bottom," he said. Turning to Karly, he explained, "Andie says the muffins on the bottom are the freshest."

"Andie told you that?" Miranda asked, popping back up. Her normally cheery face looked concerned.

Karly couldn't help smirking. It was well-known around town that Miranda didn't want her daughter dating her ex-boyfriend's son. In fact, the only time Karly could ever remember seeing a crack in her perfectly cheerful demeanor was when she overheard Miranda telling Andie that the Knight boys were no good.

If Matthew was surprised to see Miranda appear, he didn't show it. "Hey, Mrs. D'Angeli. Whoa, that baby's getting pretty big."

"It is," Miranda said with a thin smile.

"Andie and I were working on a history project together last semester," Matthew explained smoothly. "Tell her I say hi the next time you talk to her, will you?"

Miranda still looked skeptical, but she said, "Yeah, I will."

While Johnny went to pack up his order, Matthew pulled out

his wallet and dug around for a few crumpled bills. Distracted, humming along with the My Chemical Romance song playing over the speakers, he didn't seem to notice when a card slipped between his fingers and fell to the floor.

"I'll get that," Karly muttered, but she didn't think Matthew heard her. He was thanking Johnny now, reaching over the counter to grab his muffin and coffee.

"Keep the change," Matthew said, turning for the door. "See you, Mr. and Mrs. D'Angeli!"

Karly held up the card. "Wait, Matty, you—"

But Matthew had already ducked out the door into the cold. Karly glanced down at the card he dropped, wondering if it was important.

The card was thick and creamy white, a sketchy outline of mountains and a lake printed on the front.

Karly recognized it immediately: it was a Camp Lost Lake key card. And written in blocky, capital letters across the back, right above a barcode and an electronic stripe, was the name M. EDWARDS.

3

Olivia

"Pickle . . . stop it." I scrunch my nose, snorting with laughter as Pickle Rick's tiny pink tongue sweeps over my chin. "You're tickling me."

"That dog loves you," Andie says, glancing at us from the driver's seat. We're in her fancy electric car, on our way to the old Camp Lost Lake grounds. Everything around us is leather and chrome and spotless, like even the dust is too intimidated by Andie to settle. I don't blame it. My sister can be intimidating.

As Pickle's tongue slides over my nose, I close my eyes, taking a second to imagine a future like this for myself, a future of organized drawers and living spaces so clean they don't hold fingerprints. Capable and collected, I'll move through the world with effortless grace, my hair flat-ironed into a silky curtain, my clothes graceful and unwrinkled—just like Andie.

I glance sideways at her while giving Pickle Rick another ear scratch, trying to work up the courage to ask the question I've been rolling around in my head since we left. I almost immediately lose my nerve. I love my sister, I do. But it can be easy to feel overwhelmed by her.

We've never had a normal sister relationship. She's so much older than me, for one thing. And she's lived somewhere else my entire life, first in New York City for an internship that was so prestigious she somehow convinced our mom to let her leave before her senior year even ended, then undergrad at UC Berkeley, Stanford for business school and, from there, start-up land in Silicon Valley. And now she's back. For the first time in sixteen years, Andie's living in Lost Lake, opening her own company, putting down roots. It feels more like hanging out with a local celebrity than my actual sister.

It's not like she doesn't try. She's always been really nice to me, sending lavish gifts for my birthday and Christmas, texting that she was impressed when I made straight As or was elected class treasurer. But there's always been this distance between us. Sometimes I feel like I don't really know her at all.

She glances at me, and she must realize I have a question because she says, "What's up?"

Okay, Olivia, spit it out, I think. This is Andie. My big sister. Not Rihanna.

"Um, Mom used to date Jacob Knight, right?"

Andie's phone buzzes, distracting her. "What? Um, yeah, I think so."

Her casual answer encourages me to keep going. Clearly she doesn't think this is a weird thing for me to talk about. "But that was way back in high school, right? Way before she met either of our dads?"

Andie's phone's buzzing again. She doesn't pick it up, but she's spending more time squinting down at the screen than watching the road. "What?"

I hesitate, wondering if I should just tell her what I know about Dad. Andie knows how it feels to have questions about her parents. Mom got pregnant with her right after she graduated from high school. She was even married to Andie's dad for a while, before he decided he didn't want to be a dad and took off. Andie went through this phase of seeking him out and trying to have a relationship with him. Once, when she was visiting from school on break, I went through her things. While I was snooping, I found this postcard tucked between the pages of some advanced calculus textbook. There were only two lines of slanted handwriting:

I'm sorry. Don't try to fix this and don't try to find me. It's not safe. I'm starting over.

We're happy.

It didn't have a signature or a return address, and the only clue to where it came from was the mountain range on the front, the words LAKE WINNIPESAUKEE written in big block letters in the lower left corner. I'd assumed it was from Andie's dad, off with his new family, telling her to stop looking from him, so I put the postcard back and never asked about it. We were all relieved when she gave up and let Dad officially adopt her, so the four of us could be one big, happy family.

I could tell Andie the truth. She'd probably understand. I even open my mouth, trying to figure out how to word it. But something stops me. The thing is, Andie's never confided in me about how she felt about her bio dad. She didn't tell me about the postcard, and she never told me how much it hurt when he cut her out of his life.

"I'm just . . . curious about what Mom was like when she was young," I mutter, losing my nerve. It feels weird trusting her with this when I know there's so much she's never told me.

"Mom wasn't really any—" Andie's phone beeps and, like Pavlov's dog, she jerks her head toward the sound without seeming to process what she's doing. Unfortunately, she completely forgets to hit the brake when she does this, and the car keeps rolling—

Right through a stop sign.

I spot flashing red and blue lights in the rearview mirror.

"Seriously?" Andie mutters, wrinkling her nose. Even I have to admit this is bad luck. As far as I know, Andie's never gotten a ticket before. She's probably never even broken a traffic rule. What are the chances that one of the two cops in our small town was waiting at the corner the second she did?

"It'll be okay, it's just Karly," I tell her, glancing at the rearview mirror. Officer Karly Knight is a regular at Dad's diner. We've known her since we were kids.

A few minutes later, Officer Knight is smiling as she leans down to peer through Andie's car window, the crinkly skin around her eyes showing her age. She actually looks remorseful as she says, "I'm afraid I'm going to need to see your license and registration, Andie."

"Of course, Officer Knight," Andie says. She pops open her glove box and removes a sleek black folder of organized paperwork. "I've been wanting to call you, I was so sorry to hear about your mother."

Officer Knight's smile wobbles. Everyone in town knows her mother, Barbara Knight, recently died after a decades-long battle with dementia. "Thank you, Andie, that . . . that means a lot."

Officer Knight blinks, taking a second to wipe something from her eyes. "We just had the reading of her will and . . . to be honest, I'm still a bit of a wreck." She hands Andie back her paperwork and says, "I'll let you go with a warning this time. But stay off that phone. And be careful up at the campgrounds today. We've had reports of someone lurking around up there. It's probably just kids messing around, but you never know." She glances over at me and the smile slips from her face. "Olivia. I-I didn't see you there."

Something about her expression makes me feel awkward all of a sudden. Officer Knight and I have always gotten along, but now she's looking at me like she's seen a ghost.

"Is something wrong?" I ask.

She doesn't say anything for a moment, just stares, eyes narrowed, before turning to look back down the road behind her.

"Sorry," she says after a moment, shaking her head. "Déjà vu."

Camp Lost Lake's main office is built into the side of a hill. While the front of the building is level with the ground, the back sticks out into thin air where the ground gives out to a sharp incline, creating the illusion that it's precariously balanced—one false move, and the whole thing could fall. It's only when you get closer that you notice the thick, wooden stilts drilled into the ground below, holding it up. A narrow balcony wraps around the sides and back of the building, creating a shaded patio. That's where everyone's hanging out now, half-full boxes stacked around them.

"Can you walk the rest of the way?" Andie wants to know. "I forgot to pick up plates for the barbecue."

"Sure," I say, nudging Pickle Rick aside so I can climb out.

"And see if you can find out whether the phone and internet guys came by this morning to set up the landline!" Andie calls out the window. "I got confirmation that they were able to get the electric working, but no one seems to know whether the internet and phone guys were here."

I flash a thumbs-up at her rear window as she peels away and trudge up the path to join the others. Andie has a construction crew scheduled in a few weeks, but she wanted to get a cleaning committee in before then to see if anything's worth salvaging. For a long time after the murders, no one came back here. Dad said it was because the cops restricted access to the lake and surrounding areas while they searched for Matthew's body. But the lake opened back up the next summer, and people still stayed away. Andie says what happened was too sad, that no one wanted to be reminded.

Whatever the reason, leaving the campgrounds vacant for all those years just led to rumors and stories. *Don't come back to Camp Lost Lake, or the witch will return.*

The place is like a time capsule. Detectives and police officers searched the lake, but the cabins, the lodge, even my mom's old office, have been left exactly as they were that night. Mom once told me she was reading *Water for Elephants*, but she left her copy behind on her desk, and she could never bring herself to come get it. To this day, she doesn't know how the book ends.

But that was sixteen years ago. Most people don't believe the old urban legend about the Witch of Lost Lake returning, and it wasn't hard for Andie to convince people to join her cleaning committee. There are only, like, two other options for work in

Lost Lake: either you can wait tables at Dad's diner, or you can bag groceries at the general store, and there are always around thirty kids applying for each opening, so getting one is like winning the lottery. Andie's paying us all twenty bucks an hour to spend the summer cleaning out old fridges and dumpsters, which is unheard of in a town that thinks the minimum wage is a suggestion. Half my school volunteered.

It takes me a minute to make my way across the patio. First, I spend a few minutes chatting with the French Club kids, who've taken it upon themselves to handle the rancid dumpsters—or, en français, *poubelles rances*—and then I stop and say hello to Amir and Kayley, who I know from Mathletes. When I walk up, Kayley is in the middle of a joke about how the witch is coming out of hiding to attack us because we're all so bad.

"You've got the story wrong," Amir corrects her. "It's not the Witch of Lost Lake who's going to attack, it's *Matthew Knight*." He lowers his voice when he says Matthew's name, trying to make it sound spooky.

Kayley rolls her eyes. "Matthew *drowned*. The witch is the one who got away."

"Yeah, but they never found Matthew's body. People think he, like, lost his memory, and now he's some wild mountain man living off the grid, killing anyone who comes out in the woods . . ."

By the time I make my way over to Hazel, I've already been here for nearly twenty minutes.

"Finally." Hazel groans when she sees me. She's standing in the corner nearest the wall, loading things into a cardboard box. "You're too popular for your own good. I was starting to think you wouldn't be able to fit me into your busy schedule."

She's teasing me. The popular kids at our school are all athletes and cheerleaders, just like they are everywhere else. I just volunteer for a lot of different clubs and teams, so I happen to know a lot of people. And, to be honest, it seems like they only want to talk to me when they need something from me. I have a little problem saying no to things I'm not that interested in doing, so I tend to get asked for favors. A lot.

Hazel leans over the box she'd been packing up, her thick, springy natural curls swinging forward to cover her brown skin and deeply freckled face. "Pretending you're capable of doing everything all the time without any visible effort just reinforces the narrative that girls should be perfect. It's like those influencers who post 'I woke up like this' pics but fail to mention all the makeup and filters and the *two grand* they spent on veneers so they could have the perfect smile."

"Wow, Hazel," I say, shocked. She never goes off on me like this. "I am *not* an *influencer*."

"Sorry," Hazel says, blinking like she's just coming out of a trance. "That's not what I meant."

"These are my real teeth."

"I know. I've just been feeling some weird vibes all morning. I pulled the Lovers card before coming here."

Hazel pulls a tarot card every morning. It's kind of a meditation, her way of preparing herself for the day. "Does this mean you're finally going to ask Brianna out?" I ask, happy to move the topic away from me.

"What?" Hazel frowns. "Didn't I tell you? Brianna told me last week that she hates bread. She hates *all* bread, Olivia. You know I can't be with a girl like that."

I smirk. Hazel's parents run Pecky, an artisanal Jewish grocery store and bakery in town. Her dad's the one who originally opened Pecky, but her mother's family all come from the Caribbean, so when they got married they started selling cornmeal pudding and Jamaican toto alongside the hamantaschen and babka. For people who love cooking as much as Hazel's family does, saying you hate bread is like saying you hate puppies or rainbows. Like, why don't you like joy?

"Okay, then, who are these Lovers?" I ask.

"I don't know, but they were reversed, which isn't good. We're talking strained relationships, miscommunication, *lies.*"

My eye twitches. *Lies.* Without meaning to, I think of my mom, my dad, the lie they've been telling my whole life.

But I'm not even close to ready to share this drama with Hazel, so I clear my throat and say, trying to sound like I couldn't care less, "Okay . . . so what? Some couple is lying to each other. We couldn't be more single, so it obviously doesn't have anything to do with us."

But Hazel's shaking her head. "Have I taught you nothing about tarot? The Lovers don't have to be two people in love. They can represent *any* kind of relationship. Some people think the Lovers are associated with the star sign Gemini, so it's possible that they're not even lovers, but twins—"

"Oh no," I say, throwing my hands over my chest in mock horror. "*I'm* a Gemini!"

Hazel rolls her eyes at me. "If you see any deceitful twins, maybe run the other way, okay? Now, what am I supposed to do with this?" She holds up a sleeping bag. "I found it over by the trees. It was unrolled and everything, like someone's been using it."

"Creepy," I mutter, shivering. I don't know anything about sleeping bags, but the one Hazel's holding is kind of the same shape as this thousand-dollar one Dad uses when we go camping. "Here, let me take it. Andie wanted me to keep an eye out for any equipment we can resell. Apparently, some of the old camp stuff was pretty high quality."

I'm looking around, trying to think of somewhere out of the way I can stow the sleeping bag, when my eyes fall on the back door to Mom's old office. The same office she hasn't bothered cleaning out since 2008. If she left an unfinished novel on her desk, maybe she left something else behind, too. Like, for instance, a date book containing secret notes about a meetup with my real dad.

I feel a little thrill at the possibilities. But when I try the back door, it doesn't budge. "Don't bother, it's locked," says a voice behind me.

I turn. The voice came from Eric Weisel, who was my bio lab partner all of last year.

Eric is taller and skinnier than should be allowed, and he can sometimes be kind of annoying, but our joint project on cell mutation last year earned the best grade in the class, so I've mostly forgiven him for that.

It looks like he's found an old badminton racquet and birdie among the camp things. He's dribbling the birdie on the racquet, leaping around so erratically that Maggie O'Reilly and Kayley Cho keep squealing and ducking out of the way of his long, skinny limbs.

"How'd you get over here so fast?" he asks, frowning. "I thought I just saw you in a truck with some guy?"

I have no idea what he's talking about, so I ignore that, jerking backward as he lunges past me. "The door's locked?" I say, disappointed. "You're sure?"

"Yup," Eric says, grunting. "I wanted to look for sunscreen, but that guy your sister works with, uh . . . Sawyer? He told me he has the only key, and he's not letting anyone else in."

I frown. Eric's skin is very pale and covered in freckles. I have a hard time believing that he doesn't travel with his own personal sunscreen everywhere he goes.

As if reading my mind, he says, "I ran out."

I turn in place. There has to be another way inside. I study the building for a few minutes, my eyes traveling past the balcony to a row of windows directly over my head. The first is closed, and so is the next. Closed, closed, closed—

Open.

My breath catches. The window is barely cracked, broken maybe, too many years of neglect and exposure to the elements. It probably doesn't close properly anymore. Whatever the reason, it doesn't matter—it's *open.*

"Olivia?" Hazel says, coming up behind me. "You okay?

"Yeah, I just need the, uh, bathroom," I blurt. "Do you know where it is? I had this huge coffee before I left home, and I really . . . have to . . . go."

Hazel frowns at me, but after a moment she turns. "Okay . . . the only working toilets are over there." She points to a small, shed-like building on the opposite side of the grounds. "But there are spiders, so I'd just hold it."

Hazel's terrified of spiders. I wouldn't put it past her to avoid liquids all day so she won't have to brave the bathrooms. I tell her it's an emergency and then I actually walk over to the bathroom shed, just in case she's watching me. When I reach the doors, I glance over my shoulder.

Hazel and the rest of Andie's army of workers have gathered around a tall, thin guy with tan skin and a shock of purple hair. This is Sawyer, Andie's college-age intern. He's the one I have to worry about catching me, and who will definitely tell Andie I broke in someplace I wasn't supposed to be. In fact, it looks like he's in the middle of going over rules right now. I hear his voice drift toward me. ". . . be careful not to wander into the woods alone. We've had reports of strangers hanging around after—"

"It's the Witch of Lost Lake!" someone shouts, and everyone else snickers.

I turn back around, tuning them out. This is it. Everyone's distracted. I'm not going to get a better chance than this. It's now or . . . now.

My skin tingles with nerves as I walk away from the bathrooms and into the trees. I feel the temperature change the second I step beneath them. It's ten degrees cooler in the woods, the light hazy and dappled. It takes a second for my eyes to adjust, and then they settle on something a few feet away, some shape several inches taller than me and hulking.

I think of what Officer Knight said about someone lurking in the woods and flinch, my heart slamming into my teeth before I realize what I'm looking at: not some creepy witch hiding out, but a dead tree, long ago split down the middle by a bolt of lightning. I have to take deep breaths to get myself to relax.

The stairs are old, wooden, creaky. They lead up to a narrow balcony that wraps around the sides and back of the office, just above where everyone's still working. I read in a book once that if you walk along the edges of creaky stairs, you can keep them from making any noise. I try that now, carefully placing my sneakers as close to the wall of the old building as possible as I go up and up.

It actually works. I'm a little shocked. Maybe I could have a future as a spy.

I make my way up to the balcony and to the part that hangs directly over where everyone's working. It's nothing special, a wooden deck surrounded by a high guard rail, but the slats are close enough together that no one's going to see me here if they happen to look up.

The office is higher up than nearly every other structure around camp, aside from the lighthouse. From here, I can see over the tops of trees, all the way out to the archery range.

A cold feeling slips down my spine. That's where Lori Knight killed her husband. Which means I'm standing in the same spot Gia stood moments before she was shot with an arrow.

I can still make out the tattered remains of three hay bales on the range, a single white-and-red target attached to the one on the far right. Sixteen years ago, Lori Knight went to that exact spot, picked up a deadly weapon, and went to hunt down her family. If I squint, I swear I can still see an arrow sticking out of that last remaining target, the feathers long blown off the shaft so that all that's left is a splintery wooden stick.

I swallow my fear and turn back around. *Window*, I remind my racing brain. *Get to the window.*

It's an old, wooden window, the white paint peeling away in curls. One of the glass panels is cracked, but the others are all intact. And there's about half an inch of space between the bottom of the window and the top of the frame. I was right. It *is* open.

My heart thuds. It's so loud that I can't even tell how quiet I'm being, but no one looks up or shouts "Hey, Olivia, what are you doing up there?" so I'm still in the clear. I slide my hand between the frame and the bottom of the window. And then, exhaling, I try to ease it up—

It doesn't budge. Not the slightest bit. Well, crap.

I glance down to make sure no one has seen me yet. So far, so good.

I lean into the window, putting some real muscle into my attempt to move it this time. Rough wood presses into my palms, making me wince. I hear a crack that sounds like wood splintering, and I back off, anxiously glancing down. No one else seems to have noticed.

Come on . . .

I try again.

Snap.

I jerk away from the window, but it's too late. A crack splinters through the frame. I watch, horrified, as it spreads from the window to the wall, growing bigger, deeper. A piece of trim jerks to the side, sways for a moment, then drops away, crashing onto the balcony at my feet.

I have both hands pressed over my mouth, my eyes wide with horror. Someone definitely heard *that*. Every instinct in my body is telling me to run, to hide, but before I can move a muscle, my eyes land on the wall.

There's a rotted area below the newly missing piece of trim and, inside it, someone's stashed an aluminum *High School Musical* lunch box.

What the hell?

It's like a hiding place.

I act on autopilot, not thinking, just reaching for the lunch box, my curiosity blocking my fear of being caught just for a second. But, as I reach for the box, the rotted wood it's resting on gives way, and it falls.

I leap back, shocked, as the lunch box tumbles across the balcony, slides just below the guard rail, falls over the edge—

And slams into the patio below, where it pops open. Through the narrowest gap in the slats, I can see that a small, handheld video camera has tumbled out.

4

Reagan

Jack and I are ducked behind a tree just past the edge of the patio when Gia North's video camera drops from the sky and slams into the concrete.

We're about two yards away, but I've spent enough time reading the r/CampLostLake forums to know what a 2006 Sony Handycam looks like, even from this distance. The clunky silver frame, curved to fit into the palm of your hand, the Sony-branded hand strap, and the tiny display screen that flips out from the side and swivels around so you can watch yourself—or whatever else you might be recording—while you're recording it.

I'd know that camera anywhere.

According to all the reports, Gia North was an incredibly nosy gossip. She used to carry that video camera around with her, record everything, and put it all up on this YouTube channel she had. And I mean *everything*. She outed some kid in her class when she found him making out with another guy, she read people's college rejection letters when she found them in the trash, she even told her entire school when a girl was diagnosed with herpes—her dad, Dr. North, was the town ob-gyn, so she sometimes overheard these things. Truly, this girl sounded terrible.

Most armchair experts think Gia caught the killer on video, that it's why she was murdered along with Matthew and Jacob. Her camera was never found, so the theory goes that the witch murdered her and destroyed the camera to ensure that whatever she filmed stayed a secret forever.

And yet here her camera is, sitting on the concrete just six feet away from me. Not so destroyed after all.

My stomach twists. I never, in my most wildly hopeful dreams, expected Gia North's missing camera to *fall from the sky*. This is a million times better than figuring out M. Edwards's full name. This could mean finding actual proof that my mother is innocent. It could mean this whole nightmare is finally over.

I feel like I'm under a trance, like the only thing that exists is the camera lying on the ground next to some old lunch box. I stand without thinking about what I'm doing, no longer caring that one of these kids might notice me, that I'm technically not even supposed to be here. My entire brain is focused on grabbing that camera and running.

I don't fully realize what I'm doing until I feel Jack's hand wrap around my arm. He yanks me back down, hard.

"What are you thinking?" he hisses in my ear. Luckily, everyone else is too focused on the camera to notice us.

Some guy with purple hair snatches the camera off the ground. "What's this?" he says, flipping the screen open.

No, I think. Every muscle in my body tightens at the same time. The guy flips the display screen out as everyone else gathers around him. He hits the power button, but nothing happens. Of course nothing happens. It's been sixteen years.

"Must be dead," the kid mutters. He turns the camera over and, reading something on the side, says, "This says it belongs to Gia North."

A heavy, uneasy silence falls over the group. It's the kind of silence that means something, and I realize, with a sinking sensation, that they all must recognize Gia's name. Of course they would recognize her name. They probably grew up knowing this story.

"It's evidence," says a girl with freckly skin and springy brown coils. "We need to call the police."

"Don't you want to see what's on it first?" the guy holding the camera says.

Yes, I think, my heart beating in my throat. *Please watch it first.*

"Do you have a sixteen-year-old camera charger hanging around?" the girl with the brown coils asks him. The guy shrugs, and she says, "Yeah, that's what I thought. Besides, I think it's against the law not to hand over evidence in a murder investigation the moment you get it. Keeping that thing would give us, like, the worst karma ever."

"Obviously we're not going to *keep* it," says the guy. He turns to some redheaded kid and says, "Eric, can you call the police?"

Eric's already pulling out his cell phone when the dark-haired girl cuts him off.

"The lighthouse is the only spot around here with any cell reception, Sawyer," she says. "He'll have to go up there."

The guy called Sawyer groans and pinches the bridge of his nose between his fingers. "Okay . . . fine, whatever, go up to the lighthouse, but be careful. I wasn't messing around before, it's dangerous up there. I want you to go up and come right back down, is that clear?"

Eric nods.

"In the meantime," Sawyer continues, "I'm going to lock this in the lodge so no one can mess with this camera while we wait for the cops to show up. Does that sound good to everyone?"

I exhale heavily. "I'm going after him," I whisper to Jack. "I'll follow him to the lodge, sneak in behind him, grab the camera, and meet you back at the truck."

"I'm coming with you," Jack says. His voice is a little lower, a little softer, and, when I glance down, I see that he's touching me. Well, sort of. He's touching the flannel shirt part of me, but still, it's the first time he's touched me since our roadside hug, and it feels . . . different. I can't pinpoint how, exactly, but it's intimate and intentional. I don't pull away, and he leans closer, moving his hand to my elbow.

I knew this was coming. I knew it, but that doesn't mean I'm prepared for it. Not yet. It's a question I don't know the answer to, and I wasn't expecting to have to answer it so quickly.

Before I can really think about what I'm doing, I shrug his hand off. "Nope, it's fine. I can go alone."

Something in Jack's face seems to shutter. He pulls his hand away, clenching and unclenching it like he's been burned. "Right. Got it."

Crap. I basically just screamed "I'm not interested in you like that, please stop touching me forever."

"No," I say, backtracking. *What am I doing?* "I just meant . . . it'll be easier for me to get in and out without anyone seeing me if I'm on my own. Some of the people around here know you, right? They might wonder what you're doing here."

Jack still isn't looking at me, but his shoulders relax a little, and when he speaks again his voice doesn't sound quite so abrupt. "Maybe not. You know what my dad's like."

Jack's family doesn't live too far from here, sort of between this town and the next one, but Jack's dad, Henry, is kind of a reclusive shut-in. And he hates Camp Lost Lake. Jack says it's because of the murders, what happened to my parents; he's always assumed someone at camp was covering something up, letting my mom take the blame. Not that he could ever prove it.

He made sure Jack didn't have anything to do with the camp, though. And that pretty much meant that Jack couldn't have anything to do with the town. He has a few friends here, of course, but his mom didn't want him to turn into his dad, who doesn't believe in banks and was convinced the government was spying on us using our cell phones, so she made sure Jack was homeschooled by tutors out of Manhattan since he was in kindergarten, and she took him down to the city all the time, forcing him to visit art museums (which he hated) and eat authentic Chinese food (which he loved). The way he tells it, he doesn't hang out with a lot of people from Lost Lake.

"This town is tiny," I say anyway. "You're trying to tell me you're sure no one will recognize you?"

"We live closer to Auburn. Whenever we need to shop or whatever we go there."

I scoff. "C'mon, Jack."

Jack shrugs. "I guess one or two people might recognize me," he finally admits.

"So we're decided. You'll stay here."

Jack looks at me. It's such a small moment. He doesn't even move his head, just flicks his eyes over to mine, lashes low, but I feel it like a touch. "Listen," he says, "take care of yourself, okay? I'll be right here when you're done."

"I promise," I tell him.

"And Reagan? We're going to need to talk about what's going on between us." His eyebrows go up on the word *us*, leaving me without any doubt about what he means. "Maybe not right this second, but . . . eventually."

I nod, even though what I want to say is *Can we not? Can't we just keep things the way they are now? The way they've been for the last year?* But I can't say that, because it's an answer, isn't it? The wrong answer.

I look down at my knees. "Yeah," I say, slowly. "I know."

Out of the corner of my eye, I see Jack move, angling his entire body so it's facing mine. "I like you."

My cheeks burn. "Jack —"

"No," he cuts me off. "I need to say it out loud so there isn't any confusion. I like you a lot. And if you don't like me, that's fine. I just . . . I need you to be honest with me. I can take it."

Honest. It's just like Jack to think it's that easy.

I swallow. I can't do this now. It's too much pressure. Too much *everything*. I need more time to sort out how I feel, what I want and don't want, and what's stupid to even think about wanting, considering how ridiculous and messed up my life is. Jack was there for me at the lowest point of my entire life. That means something. I just don't know *what* it means.

"We'll talk when I get back, okay?" I blurt. And then, before Jack can say anything else, I duck out from behind the trees as quietly as I can manage, praying no one hears me.

I've only known Jack for one year, but it feels like longer. His dad, Henry, was the Camp Lost Lake groundskeeper back in the day. Apparently, his parents and my parents were close. To hear Henry tell it, Lori "was one of the only shitty camp people I could actually stand." High praise, coming from him.

Jack and I met back when Mom and I first went on the run. Jack's family are all these outdoorsy, off-the-grid types, all except for his mom, Nora Choi, a famous New York City artist who moved upstate to "find her light." They own a bunch of land and half a dozen old trailers in between Lost Lake and Scarsdale. Henry let us hide out with them for a few weeks while Mom tried to figure out a plan. Mom claimed we couldn't stay any longer than that; she didn't want to get Henry or Nora into any trouble. Call me cynical, but I don't think that had anything to do with it.

I think we left because of the photo albums. Henry and Nora have an extensive collection of photo albums. Nora paints the albums and decorates each page, and not in some basic scrapbook way, either, but like they're actual works of art. We're talking elaborate paper collages, intricate sketches, watercolor paintings. They're breathtaking. I started looking through the albums because of how beautiful they were—and then I realized how far back they went.

All the way back to 2008. The year of the murders.

The year I was born.

While Mom and Henry were in the other room, making dinner and talking, I found the 2008 album and looked through every page. I didn't even know what I was looking for until I found a picture of Mom and a man I didn't know with their arms wrapped around each other, seemingly in love. I recognized the shape of the man's brow and the slope of his nose almost immediately. I see them staring at me from the mirror every morning. *My dad.* I pulled the photo out of the album and flipped it over: *Lori and Jacob.*

By now everyone else in the world knew Lori Knight and Jacob Knight had been married, but I was still refusing to listen to the podcast at that point and Mom had never told me a thing about my dad, no matter how much I begged her. I always assumed it was because he wasn't important, a one-night stand, maybe someone she didn't know very well. But the man in this picture was clearly important. I could tell from the way they looked at each other, how they held each other. I dropped my gaze to their entwined fingers and felt another jolt. Rings. My mom and dad had been married.

I already wanted to lie in a fetal position on the floor, but it was like someone had kicked me while I was down when I flipped to the next page. There was my mom and my maybe-dad. And, between them, a teenage boy with a wide-open smile and floppy blond hair. A brother no one had told me about.

For the first time in my life, I understood what my mom meant when she called me her second chance. I was her second chance at having a family, at being a mother.

That's when Jack found me. He took in the albums scattered around me, the way I was breathing, like I was about to have a full-on panic attack, and he swept me out of there, taking me to his secret spot in the woods, an old tree house his dad built him when he was a little kid. It was a small space, meant for little bodies, not teenagers, but it was cozy. So surrounded by trees, it was hard to remember that other people existed. There, I told him all about finding the photos, learning about a family I never realized I had, all while staring at my hands so I wouldn't start blubbering all over again.

"How could you not know about Jacob and Matthew?" Jack asked, once I'd finished. "Didn't you listen to the podcast?"

No, of course I hadn't listened. I'd done a really good job of avoiding it, too, and the few details I'd gleaned from overhearing other people talk about it were about Gia. Mom's middle-of-the-night confession hadn't mentioned much about the identity of her so-called victims, and if someone had said the names Jacob or Matthew, I hadn't put together that they'd had anything to do with me.

When I told Jack, he sighed, all slow, like he was making a difficult decision, and then he dug his secret cell phone out from under the milk crate where he hid it from his parents, who wouldn't have approved even though Jack paid for it himself.

"This is your story," he told me, pulling up the podcast. "I get that it's scary, but I think you need to listen. You need to know the truth, Reagan."

That was the first time I ever heard the podcast. Jack and I stayed up there for the next four hours, listening to every episode.

That's how I learned all about how my dad, Jacob Knight, had supposedly cheated on my mom. How she'd supposedly killed him in a fit of jealousy, then killed her son—my older brother, Matthew—before going after Gia. *Supposedly*.

It was too much, all of it. The fact that I'd had a family. That someone had taken them away. That the entire world blamed my mother, who I could never in a million years imagine doing the things she'd been accused of. That was the moment I decided I wanted to exonerate her, that I needed to know the real culprit was behind bars. When I started to cry, Jack held my hand, so I'd know I wasn't alone.

Jack and I have been texting pretty much nonstop since that night in the tree house. Even before he said it out loud, I could tell there was something there, something more than friendship. But I have a hard time imagining taking the next step. It's not that I don't think Jack's hot or smart or funny. He's just such a . . . *guy*. He fishes and chops wood and watches sports—and not just the swimming events at the summer Olympics, like my old friends did, but *all* sports. Basketball and baseball. He once texted that he rooted for the Cornhuskers since his dad's family was all originally from Nebraska. I had to google that entire sentence before I understood that he was talking about college football and not, like, actual corn.

It's all so different from what I'm used to. I don't have the most extensive dating history. There was a guy I met at the community pool during the summer between middle and high school and a girl on my swim team freshman year. But that was all pre-podcast. Maybe I'd be willing to take a chance with Jack if I lived anything even remotely resembling a normal life. But with how things are now, me and Mom always on the road, what would getting together be like? One awkward hookup in a car, followed by months of trying to have some kind of relationship over *text*? Always knowing I was competing with every girl he met in real life? Girls who actually shared his interests, who he could date and talk to and kiss? That sounds like torture. My life is *already* torture.

I like Jack. Maybe I even more than like him. But I'd be lost if we hooked up and things didn't work out. I have exactly one friend. Right now, I need him to stay a friend. Even if my skin warms every time he looks over at me.

There's an ancient-looking sign attached to one of the trees up ahead. I squint at the faded words, only just able to make them out beneath all the grime and dirt.

LODGE, the sign reads, and there's an arrow pointing down the trail to the left. I stare at it for a long moment, feeling my breath get short and shallow.

There's a splintery hole right through the middle of the sign. It's small, diamond-shaped, like it was shot through with a real arrow.

There are so many things these woods could be hiding.

I walk slowly past the sign, holding my breath as I duck into the dark. All the while, I'm imagining the trees snapping closed behind me. Like teeth.

The Day Before
the Murders

The last day of junior year ended twenty minutes ago, but Gia North was still perched on a bench just inside the school's double doors, holding her Sony Handycam.

"Summer break is finally here," she said into the camera, "and I hope you're all ready for more of your friends' deepest, darkest secrets, because I've been watching our town very closely this year, and let me tell you, the stuff you're all doing is *scandalous*." She forced a smile that she hoped came across as mischievous but approachable: the girl at the party you wanted to hang with in the corner, casually ripping on everyone else.

Gossip was her thing. Maybe it was a little shady that her "thing" was talking about people behind their backs, but other people were into it, too. Look at Perez Hilton. And those Gossip Girl books. Gia hadn't told anyone this, but she was secretly hoping the videos she was making about everyone in her small town would turn her into a real-life Gossip Girl. She just had to find the right story. Something really scandalous. Something people couldn't help watching.

She took a breath and continued. "The question on everyone's minds as we go into the summer is where all the outgoing seniors are headed off to this fall. *I* heard—"

A door slammed in the parking lot outside, loud enough that it cut her off. Her face dropped into a scowl. *Eff.* Now she was going to have to start over. She switched her camera off, glancing up just as the most popular senior in their class, Matthew Knight, climbed into an old white Toyota that was definitely not his car.

Gia squinted to see the driver. She wasn't wearing her glasses because the light from her camera reflected off the lenses, and whoever it was peeled away before she could make them out. It didn't really matter. She knew what everyone in town drove. Matthew drove his parents' black Jeep. That white Toyota belonged to—

"Gia?"

The voice startled Gia, and she jumped a little, whirling around. It was Officer Knight, Matthew's aunt.

"Officer Knight!" she said, snapping her video camera shut. It wasn't illegal to film gossip videos about your friends, but she still didn't want some grown-up lecturing her about the morality of what she was doing. "What are you doing here?"

"Looking for Matthew," Officer Knight said after a moment. "Have you seen him around? He dropped something at the diner this morning."

Gia dropped her eyes to Officer Knight's hands, noticing that she was holding a small white card, kind of hiding it in her palm. It was the wrong color for a credit card, and it didn't look like a driver's license.

Gia's curiosity surfaced, loyal as a dog.

"I just saw Matthew leave," Gia said, "but I'm happy to pass on whatever he dropped. Let me—"

She grabbed for the card. Officer Knight was clearly unprepared for this and let it go with a surprised "Oh."

Gia's shoulders drooped when she saw what it was: just a dumb Camp Lost Lake key card. Everyone who'd ever been a counselor or a camper had one of these. Nothing scandalous here.

"Gia," Officer Knight was saying, "could I have that—"

But Gia wasn't listening. Her eyes had moved over the sketchy lines of the mountains to the barcode, the name—

Oh.

This key card didn't belong to Matthew. It belonged to *M. Edwards.*

As in the *M. Edwards* whose car Matthew had just climbed into.

5

Olivia

I'm crouched on the balcony above my friends' heads, staring down at the camera.

I know who Gia North is. Everyone in our town knows. Her murder might've been sixteen years ago, but it's the kind of thing a small town like ours doesn't just forget. So I also know what camera I'm staring down at. Gia North's lost camera is almost as famous as she is.

I don't bother walking on the sides of the stairs as I make my way down from the balcony. Everyone's distracted, so consumed by the camera that there's no way they're going to notice me. They don't even seem to have registered that the camera isn't the only thing that fell out of the lunch box. A couple pieces of paper have scattered across the patio, all of them faded and yellowed with age. They probably would've disintegrated by now if the lunch box hadn't protected them from the elements.

I chase them down before they blow away, finding a rejection letter for someone called Quinn Cassidy from Brown University, one of Andie's old homework assignments, and—

The back of my neck prickles.

And an ultrasound.

I lean down to pick it up, feeling like my heart has stopped inside of my chest. The name at the top of the ultrasound is MIRANDA D'ANGELI. My mother's name. And it's dated March 18, 2008.

I'd forgotten until this moment that Gia was Dr. North's daughter. As in our town's only ob-gyn, Dr. North. Mom would've had to see him to confirm her pregnancy.

The cloudy, black-and-white mass doesn't even look human yet. It's a whitish bean in a sea of black, the yellow arrow labeling it FETUS the only thing that indicates it's a person. That it's *me*. I frown, confused. I've seen ultrasounds on television, clear profiles of tiny faces and noses, some kicking legs. And this ultrasound was taken pretty far along in my mom's pregnancy. If she gave birth at thirty-seven weeks in June, then on March 18, she would've been— I quickly do the math in my head—around twenty-four weeks pregnant. Shouldn't I have looked a little more . . . developed?

I move my gaze from the fetus to the row of numbers running along the side of the image, trying to find anything that might indicate how far along my mom was when it was taken. Right below the date are the words SIX WEEKS.

"What?" I murmur. Mom couldn't have been six weeks pregnant on March 18. I was born only three months later. If she'd only been six weeks along in March, she would've given birth to an eighteen-week-old fetus. That's not possible. I wouldn't have survived.

My heart is beating hard and fast in my rib cage now. I'm missing something. This doesn't make sense. Did my mom lie about when I was born? She couldn't have . . . people *saw* her go into labor the night of the massacre. They found her with me in her arms. It's in a police report!

What the hell?

My eyes swivel from the ultrasound to the camera in Sawyer's hands. Gia had the ultrasound. Maybe she knew something else, saw something else—*filmed* something else. If there's even a sliver of a chance there's something about my family on that tape, I need to see it.

This could be the exact piece of proof I was hoping to find, something that forces my mom to tell me the truth. I have to get that camera.

I'll just have to head Sawyer off before he gets to the lodge and . . . come up with something brilliant to convince him to give *me* the camera instead of waiting for the cops.

I duck into the woods before I can second-guess any part of this plan. I haven't spent a lot of time in this specific stretch, but there's a framed map of the campgrounds in the downstairs bathroom back home. About a year and a half ago I got a nasty case of food poisoning after eating these fish tacos from a less-than-sanitary taco truck. I spent two days on the floor of that bathroom, and the only thing I had to look at was the map on the wall. I have a pretty good idea of the layout of camp.

Sawyer's heading to the lodge, which used to be where they hosted big group activities like the annual talent show, the arts and crafts fair, and the end-of-camp dance. It's all the way on the other side of camp. Someone unfamiliar with the grounds might go around the trees to get there, but I know there's a little dirt path that cuts straight through the woods, leading directly from my mom's office to the lodge's double doors. I should get there before Sawyer, with minutes to spare.

Except the trees out here are much thicker and more over-grown than I was expecting. I feel myself getting more anxious the farther I get from camp. Despite Mom's insistence that camping is in our blood, I've always felt uneasy in the woods. I think it spans back to when I was eight years old, camping with my parents for the first time. We'd had so much fun during the day, hiking and building a fire and making s'mores, but when it came time to go to sleep, I couldn't do it. Everything was *too* quiet. Mom wanted to help, so she crawled into the tent with me and told me that it wasn't actually quiet at all and, if I listened close, I could hear the wind shaking the tree branches, and owls hooting, and all the nocturnal animals waking up and scurrying around in the brush to start their day.

The idea that there were a ton of creepy night animals wander-ing around in the dark freaked me out even worse than the quiet had. I stayed awake the whole night, convinced I heard them wan-dering around our campsite.

And then I was sure that what I was hearing wasn't just animals. The noises sounded like footsteps in the underbrush, like the low, even sound of a man breathing.

I didn't sleep for a week afterward.

I think about that now as I creep through the trees. Everything is still and silent—except when it's not. I've just gotten used to the muffled sound of my own footsteps on the dirt path, the light brush of the wind in the leaves, when there's a rustle right behind me, much closer than I'm expecting.

I jerk around, my hands flying to my mouth involuntarily. For a long moment I stay still, trying to steady my breathing.

Something scurries through the brush. A moment later, there's a strangled yelp that makes my stomach turn over.

It's got to be an animal, a predatory bird that just caught his lunch, maybe. But I picture a man hiding in the trees, just outside of the sunlight. Watching me.

I shiver and push the thought out of my head, hurrying forward. All I have to do is get the camera from Sawyer. Then I can get out of these creepy woods and back to where the people are.

But uneasiness continues to creep over me as I make my way deeper into the trees. I feel like I'm ten years old again, huddled in my sleeping bag while Maeve tells the story of the Witch of Lost Lake, that silly fire crackling on her iPad. I can practically hear her whispering about how the witch still wanders around out here, waiting for another teenager to step out of line.

After a few minutes the ground flattens out, becoming a wide, muddy field pockmarked with tufts of overgrown grass, dandelions, and weeds. It's barely three, but the sky is already growing dark, and when I look up I see that storm clouds have blown in, obscuring the sun. Everything is gray.

A sort of shelter stands to my right, hunched low to the ground, flat roof, the walls bare wooden planks. I stare at the shelter for a moment longer than necessary to convince myself there's no one hiding inside where I can't see them, and then I look across the field.

It's not just any field; it's the archery range that I was just looking at when I stood outside my mom's office. Which means that's not a shelter, it's an equipment shed where they stored all the archery stuff.

I stop walking at once. I'm not in the woods anymore; I'm in Maeve's living room, my knees pulled up to my chest, hearing the story of the Camp Lost Lake murders for the first time. Maeve's high, little-girl voice sounds as clearly as if she were speaking directly into my ear: "Lori's husband, Jacob, used to teach archery at Camp Lost Lake before he died. Lori confronted him on the archery range at camp and killed him with his own arrows."

Blood thumps in my temples and, for a moment, fear rises inside me, so strong I can't think of anything else. I'm alone out here. Far enough from my friends that they wouldn't even hear me scream.

I've just about gotten the fear under control when I sense movement from the corner of my eye. I whip my head around, breathing hard.

The equipment shed. Something moved inside the equipment shed.

I bring a hand to my mouth, breathing hard. I wait for one moment. Two.

Nothing moves again.

I take a step toward the shed. It's dark in there. Half the shed is open air, no walls, just one long bench stretched across a concrete floor, and the other half is a small square room, one door, no windows.

I lick my lips, eyes on the shed. The door is open, I notice. A thick padlock hangs from the doorknob, but it's not locked, just dangling.

I take another step forward. I can see inside now. There's an old gas lantern on the floor, a tin coffee cup with a ring of brown still sitting on the bottom, a pocketknife, and a camp stove. All things someone could find on campgrounds.

My heart starts beating faster. I think of the sleeping bag Hazel found. She said it was unrolled. Like someone had been *using* it.

The shed door sways slightly, and I jump backward, releasing a little scream. But it's just the wind. There's no one there.

I watch that door for the length of one breath, my heart thrashing around inside my chest like a caged bird. I want to know how *long* these things have been here. Has it been like this for sixteen years? Or has someone been here more recently?

"It's nothing," I murmur under my breath. It's just an open door and a few camp supplies. No reason to freak out. Even if there was someone here recently, it was probably just some kid messing around, like Officer Knight said.

But when I take a step back toward the field, I notice the footprints. They're all across the ground.

Fresh footprints.

The witch's footprints, a voice in my mind whispers. I shiver, feeling like I've just been touched by something gross that I desperately want to shake off.

Stop it, stop it, stop it.

I keep my head ducked and hurry across the range, back into the woods. I can't have gone more than a dozen feet when a shadow slides out from behind a tree.

I jerk backward, my heart suddenly in my throat. I want to scream, but it's like my voice has dried up inside of me.

The shadow's hands come up. "Hey, calm down, it's just me." The shadow—now a fully formed guy—steps onto the path in front of me, his hands held up in a classic "good guy" stance. I'm startled enough that it takes a second for my heart to stop rattling and my eyes to travel up to his face. And then—

Whoa. Okay, yeah, this guy is . . . distractingly attractive. I was not prepared for that. He's tall and lean, with longish black hair and a good, strong jawline. He appears to be East Asian.

"Hi," I say, dumbfounded. He's maybe the hottest guy I've ever seen in real life.

"How'd you get back here? I thought you were a few yards ahead," he says, turning to point deeper into the woods.

"You . . . what?" This makes no sense. Unless . . .

My throat feels suddenly tight. Was he *following* me?

The guy frowns at me, those frustratingly beautiful eyes moving over my face, my clothes. "Did you change your shirt?"

I touch the hem of my Antlers polo. This is getting creepy. I'm all alone with some guy, in the middle of the woods, far enough from my friends that I can't exactly call for help if this interaction goes south.

I swallow, nervous now. I wonder if he was the guy who put all that camping stuff in the archery shed. Mom once told me that she knows people sneak into the camp sometimes, weirdos coming to the site of the murders to see "where it all happened." I suddenly want to put some distance between the two of us.

"Excuse me," I say, skirting the edge of the trail. The boy kind of blinks, and then shuffles out of my way. For a second it looks like he might follow me, but he doesn't. I hurry down the dirt road before he can change his mind, the back of my neck itching. He's definitely watching me walk away.

He *was* cute, though. I allow myself a fraction of a second to be thankful that I wore my jean shorts that make my legs look super long, then immediately shake myself out of it. For all I know, this guy's some murder fanboy.

Once I've gone a few yards, something hits me: I changed my shirt at home, in my bedroom. How could he know about that?

I stop walking and quickly check behind me to make sure he isn't following me. He isn't. The dirt road behind me is long and empty, stray weeds and dandelions blowing lightly in the breeze to either side. No sign of life.

A nervous flutter skims my neck. I start walking again, faster now. Luckily, the lodge is right up ahead, a long, low building with a pitched roof and tons of dark windows. I look around for Sawyer, but don't see him anywhere, which means my delay with the hot, creepy stranger made me too late to head him off before he went inside. Crap.

I try the front door—thank God, it's unlocked.

"Hello?" I call and step into the dark.

6

Reagan

I've spent the last few months memorizing old maps of the camp-grounds I found online and locate the path through the woods easily. Five minutes later, the lodge rises from beyond the trees like a mirage.

I stay out of sight for a while longer, considering my strategy. There's the front door, but that's probably how the guy with the camera's planning to get inside. If he sees me, he'll bolt and take the camera somewhere else.

I walk the perimeter of the lodge instead. There's no back door, but there *is* a row of dusty windows. I try to open the first one, but it doesn't budge. Either locked or rusted closed. Same with the next and the next. Great.

The way to break a window is you don't let yourself think about what you're doing. If you think about it too hard, you're going to psych yourself out. I close my eyes and count down—*three, two, one*—and then jerk my elbow back as hard as I can, bracing myself for impact. My arm slams into the window with a sharp *thwunk!* and there's a crash of breaking glass as it shatters like brittle candy. Pain vibrates up my arm. Luckily, my flannel's thick enough that none of the broken shards pierce skin.

I shrug my sleeve down over my hand and use it to carefully brush the rest of the broken glass away from the frame. Once the glass is gone, I haul my body up and through the window.

I stay near the window for a long moment, blinking. The storm clouds outside have almost completely obscured the sun, and in here it's so dark that it takes a long moment for my eyes to adjust. When they do, a chill creeps up my spine. It's unnerving. The air in here feels wrong. Too still. It's like time stopped back in 2008, like this air hasn't been disturbed since the day Gia and Jacob and Matthew were murdered.

I'm in a smaller room—an office, maybe—that's been sectioned off from a much larger area. You can tell because the eight-foot walls don't even come close to reaching the soaring ceiling, and it gives the space a cubicle feeling. There's another window on the wall adjacent to the one I just broke, but it's layered with years of thick, yellow dust, and any light that filters in through the glass is muddy and dim. A heavy, wooden desk leans against another wall and, if I squint, I can make out the hulking outline of an ancient iMac sitting on top of it, the kind made of clear, teal plastic that you can see all the wires through. The air smells like old newspaper.

I cross the room, push the door open. There's not a wide-open room on the other side, like I was expecting, but a narrow hallway. I feel something cold move down my neck. We did a Greek mythology unit at my old school. My final day in class, we were discussing a story about Theseus, who gets trapped in a huge labyrinth with a monster hunting him.

I can't help thinking about poor old Theseus now, as I stare down the dark, dark hall. Did he ever get out of that labyrinth?

Did he even survive? Mom pulled me out of school before I got a chance to finish the story.

I really wish I could think of something other than Theseus and the Minotaur right now.

"Get it together, Reagan," I murmur, forcing myself to take one step forward, and then another. Deeper and deeper into the labyrinth.

My eyes are drawn to faded snapshots hanging on the walls, campers engaged in idyllic summer activities, canoeing and building elaborate art projects from Popsicle sticks, roasting marshmallows around a fire. Occasionally a member of the staff will be in the shot, too, standing shoulder to shoulder with the campers, grinning at the camera. You can tell when it's someone who works at camp because they wear narrow gold name tags. I find myself squinting in the dark, reading the names as I walk:

L. RUBIN, A. MURRAY, R. WHITMER, M. EDWARDS.

I jerk to a stop.

M. Edwards? *My* M. Edwards?

I look from the name tag to the woman who's wearing it, and all the air leaves my lungs.

M. Edwards is a white woman with chin-length blond hair and wide blue eyes. She doesn't exactly give violent killer.

Except that she's holding a bow and arrow.

And she's not just holding it. She's gripping the bow expertly, one hand aiming, the other pulling the string taut, her arm lean and muscled in the sunlight. There's an arrow nocked and aimed. Whoever took the photo caught her a moment before she let it fly.

I've started breathing again, but each inhale is shallow and short. This photo, it proves that M. Edwards had the ability to kill with a bow and arrow. And the key card evidence proves she was at camp when the murders were committed. All I need now is motive. Hopefully that's what Gia caught on tape. The reason this woman killed her, too.

A sudden, sharp sound cuts through the quiet.

I go still. Somewhere deeper in the lodge there's a click of metal on metal, the creak of old hinges: someone's opened a door.

It's that guy, I tell myself. *The one with the camera.* But my hands have gotten sweaty, and a rash of goose bumps rises on my arms.

As quietly as I can, I take the frame down from the wall and remove the back. Then, I slip the photo of M. Edwards out of the frame and into my pocket.

I hear a telltale click—a door closing—and a shuffle of footsteps as someone walks into the building. Whoever it is isn't trying to be quiet, which calms me down some. This isn't someone planning to sneak up on me. They don't know I'm here.

I hold my breath and lean forward, peering around the corner—

My breath catches in my throat.

I can tell, immediately, that whoever just came in is *not* the dude with the camera. It's dark in here and, from where I'm standing, I can only make out the outline of a body, but that body is small and slight and much shorter than the dude with the camera's had been. It looks more like a girl about my size.

My chest clenches. I think of the photograph in my pocket. *M. Edwards.* Could it be her? Is she after the camera, too?

Whoever it is, she doesn't appear to be armed. I'm not a fighter, but I used to train for an hour a day to stay in shape for swim. It's been a year since I was in a pool, but I haven't completely fallen out of shape. I think I could take her.

The girl doesn't turn on any lights but moves quickly down the hall, the sound of her footsteps echoing off the walls and floor.

"Hello?" she calls. Her voice is loud and clear, not the voice of someone who's afraid there's a stranger waiting for her in the dark. "Sawyer?"

She's still walking, but it looks like she's got her phone out now, and if I squint a little, I can see that her head is all hunched over it. She's heading my way, but she still doesn't look up, which is good, because if she did, she'd definitely see me peering around the corner at her. Any second, she's going to round the corner and walk right into me. I glance over my shoulder, but there's only the narrow hall and that office room behind me. Dead end, unless I'm planning to call it quits and climb right back out the window I just broke. If I want to get the camera, I'm going to have to go through her.

Okay, here goes nothing.

I take another deep breath and step forward.

The girl is still fumbling with her phone, but my sudden appearance seems to scare the shit out of her.

"Oh my God," she shouts, and jerks away from me, raising the hand that's still holding her phone, like she's planning to throw it at me.

She must've been trying to turn her flashlight app on because, in a weird twist of fate, a white beam blinks on at that exact moment, illuminating her.

It's dark enough in here that I only catch the girl's face in pieces, at first. There's her pale skin, blue-green eyes that are just a tiny bit too close together on her face, nose dusted in light freckles. Her honey-blond hair falls a few inches past her shoulders—longer than mine, but not by much—and her face would be heart-shaped, except that her chin is short and a little square, a heart with the bottom corner snipped off.

I inhale, déjà vu twisting through my gut as I stare.

I know that face.

I know that when her freckles get too much sun they get darker and more pop up on her forehead and cheeks. And her eyes, I know they're so exactly halfway between green and blue that it's impossible to know what to write on forms that ask what color they are. I know her cheeks are so round she has a hard time finding flattering sunglasses and her hair is wavy in strange places, wavy enough that it seems like it would curl, but when she gets it wet and scrunches it up like everyone on TikTok says to, it just falls flat against her shoulders, all limp-looking and sad.

The girl standing in front of me is . . .

Me.

I exhale and words explode from my lips. "What. In the actual. *Hell?*"

"The . . . hell?" the girl repeats, sounding confused. Her mouth is wide and full and turned down at the corners, just like mine, and even though she isn't smiling, I can see the bottom edges of her two front teeth beneath her top lip, in an expression so creepily reminiscent of one I've seen on my own face in pictures or the mirror that I actually shiver. She moves the light to my face.

For a moment I can't think, can't speak, can't move. This doesn't make sense. This isn't *possible.* I can't manage to catch my breath. My head feels light and full of hot air, like if it weren't attached to my body, it would just float away. The room around me blinks in and out of focus.

"Who are you?" the girl asks.

"Reagan." The name slips out before I can consider whether it's a good idea to give it to her. I bite my lip to hide my nerves and add, "Who the *hell* are *you*?"

The girl doesn't answer. She looks skittish. Her eyes keep jumping from my face to my arm to the wall. She reminds me of the character in the horror movie who screams when she should be keeping her mouth shut, who gets the whole group caught by the axe-wielding psychopath. It makes me nervous.

"Don't move . . ." I tell her. My body feels tight and hot, like a live wire. "Don't . . . don't do anything."

"I-I think I'm going to faint," the girl murmurs.

"Do *not* faint!"

"It's not really something your body gives you a choice about one way or another," she says. Then, her eyes moving off my face, she adds, "I know this is jarring, but I don't think hitting me is going to help with anything."

I frown and drop my arm. I had no idea I'd even made a fist. "Sorry. Instinct."

"*Punching* is your instinct?"

"*Fainting* is yours?" I throw back at her.

"This isn't possible," the girl says, ignoring me. She's doing her skittish thing again, bouncing from one foot to the other, squeezing her hands together, then relaxing them. I want to grab her by the shoulders, tell her to *hold still*.

"Yeah, obviously," I say, instead.

She looks like she's going to say something else when a door suddenly slams open, interrupting her. We both jerk around to stare into the darkness.

Someone stands at the end of the hall. I can't quite make them out. Whoever it is appears to be wearing a large black coat, and is all in silhouette, just a shadow backlit by the watery gray light streaming in from the windows behind them.

"Who's that?" the other girl says softly.

"That guy—" I start, but she's already shaking her head.

"That isn't Sawyer," she murmurs.

Whoever it is doesn't speak, but I have a feeling they're looking straight at us, that they can see us clearly in the dim light.

This isn't okay. Something feels very, very wrong.

"Hey, you," the other girl calls, her voice all false bravado. "What do you—"

I grab her arm. "Shut *up*," I hiss through my teeth. Out of the corner of my eye, I see her head swivel around to face me, but I can't explain why she should be quiet. I know something's off, even if I can't find the words to explain *why*.

Slowly, I pull my phone out of my pocket and hold it before my face. My hands are shaking, badly, and it takes me two tries to turn the flashlight on. A dim white glow appears, illuminating me and the other girl and a circle of dark floor.

I squint, making out the face of whoever's standing at the end of the hall, just inside the edge of the illuminated circle. They're old, haggard, with green-tinted skin and long, stringy gray hair. Their eyes are black and sunken, surrounded by deeply lined, rubbery skin, and their nose is long, hooked, covered in warts.

"The Witch of Lost Lake," I murmur. I wouldn't have realized I'd said the words out loud, except the other girl looks at me, frowning like she wants to argue, but I know I'm right. Whoever's standing at the end of the hall is wearing a Witch of Lost Lake mask.

My heart leaps into my throat. I look down and see the sharp point of an arrow aimed right at us.

Something twitches at the corner of my eyesight: *movement*. I jerk around.

It's that guy, the tall, thin guy with the purple hair, the one who took Gia's camera. *Sawyer?* He must've come in through the front door, after the girl. Now, he steps out from the hallway, frowning at us.

"What's going on? Olivia?" He stares at the girl who looks like me for a moment, and then his eyes move to my face, and he blinks a few times. "Wait—"

There's a soft *thwup*, followed by the sound of something flying toward us, fast. A second later, a small, pointed object shoots into Sawyer's neck, spraying blood across the wall.

Sawyer blinks at us few times, then grasps for his neck with both hands, eyes widening in terror. Blood spurts from between his fingers and runs down his chest. When he opens his mouth again, his teeth are slick and red.

"He . . . lp," he groans, his voice a rasp. I leap backward as he drops to his knees on the floor, blood pooling around him. He lurches forward, collapsing onto the ground.

Fear floods through me. This is a joke. It has to be. These dumb camp kids have turned the Lost Lake murders into a game, with a fake bow and arrows and a cheesy Halloween mask and fake blood and . . .

But it looks so *real*.

It's like roots have sprouted from the bottoms of my feet, holding me firmly in place. I can't breathe, can't move. That kid was *just* alive. He was *just* moving. And now . . .

The girl with my face grabs my arm. "*Run,*" she says.

Down the hall, the witch nocks a second arrow.

My hands have started trembling. It's hard to breathe. I can't believe this is happening. It's as if I'm living the urban legend. I went someplace I wasn't supposed to, I went to Camp Lost Lake, and the witch is here to punish me.

The girl who looks like me—Olivia, apparently—pulls me down the hall Sawyer just came through, yanking so hard that I feel a flare of pain through my shoulder.

It's a strange sensation, trying to run on shaky legs. It feels like I'm going to lose my balance and go sprawling, face-first, onto the floor. And then that woman, the witch, she'll find me and . . .

No, I tell myself, pushing the image out of my head. *Don't think about that.* I'll never be able to stay upright if I let myself think about that.

Behind me, I hear footsteps. Slow, even, unhurried footsteps. The sound freaks me out even more than if the witch had been running. This is not someone who's worried we're going to get away.

Olivia must be taking us back to the main entrance. We round a corner, spilling out into a bigger, more open room. Dim sunlight filters in from the dirty windows, dancing over wood-planked walls. Boxes tower around us, and there are shelves filled with books and sports gear and art supplies.

I see the front door at the same time Olivia does.

"Thank God," she sobs, stumbling forward. I pause for a second to catch my breath, and that's when I see it.

Gia's camera sits on the table under a window on the far side of the room. It's right there, in front of us, the camera that could change my entire life.

I stumble forward, reaching for it—

But Olivia snatches it first.

"Let's *go*," she says, and races outside.

The Night Before the Murders

The evening was thick with summer, crickets humming in the tall, dry grass, the setting sun dusting everything in gold, the smell of bonfire reaching through the air like a crooked finger.

Miranda D'Angeli, who usually loved everything about camp, all the sounds and smells, felt sick to her stomach. She had her head ducked over her Camp Lost Lake tote bag, her long blond hair spilling forward to hide her face as she scavenged around inside for her car keys, worn-down flip-flops kicking up dirt in the parking lot. She didn't normally wear flip-flops to work, but her ankles were swollen, her butt ached from sitting all day, and her joints were sore. But that was nothing compared to how depressed she felt. She'd been trying to put on a happy face, smiling to everyone who came into the diner and everyone she saw at camp, but it was all a lie. After what happened two days ago, she doubted she'd ever truly feel like smiling again.

The only thing she wanted in the entire world was to climb into her car and blast the air conditioner as high as it would go.

Maybe she'd fall asleep right here, in the camp parking lot, under the shadow of the old lighthouse.

But when she reached the parking lot, her car wasn't where she remembered leaving it. It was parked all the way on the other side of the lot, near the woods.

Miranda stopped walking, frowning. That was odd. Had she parked it over there this morning and just forgotten? To be fair, that sort of thing had been happening to her a lot lately. Her memory had been complete crap. Her doctor said it was normal, that she needed to give herself time.

She took a single step toward the car. She heard a rustle in the bushes, a sound like someone trying to muffle a cough. She jerked her head around—

No one there.

"Lori?" Miranda called out. She wondered if she'd left something on her desk, if her assistant had chased after her, knowing there was no way she was hauling herself back up to her office. But no one answered.

Wind rippled over the grass like it was water, and the crickets seemed a bit louder than they'd been a minute ago, the white-noise sound of their hum filling Miranda's ears.

It was just before sundown, two weeks before camp opened for the season. Normally, this was Miranda's favorite time of day during her favorite time of year. She was the director of Camp Lost Lake, and she loved how peaceful the grounds were before they were overrun with children. The wind in the trees and the softly lapping lake in the distance, every cabin scrubbed to within an inch of its life.

But, tonight, she could only focus on how miserable she felt.

It was already dark in the shadow of the lighthouse, and she was so alone out here, just her and the trees and lake and mountains for miles. There was no one around to hear her scream—oh God, why would she even think that?

She let her eyes move over the tall, leafy trees, the empty cabins, the distant archery range, and the stables—hesitating when she saw movement. People had mentioned seeing someone sneaking around the woods. But the campgrounds were private property. No one was allowed here. But she just saw a flash of gold. It looked like . . .

"Andie?" Miranda called, confused. Her daughter, Andie, was a high school senior, but she'd left school a semester early. Right now, she was at her internship down in New York City. She'd been there since January.

And yet Miranda could've sworn that was her blond hair she'd just seen flickering through the trees.

7

Olivia

Gia's camera thumps in my pocket as I run, reminding me with every step that I'm close to getting answers, if only I can stay alive. I focus on the weight hitting my hip so I won't think about how it might feel if the sharp point of an arrowhead burrows into my shoulder. I imagine that bright heat ripping through my skin and muscle, and an ugly sob escapes my lips.

Oh God. I'm going to die. I'm going to die *here*, in the woods.

Another victim of the Witch of Lost Lake.

Cool air burns up my lungs as I weave through the trees surrounding the lodge. The other girl is right behind me, easily keeping up with my pace despite how catatonic she'd seemed just a moment ago. She's in amazing shape, not even breathing heavy, though I'm already gasping for air.

She's going to get away, I realize. She's faster than me, stronger. I picture the witch following, reloading the bow she just used to kill Sawyer. Of the two of us, *I'm* the easy target, the one stumbling over rocks, struggling to keep up.

Panic corkscrews through me. The trees give way a few yards ahead, the thick canopy of leaves and branches opening up to reveal the larger clearing where the cabins and offices and people are. A fresh sob bubbles up my throat, but this one is relieved: *safety*. I'm so close.

Before I can get even one step closer, I feel a hand on my elbow, jerking me back. Every muscle in my body seizes as I whirl around, expecting the archer. *The witch.*

It's not, it's the girl who looks like me. *Reagan.* "This way," she gasps, trying to tug me deeper into the trees.

I hold my ground. "No! We have to get back to camp." Everyone knows you head for people when there's a killer on the loose.

"She could've circled back there already." Again, the girl tries to pull me toward the trees. "We need to *hide*."

There's a crack behind us, the sound of a footstep.

My fear is immediate and all-consuming. I shriek and dart for the clearing, hoping the other girl is smart enough to follow me. The ground is rocky and uneven, hard to navigate. I nearly trip on rocks a few times, only managing to right myself at the last second. Falling now is the difference between living and dying.

The clearing seems to be getting farther and farther away. Is the witch right behind me? Is she going to shoot another arrow? What is she waiting for?

When I'm close enough to make out the parking lot, I nearly sob out loud in relief: Andie's car is here. She's back from the store, and I'm sure she'll know how to fix this. Andie knows how to fix everything.

It's less than a yard to the clearing now. I'm going to make it. Once we reach the cabins, once we're surrounded by other people, we'll be safe. I'm almost there—

And then the witch steps out of the trees right in front of us.

Her appearance shocks me so badly that I immediately start

backtracking, stumbling down the path that leads back toward the lodge. *Oh no oh no oh no.*

The other girl takes a different tack, banking left, deeper into the trees. I want to scream at her, tell her that she shouldn't go into the trees, that she's making it way too easy for this woman to chase after her, but it's too late for that.

And, anyway, the witch isn't following her.

She's following *me*.

Now that we're outside, where it's a little brighter, I have a clearer view of what she looks like. She's medium height and slim through the arms and shoulders. The witch's mask looks like it truly is sixteen years old, with something splattered across the chin and nose. Something reddish brown . . .

My stomach churns. There's *blood* crusted onto the mask. I drop my eyes, and now I see that she's still holding the bow and arrow.

I feel my pulse throbbing in my temples. It fills my head with the sound of rushing blood and static, making it impossible to hear anything else. I stagger backward, nearly stumbling over an old root, and manage to grab hold of the tree to steady myself. I release a low, hitching sob.

Where do I go now? I have no idea. I can't go back to the lodge, and the witch is blocking the way to the cabins. I'm trapped.

She tilts her head, examining me. Then—moving slowly, unrushed, she knows I have nowhere to run—she reaches into the quiver on her back and removes an arrow.

I turn and throw myself deeper into the trees, screaming when I hear the bark on the tree nearest me explode, an arrow slamming into it.

A twig breaks behind me. I glance over my shoulder, a scream ripping up my throat: the witch is *right there*. She's not even two yards away, running fast and silently through the woods, easily ducking below tree branches and darting around rocks. Her eyes are dark and unfathomable behind that old, drooping mask.

I head deeper into the woods. Tree branches whip against my cheeks and I can feel the sharp points of rocks through the soles of my shoes. My calves scream with pain and my chest feels tight, making it impossible to breathe. My heart is pounding so hard it feels like my chest might explode.

A barn appears from between the trees, glimpses of red wood and a steepled roof flickering here and there behind branches and leaves. It's my only choice. I can't keep running—she'll catch me. At least in the barn I might be able to find a weapon.

I burst through the doors at a run, gasping hard. The barn is dark, with faint strips of sunlight peeking between the gaps in the wood, striping the dirt-and-straw-covered floor. The smells of mildew and manure hang heavily in the air.

Weapon. I have to find a weapon.

There isn't much to choose from. A rusted shovel that looks like it'd snap in half if I used it to hit anything, a pile of rope, a lantern . . .

My eyes move away from the wall, over to a bale of hay, and—*there*.

A pitchfork.

Thank God. I race across the barn and grab it, my hands tightening around the splintery wood.

And then I wait, breathing hard, watching the doors, knowing the witch is going to burst through them at any moment.

8

Reagan

Faster.

The word circles my head until it loses all meaning.

Faster. Faster.

Faster.

I exhale, my throat and lungs beginning to burn. My leg muscles are tight springs. They scream each time my foot slams into the packed dirt, the shudder of the impact trembling through my body. One wrong step, and I'll go flying.

The skin along my neck and the backs of my arms tingles, anticipating the hand I'm sure is going to reach out and grab me at any moment.

Finally, I burst through the trees, stumbling into a flattened grass clearing. Little wood cabins wink at me from the trees, looking warm and normal and safe. There are people, too. The kids I saw packing up boxes on the patio when Jack and I first arrived have migrated here and lined up around a grill holding cans of soda and paper plates. It must be close to dinnertime because the smell of cooking meat hangs in the air like smoke.

Relief washes over me. Maybe my instinct to avoid these

people was wrong. Even with a bow and arrow, there's no way the murderer can take all of us out.

Can she?

I hear the snap of a twig behind me and spring forward, my heart leaping into my throat.

"There's . . . there's a killer!" I scream. The effort steals the last of my energy and I double over, my hands cupping my bare knees. *Inhale.*

I'm vaguely aware that everyone gathered around the grill has turned to look at me. I hear confused murmurs, but I don't have the oxygen left in my lungs to keep talking.

She's right behind me, I think.

I stumble forward a few more steps, wheezing hard. "Please . . . please . . ."

To my utter disappointment, no one is racing to call the cops or grab weapons. They're just *looking* at each other, frowning like they think I'm making stuff up. A few of them try out tentative smiles and nervous laughter. Do they think anyone would actually *joke* about this?

The crowd parts as a blond, white woman steps forward—a tiny, oddly shaped dog following at her heels. She doesn't look like someone who belongs in the woods. She's too chic, with sleek, iron-straight hair and the kind of makeup that's so tasteful you can hardly tell she's wearing it. There's not a single smear of dirt on her black clothes.

She's frowning at me. In a low voice, like she doesn't want to embarrass me, she says, "That's not funny. You're scaring people."

"Not . . . *joking.*" I'm still doubled over, breathing hard, and so my explanation comes out all jumbled and confused. "She's . . . she's . . . behind me . . . *arrows* . . ."

The energy coming off the crowd grows anxious. Someone calls out, "Who's behind you?"

And someone else answers, his voice light, still trying to make this a joke, "Is it the Witch of Lost Lake?"

This time, no one laughs.

In front of me, the blond woman's frown deepens. I expect her to get annoyed, tell me to knock it off, maybe.

Instead, she crouches beside me, her hand going to my back. "Shh, it's okay," she says, her hand moving in slow circles. "Just breathe."

I'd forgotten how nice it feels to be comforted. In the past year, the only person whose touched me like this has been my mother and, once or twice, Jack. I part my lips and air whooshes out. I can feel my heartbeat steady.

"Okay, Olivia," Blond Woman says, "now tell me what happened."

Olivia.

That was the other girl's name, the one who looked like me.

I glance over my shoulder, expecting to see the real Olivia burst out of the trees. But she doesn't. The trees are still, a slight breeze rippling through the branches, turning over the leaves. Light flashes in the low hanging clouds and a crow caws and leaps off a branch, making me flinch.

But no one comes.

My heart starts beating fast again, a new fear rippling through me.

Oh my God, where did she go?

"Olivia?" Blond Woman is saying. "Hey . . . can you talk now? Can you tell me what happened? Who was chasing you?"

I blink at her, too confused and freaked out and oxygen-deprived to make words come out of my mouth. She thinks I'm Olivia. Of course she thinks I'm Olivia. The other girl, the real Olivia, she looked like me and she's not here and why would anyone expect *two* Olivias to be wandering around in the woods for no obvious reason?

For long moments, I can't speak. This nice blond woman clearly knows the real Olivia, and she probably cares about her, and the real Olivia is back in the woods. With the witch.

And I left her. I just *left* her behind with a murderer. What kind of person does that?

"There-there was someone," I manage to blurt out. "She was wearing a black trench coat and a witch's mask, and she had a-a bow and arrow . . . she *shot* this other guy, the one with the purple hair and . . . he . . . he . . ."

"Sawyer?" Blond Woman says abruptly. "You saw someone shoot Sawyer?"

I nod.

She blinks twice. It's the only sign she gives that she's scared. "And you're sure it was real? He, she, whoever it was wasn't playing a trick on you?"

Am I sure? It looked real, but I don't know this Sawyer guy. Maybe he's an elaborate prankster who thinks this kind of thing is funny. Maybe all of this was supposed to be some sort of joke.

I'm staring down at my legs, at my fingers wrapped around my knees, and I'm about to straighten when I notice the spray of blood across my jeans. I start gasping again, coming dangerously close to hyperventilating. I remember the arrow shooting out of Sawyer's neck, the spray of blood, how he looked at me, desperate and scared, the strangled way he said *help*.

There's no way in hell that wasn't real.

"It was a real arrow," I tell Blond Woman, pointing at the stain on my jeans. "*This* is real, I'm sure."

Blond Woman looks at the blood spray, and I see the exact moment the truth registers in her brain. Her eyes widen, and the muscles in her throat tighten as she swallows.

"Okay," she says this quietly enough that I hear it, but I don't think anyone still gathered behind her does. "I believe you. Did you see who it was?"

"She was wearing a mask."

"Did you see anything that could help narrow it down?" When I don't answer right away, she adds, "Did you notice anything about her? Her height or general size, maybe? Her hair color? What shoes she was wearing?"

"I-I couldn't see her hair, and she was . . . average size, I guess? She wore a loose coat, so it's hard to tell and, I think . . . boots?" I think of the picture in my back pocket, the mysterious M. Edwards holding a bow and arrow, smiling at the camera.

I shiver, hard. I have no evidence that the woman in the witch costume is the same person. Out loud, all I say is, "She was using a bow and arrow. And was really good with it."

Blond Woman presses her lips together, looking like she's gearing up for something. "You know what to do in an emergency," she says in a low voice. "You need to try to stay calm so we can make sure everyone gets out of here safely. These other kids are going to be really freaked out and we don't want to cause a panic, so no more screaming, okay? We're going to tell them all that Sawyer got hurt, and that we need to get out of here before anyone else does, too."

I stare at her. I don't think she fully understands what's happening. Didn't she see the blood? People *should* be panicking. The Witch of Lost Lake is back. This isn't the time for single-file lines and keeping calm. "You don't understand, she had a bow and arrow, she-she . . ."

I grab Blond Woman's arm, and the tiny dog that had been waiting quietly at her feet releases a low warning growl. I look down and see that his eyes are fixed on me, his lips pulled back to display a row of sharp teeth.

I drop her arm, imagining those tiny, sharp teeth sinking into my skin.

The woman looks at the little dog, frowning. "Pickle . . . why are you growling at Olivia?"

I swallow, suddenly nervous. But, before I can get another word out, Blond Woman is straightening and ushering me into the largest of the cabins. "In," she says, firmly. Then, raising her voice, she adds, "You hear that, everyone? I want you all inside the cabin. *Now.*"

For the next fifteen minutes or so, my brain doesn't work the way it's supposed to. It keeps blinking in and out, so that everything seems to be happening out of order.

Someone's draping a blanket over my shoulders and asking

if I want a glass of water, and then someone else is pushing me into a small cabin along with all the other teenagers, and then Blond Woman is locking the door behind us, explaining in a calm voice—too calm, in my opinion—that Sawyer got hurt in the woods, and that we need to call an ambulance and quickly vacate the premises. She sends some kid called Eric out to the lighthouse to see if he can get cell service and call the cops.

"The landline in the office won't work," she reminds him. "It was cut sixteen years ago."

Outside, the sky grows darker. Rain begins hitting the windows.

Blond Woman's attempt at maintaining the peace doesn't work. The others are bombarding her with questions. *How did Sawyer get hurt?* and *Who was chasing Olivia?* and *Was it the Witch of Lost Lake; was it?* Some girl is crying, saying, "We shouldn't have come back here, Andie" over and over, which isn't helpful, but at least now I know Blond Woman's name. *Andie.*

"Everyone knows the Witch of Lost Lake doesn't want people here," the girl says when she catches me looking at her. "That's why she came back. She's punishing us."

I quickly look away. I hear my mother's name a few times, said in equal parts awe and disgust, and I immediately close my eyes, wanting to block it all out.

I can't stop picturing the woman I saw. And I'm pretty sure it was a woman, the shape of her body beneath that trench coat was slender and short. I think of the photograph tucked in my back pocket. *M. Edwards.*

Was that who I saw? The mysterious M. Edwards in the flesh, finally? There aren't many people in the world who know how to shoot a bow and arrow with that kind of accuracy. Did she come back, just like Jack said she would, to keep me from finding Gia's camera and learning the truth about what really happened that night?

I feel suddenly lightheaded. It's like there's not enough oxygen in this small, unventilated room. There are too many people and they're all breathing at the same time and there's not enough air to go around.

Panic attack. The word blazes neon in my head, a lit-up sign. I'm having a panic attack.

I sit on the edge of the cot and stick my head between my legs and take big, gulping breaths until my brain starts to clear.

Dimly, I realize that some girl is sitting next to me, squeezing my shoulder. It's the kind of thing you only do for someone you know well, and I have to resist the impulse to shrug her off of me. She probably knows Olivia. She probably thinks *I'm* Olivia.

I left Olivia in the woods, I think again, a fresh wave of guilt washing over me. And she's not the only one I left behind. I picture Jack in my mom's truck, probably playing his music too loud, drumming his palms on the steering wheel, waiting for me. Jack has no idea there's a murderer wandering around the trees. Jack could be her next target.

I can't stay here. I need to go back out there and find the real Olivia, and then I need to get back to my truck, back to Jack, and two of us need to get the hell out of here before M. Edwards comes back for round two.

I must look really freaked, because the girl who's been rubbing my back suddenly reaches out and squeezes my arm. "Hey, are you okay?"

She's very short, I notice, with brown, natural coils and freckly brown skin. I think I saw her earlier, right after we found the camera. Did anyone ever say her name? I can't remember.

"I'm fine," I say, shrugging her hand off me. Some emotion flashes across her face.

Hurt?

I push the flicker of concern I feel to the back of my head. I don't have time to worry about hurt feelings. I need to get out of here.

The cabin we're hunkered down in is bigger than a normal campers' cabin, one main room with several smaller rooms branching off, each holding a bed, a dresser, and a desk, everything covered in a layer of dust so thick you could write a haiku in it. There's also a tiny kitchenette and a stairway leading to a lower level. And across the room is a back door.

I stand and, as I do, I feel the photograph shift in my back pocket. It's a small feeling, the slightest crinkle, but it makes me pause, my heart beating in my ears.

M. Edwards worked here sixteen years ago. Sixteen years is a long time, but this is a small town. There's a chance someone in this room might remember her, that they would recognize her face if I showed them her photograph.

Gia's camera is long gone by now, lost somewhere in the woods with the real Olivia. But I can still figure out what the M stands for, I can google the woman in the photograph, maybe even figure out where she's been hiding.

I swallow and look again at the back door, thinking of Olivia and Jack. The longer I wait to leave, the more likely they'll get hurt. Am I really going to hang around here, playing detective?

My brain offers an immediate counterpoint: *Am I really going to leave now, when I'm so close to learning the truth?*

My need to know the truth wins out over my guilt. I'll just have to do this fast. I slide the picture out of my back pocket and turn to the girl who'd been touching me, trying my best to sound casual as I ask, "Can I show you something?" Before she can answer, I thrust the photograph of M. Edwards in front of her and say, "Do you recognize this woman?"

The girl frowns, taken aback. Her eyes flick down to the photograph, then back up to my face.

"Uh . . . yeah?" she says.

I was expecting a no, sure it couldn't possibly be this easy, and so it takes me a moment to process what she said. My heart gives a double thump inside my chest. "You do?"

The girl seems genuinely confused now. "Well . . . yeah, of course I do."

My fingers feel sweaty all of a sudden, the photograph slick to the touch. I breathe in, slowly, trying to steady my racing heart. "Okay. Can you tell me what the *M* on her name tag stands for?"

The girl pops an eyebrow. I have to fight the urge to grab her shoulders and shake, demanding she just spit it out already. After months of research, months of theorizing and wondering, I'm finally close to answers. I don't want to wait another second.

"It stands for . . . Miranda?" the girl says slowly.

Miranda? I blink at her, the wind knocked out of me. I've read through every piece of evidence in this case at least a dozen times and there was only one Miranda ever mentioned. "You mean like Miranda D'Angeli? The camp director?"

"Well, yeah," the girl says.

No, that can't be right. I look back down at the photograph, at the name Edwards emblazoned on her name tag. And, suddenly, it clicks.

Miranda had just gotten married. She must have changed her name. "Edwards was her maiden name?"

The girl's looking at me like I've told a joke and she's still waiting for the punchline. She's quiet for a long moment, and then she blinks and says the last thing on earth I expect her to say. "Olivia, come on, you know your mom's maiden name."

The Day of
the Murders

Gia went straight to Mrs. D'Angeli's office at Camp Lost Lake the next morning. The director's old key card was practically burning a hole through her pocket, scorching her upper thigh. It felt particularly scandalous that it was her *old* card, the one that still had her maiden name on it. What possible reason could *Matthew* have for dropping that? And after climbing out of her car?

"Can I help you, Miss North?" Matthew's mom, Lori, asked when Gia stepped through the door.

Gia hesitated. Lori had always made her nervous for reasons she could never quite pinpoint. The way she looked at her was strange. Her gaze was heavier than other people's, like it had a physical weight to it that Gia could feel on her skin, like touch.

"I'd . . . er, like to speak with Mrs. D'Angeli, please," Gia said, her voice overly polite. Most adults ate it up, but Lori only stared at her. It made Gia squirm.

"Mrs. D'Angeli's on the phone right now," Lori said. "Why don't you take a seat?"

Gia slunk down into a chair; arms crossed over her chest. Lori was still watching her. Gia squirmed again, suddenly wishing she wasn't sitting here, in this uncomfortable chair, in this over-air-conditioned office. She should've waited to come up here while Lori was at lunch. Mrs. D'Angeli was a total pushover. She loved talking about the history of Camp Lost Lake and the outdoors and the proper gear you needed for a hike. All Gia would've had to do was pretend she had a question about something out-doorsy, and Mrs. D'Angeli would've invited her right into her office. Then, she could've ambushed her with the key card when the two of them were alone, that way she might've gotten her full, honest reaction when she told her everything she'd pieced together.

I saw Matthew sneaking out of your car, she imagined herself saying. And just when Mrs. D'Angeli tried to deny it, Gia would whip the key card out of her pocket, her gotcha moment! *Are you missing this? Officer Knight told me it fell out of Matthew's pocket. What was* he *doing with* your *old key card?*

Gia felt giddy imagining it. It was so scandalous, the most vi-cious piece of gossip she'd ever uncovered. She bit back a smile. Soon, everyone in town would be talking about Miranda and Matthew. And they'd all know *she* was the one who found them out.

Gia was just starting to rise from her chair, planning some excuse for why she had to go, when the door to the inner office opened and Mrs. D'Angeli herself stepped out, a phone pressed to her ear.

Gia couldn't help but notice how pretty she looked. Pregnancy clearly agreed with her. It had left her blond hair thick and shiny, her skin clear, glowing, and she had the most adorable baby bump. She looked the way pregnant women look in movies.

"Yes, yes, I found it," Mrs. D'Angeli was saying into a cordless phone as she stepped into the main room. Something was off about her voice, but Gia couldn't exactly place what it was. Was she happy? Angry? It was impossible to tell. "I can't believe you didn't tell me this earlier, I had no—"

Gia dropped back down in her seat and leaned forward, craning to hear what she was talking about.

Unfortunately, that was the moment Mrs. D'Angeli seemed to register that she was sitting there. "Hold on," she murmured, glancing at Gia as she lowered the phone from her ear. "Gia, dear, what can I do for you?"

Gia couldn't stop staring at the phone. Who was she talking to? It couldn't be Matthew, could it? Her eyes flicked to Lori. Not with his mother *right there*.

"Oh, I . . . uh, just needed to ask you something," Gia blurted out. She smiled, a beat too late.

"I'll be back in a minute. Why don't you wait for me in my office?" And then she crossed the room, taking her phone call outside. "Are you here now? I can come and—" The door closed behind her before Gia could hear what she was planning to come and do.

"Go on," Lori said, nodding to Mrs. D'Angeli's office. Gia stood and shuffled into the room feeling that she would rather be following the camp director out to her car, listening in on the rest of that conversation. Did cordless phones even work in the parking lot? She had no idea.

Still, she wasn't about to let an opportunity to snoop through

Mrs. D'Angeli's private office slip through her fingers. As soon as the latch clicked closed behind her, Gia crossed the room to the desk and started yanking open drawers.

She was hoping for something good. Love notes from Matthew, perhaps. Dirty Polaroids. But all she found was an ultrasound, which wasn't scandalous at all considering everyone in town already knew that Mrs. D'Angeli was pregnant. Gia had seen plenty of her ultrasounds before, back at her dad's office. She even had one stuffed in the old lunch box where she hid all of the things she collected. She'd fished it out of the trash after one of Mrs. D'Angeli's appointments. She did that sometimes. Not just with ultrasounds but with lots of stuff, old homework and receipts and notes. You never knew what could be useful.

But something about this particular ultrasound was different than the others. Gia stared at it for a long moment, trying to put her finger on what it was, exactly. There was Mrs. D'Angeli's name, and the date, and—

And now Gia clamped a hand over her mouth, shocked, as the pieces slid together in her head.

Oh.

Suddenly everything made sense. The key card. The car. This ultrasound. Even the phone call. It was *obvious* what was happening here. Gia couldn't believe she hadn't put it together before.

This was too, *too* good.

9

Olivia

I don't know how long I've been hiding. There is only me, the barn door, and the pitchfork trembling in my hands.

A minute passes.

No one comes through the door.

My heartbeat begins to slow. I'm no longer shaky with adrenaline. Everything has gone still, even my breathing. I inhale. Exhale. Swallow.

The air in the barn is stale and warm. There's a sound in the woods on the other side of the thin plank walls: a soft rustle, followed by a light tapping. Rain.

My arms are getting tired from holding the pitchfork. It's heavier than I thought it would be, and the handle is all splintery. I tighten my grip and inch away from the wall.

I can't just hide out here all day, waiting for the witch to find me. I'm going to peek outside. Maybe she's not there. Maybe she ran in the opposite direction.

Quietly, I inch toward the door. I need to be brave. I take three quick, shallow breaths, trying to psych myself up. Then I reach for the door handle, swing it open, and peer out.

The woods are still. Trees surround me like dark sentries, their leaves shuddering softly. Rain spills through the branches, spotting the dirt ground with darker wet spots. Thunder rumbles somewhere in the distance.

My shoulders have just dropped away from my ears, relief falling over me like a blanket, when some deep, primitive instinct perceives a change:

Shuffling grass. A snapping twig. The soft, padded sound of footsteps.

Oh God, no. I shrink back into the barn doorway, my fingers tightening around the pitchfork. The faint noises grow more distinct. I hear a thump, the sound of someone swearing under his breath, the voice deep, like a man's. My breath has gotten shallow and loud again, my thoughts pinging wildly around inside my head.

I grab for the door, nearly dropping my pitchfork in my hurry to duck back inside, but a guy steps out from between the trees before I can get the door closed again. It's the same guy from earlier, the ridiculously attractive one who was looking for the Lost Lake murder site.

My body starts to relax—*I know him, it's fine*—which is totally stupid because, of course, I don't *know* him. I saw him once, and he was acting suspicious AF.

My eyes sweep over his body. He's taller than me, but not *tall*, and his shoulders are slender, his body thin. It's not impossible that he was the one dressed up in a witch's mask and black trench coat, shooting arrows just a few minutes ago. I can't rule him out.

I hold my pitchfork up a little higher and say, "Don't come any closer!"

"Reagan?" the guy frowns. He looks not at all concerned about my pitchfork. "What are you doing in there?"

Reagan? He thinks I'm that other girl, my look-alike.

But . . . but that means he's safe, right? Reagan was just as freaked out by the witch as I was.

My heartbeat starts racing again. I don't know who to trust.

Oh God oh God oh God . . .

"What's with the pitchfork?" the guy asks. And then, to my horror, he reaches out and *takes* it from me. It's that easy for him. He just plucks it out of my hands. I couldn't have made it any simpler if I'd handed it to him myself.

I hug my arms around my chest, trying not to completely lose it. "There was someone in the woods," I blurt, fear rushing my words. "She was wearing a mask and she . . . she killed Sawyer."

The guy tilts his head, that frown still on his lips. "Who's Sawyer?"

"He's-he's—who cares who he is?" I snap. I take a shaky breath, trying to calm myself enough to explain what happened. "Listen, there's someone out there, and I-I saw her kill someone. We need to call the cops!"

"*You* want to call the cops?" The guy looks deeply confused. He glances over his shoulder, like he expects whoever I'm talking about to suddenly appear from among the trees. "Where did she go?"

"I don't know!" I blurt, gasping. I'm seconds away from seriously losing my cool. I lean close to the guy and say, in a hushed whisper, "But we have to do something, run or-or something. We can't just wait around for her to come back!"

The guy is still looking over his shoulder, but he turns to me when I start talking, irritation clouding his face. "I told you this would happen," he says, his voice low. "I told you that if you tried to clear your mom's name, the real killer was going to come after you."

Time pauses. For a moment, I forget my fear. In fact, I forget everything that happened before the words "if you tried to clear your mom's name" came out of this guy's mouth.

"My-my *mom*?" I know I need to breathe, but I can't remember whether I've inhaled or exhaled last.

If you tried to clear *your mom's* name.

Why would Reagan be here, trying to clear her mom's name, unless . . .

"Is Lori Knight my *mom*?"

The mystery guy's forehead furrows, his eyebrows practically touching. "Are you feeling okay?"

I shiver, thinking *No, I'm definitely not feeling okay*. Instead, I say, "Please, just answer the question. Is Lori Knight my mom?"

The guy looks visibly confused now. "Why are you acting like you don't know who your mom is?" Which is basically the same as saying *yes*.

Lori Knight is Reagan's mom. And Reagan looks like me.

No, not just like me. *Exactly* like me.

Identical.

I think of the ultrasound I still have shoved in my pocket. The paternity test. The photo of Jacob Knight staring at my mother.

All this proof that my parents lied to me about who they are. Who *I* am.

One of my favorite mathematical concepts is called Occam's razor, which says that, among competing hypotheses, the one with the fewest assumptions is probably correct.

In other words, it might be *possible* that I have an identical doppelgänger who I just happened to run into on my family's campgrounds, on the same day I learned that my mom lied about who my father was and, possibly, when I was born. It could just be random. A coincidence. One of the many mysteries of a chaotic universe.

But the simpler explanation is that Reagan and I look alike because we're sisters.

Twins.

But Lori Knight isn't my mom, I think. I need this to be true. My dad might not be my dad, but my mom *has* to be my mom. And I have proof, I did the DNA test.

And then the bottom drops out of my stomach as something horrible occurs to me: I never tested mom's DNA. I sent *my* DNA sample into the ancestry place, and then I did a paternity test to see whether my dad was actually my dad. But I never even considered doing a maternity test. It never occurred to me that my mom might not be my mom.

I raise a hand to my mouth, trembling now. If the ultrasound I found is real, if my mom was only eighteen weeks pregnant on the night I was born, then she *can't* be my mom. It wouldn't be possible.

After a moment the guy frowns and says something, but I don't hear what it is. I can't hear anything over the buzzing in my ears, the sound of blood pounding in my temples. I don't know who my real parents are. Which means I don't know who *I* am. Everything I thought I knew about myself was based on a lie.

"Reagan!" the guy says, loud enough that I finally jerk my head toward him, blinking. I look at him, *really* look at him, like if I stare for long enough, I might be able to see past his skin and eyes and skull, all the way to the squishy pink center of his brain.

He's still holding my pitchfork, I realize.

Why is he holding my pitchfork?

My surroundings slam back into focus, everything louder and closer than it felt a moment ago. I'm alone, in the middle of the woods, in a dark, abandoned barn. The only person who knows where I am is this stranger, this stranger who just admitted to knowing Lori Knight. As in, serial killer Lori Knight. Witch of Lost Lake Lori Knight.

And I just saw someone murdered. I was *just* running for my life through the woods.

What the hell am I still doing here?

"We have to call the police," I blurt. I'm still staring at that pitchfork, imagining those sharp prongs sliding through my chest, piercing my lungs, my heart. I swallow and force my eyes back to the guy's face. "Do you have a phone?"

Mine is back on the porch where we were all cleaning, along with my bag and the rest of my things.

"Yeah," the guy says. "But it's not going to work out here. The only place with cell service is—"

"The top of the lighthouse," I finish for him, remembering. "Right. I knew that."

"The truck's not too far," the guy says. "We can head back there and drive around to the other side of the woods. I think service is less spotty around there."

He moves toward the door, taking it for granted that I'll follow him. I swallow. I don't want to be a total bitch, but getting into a truck with someone I don't know when there's a murderer on the loose seems like a wildly bad idea. But my only other options are to either stay hidden in the barn or make my way back through the woods by myself. And I'm not loving either of those.

The guy holds the barn door open for me, standing aside to let me take the first step into the woods. I want to insist that he walk out first, so I can keep an eye on him, but I really don't want to piss him off. He's still holding that pitchfork. I walk ahead hesitantly, so nervous I feel like I might pee. He's behind me, now. Every inch of my skin hums.

Please don't be the murderer, I think. *Please don't kill me.*

Rain hits my arms and the top of my head. It seems dumb to head for the dirt path, so instead I cut to the left to walk through the tall grass and trees. I move fast, wanting to leave this guy behind. He doesn't seem to notice. He's walking more carefully, checking behind us every few feet to make sure no one's following.

It's impossible to see the ground, but the earth is soft beneath my feet, and it feels sodden and muddy from the rain. I speed up a little more, considering breaking into a run . . .

I can't have gone more than three feet before my foot catches on something beneath the grass, and then I'm falling, the ground slapping me in the face, grass and mud filling my mouth, pain everywhere.

"Reagan!" the guy shouts, and I hear his footsteps crashing through the brush behind me. I glance over my shoulder to see what I just tripped over—and all the air leaves my lungs.

The thing half-hidden in the grass, it's not a thing.

It's a body.

It's *Eric Weisel's* body.

Eric is gazing up at the sky, unblinking. The tall grass hid him from view while I was walking toward him, but from this angle his body is clearly visible, his limp arm and leg mashing down the grass around him, his head jerked at an awkward angle, dirt smeared across his pale cheek. His lips are slightly open but they're not red anymore. They're a strange, sickly color that reminds me of meat gone bad. Purple and brown and blue bruises circle his neck, shaped like fingers pressing into his skin.

He's been *strangled*.

I . . . I think I'm going to be sick. I bring my hands to my mouth, breathing hard against my fingers. I've known Eric Weisel since we were both about five years old. He can't be dead. I was *just* talking to him. He was playing with that stupid badminton set, hitting the birdie all over, forcing people to jump out of the way of his ridiculously long arms. We were talking about sunscreen. This *can't* be happening.

That guy is right behind me now. I flinch when I see him, heartbeat slamming against my ribs.

"Reagan, what—" Like me, he didn't notice Eric while he was walking toward me, but once he reaches my side, his eyes slide from my face to the dead body lying in the grass. He jerks backward. *"Shit."*

I reach for Eric's neck, stomach churning as I press the pad of my finger to the skin just below his ear. It's not warm anymore. That realization sends horror squirming through my body, but I keep my finger where it is, just in case. His skin could be cold because of the rain. He could still be okay. For the rest of my life, I'll never forgive myself if I leave him here. Not unless I'm sure that he's . . . gone.

The rain was coming down hard for a second, thick sheets that immediately soaked my clothes and plastered my hair to my skull. It's slowed to a drizzle, but I still feel it in my sneakers and soaking through my shorts. Goose bumps have sprouted up my legs. I want to be back in the cabin with my friends, wrapped in a blanket and waiting for the cops to finally show up. But I stay where I am, fingers pressed to Eric's neck.

There's no pulse. There's nothing. He's dead.

I jerk away and double over, heaving. A shadow falls over me as the guy leans closer, making sure I'm okay.

I feel suddenly cold. This guy looked surprised to see the body. But he could've been faking. I don't know him. All I do know is he's the only other person I've seen in the woods, that he found me moments after the killer left, that Eric is lying on the ground in front of us, dead.

He's slender enough to have been the person wearing a witch mask and chasing me. He knows Lori Knight. And he certainly looks strong enough to have strangled someone.

I don't care about being nice anymore. Nice girls die in situations like this. I stumble to my feet, backing away from him. "Get-get away from me."

He looks at me and his eyebrows come together, creasing the skin of his forehead. "What?"

"Please." I need another weapon. Making sure not to take my eyes off this guy, I quickly kneel and snatch a stick from the forest floor. It's not long, but it's thicker around than my wrist and I think I could do some real damage if I put some muscle into it. I hold it in front of me in an attempt to ward him off. "Please . . . don't come any closer."

The guy's still frowning but, to his credit, he lifts both his hands over his head. He's still holding the pitchfork, but it doesn't seem to occur to him to use it to ward off my pathetic stick.

"Reagan," he says, his voice very calm, "what's—"

"I'm not Reagan," I blurt out. It seems silly to keep up this charade now. "And I don't know who you are, but if you come any closer I-I'm going to hit you with this, so just back off, okay?" I swing at him with my stick. It's such a pathetic attempt at defending myself that, if this were a movie, I'd be groaning and rooting for me to die.

The guy looks really confused. "What?"

"*Don't* follow me," I warn.

And then, unsure of what else to do or how else to get away, I turn and dash into the woods.

10

Reagan

M. Edwards is Miranda D'Angeli. Miranda is Olivia's mother.

And Olivia . . .

Olivia looks just like me.

All this means something. These new facts, they're like puzzle pieces, each showing a tiny slice of what happened the night of the massacre. If I can be smart and figure out how the pieces fit together, then I'll finally see the whole picture.

I let my breath out in a slow trickle thinking, *Okay, time to be smart.*

What do I know?

I know the story everyone knows: that my mom found out Jacob Knight, my dad, was cheating on her, and killed him in a fit of rage and jealousy. And yeah, I guess I thought it was a little strange that no one seemed to know who he'd been cheating *with* or even how my mom found out he'd been cheating in the first place, but that was the story.

Sixteen years ago, Miranda was a newlywed. She was pregnant the night of the murders, she gave birth moments after Gia's death—to Olivia, apparently. And now I've met Olivia, and I know she's my exact age, with my exact face.

If Jacob had been cheating with Miranda, if he'd gotten her pregnant at the same time my mom was pregnant, would that explain why Olivia and I look so much alike? Because we're half sisters, born the same year, with the same father and two different mothers?

I frown as I turn this theory over in my head, realizing it can't possibly be the truth. I've never seen sisters that look as much alike as Olivia and I do, even sisters with the same mother *and* father. What we are is something else.

Twins.

I close my eyes, feeling suddenly dizzy. That would mean at least one of our mothers is not actually our mother. One of them stole one of us. Pretended we were hers. It's like a really messed-up fairy tale.

And, speaking of fairy tales, there's the witch, the masked woman who chased us through the trees. A new killer? Or the old killer returning to . . . what? Why would the old killer come out of hiding sixteen years after getting away with murder?

I don't want to think about this anymore. I force my brain to move on to another topic, another clue: the key card, issued to Miranda Edwards. It's not exactly the smoking gun I'd hoped it would be. But the records show that Miranda had been using her *Miranda D'Angeli* key card the morning of the murders. She swiped into buildings all over camp. So why would another of her key cards be found just a few feet away from where Gia was murdered?

I shiver in my flannel, even though it's warm in here. For the first time since I heard the podcast a year ago, I can almost picture it: my mom finding out about her husband's betrayal, about the twins he was having with another woman. I imagine her killing him in a fit of rage. And after, when she realized what she'd done, going after Gia, the one girl who'd seen her, who had proof.

But would she actually kidnap me? Pretend I was her daughter?

All those times she told me I was her second chance, her fresh start, was this what she meant? Did she take me as a messed-up replacement for Matthew? Her way to be a mother again?

I squeeze my eyes shut, every nerve inside my body screaming *no*. That can't be what happened. Even if I were to accept that my mom killed my dad, that she kidnapped me, I could never believe that she'd kill Matthew, her own *son*. She's always told me that becoming a mother was the best thing she'd ever done with her life. She wouldn't have hurt her own child, no matter what. It doesn't make sense.

And it doesn't explain who's here now, today, killing that boy in the lodge, chasing me through the woods. Even if Mom had hopped on a bus the *second* she saw that I was gone to get here in time, she never would've been able to shoot a bow and arrow, not with her arthritis.

There has to be something I'm missing.

The lights in the cabin suddenly blink out. A girl shrieks and drops something. A boy laughs nervously. Outside, thunder rumbles like a car engine.

A moment later, the lights turn back on again. Everyone looks a shade paler than they did a second ago. Anxious murmurs erupt around the room. I look around for Andie, since she seems to be in charge, but she ran out to look for Eric a few minutes ago and hasn't returned yet.

I exhale, shakily. Maybe Jack and my mom were right, maybe I don't really want to know the truth about what happened that night.

Maybe I just need to get out of here.

Over the last year, I've learned that no one pays attention to you if you move confidently, if you look like you're doing what you're supposed to be doing. So I don't creep or duck my head, but walk across the room with my chin high, easily meeting people's eyes as I pass. Hardly anyone even notices me. They're all talking over each other, their voices anxious, rushed.

"This is a joke," I hear a tall boy with dark brown skin say. "Sawyer's just messing with us."

"But didn't you see the blood on her jeans?" a girl with long red hair whispers back.

Everyone's distracted. None of them are looking at me, and so no one notices me cross the room and casually pull the back door open.

I exhale as soon as I step outside, thinking I'm home free. I carefully ease the door closed behind me—

And the back of the door leaps out at me, knocking the wind from my chest. Someone's written a message on it, carved it into the wood in thin, spiky letters:

I KNOW WHO YOU ARE, it reads. LEAVE NOW, OR THEY ALL DIE.

My mouth goes dry. My legs, my hands, everything starts to shake. Those letters, they look like they were carved into the wood with an arrowhead. The sound of the rain must've masked the scratching sounds, because the words look fresh. There are still splinters clinging to all the lines.

The witch followed me here.

I take a single, trembling step toward the trees, breathing hard. And then I stop, fear roaring up inside me. I should go back. I was safe in there. You don't leave the group when there's a killer on the loose. Everyone knows that.

But . . .

Leave now or they all die.

How can I go back into the cabin without putting everyone else at risk? And Jack and Olivia, they're both still out in the woods, alone.

Something touches the top of my head. I scream and whirl around—

It's the rain. It's been drizzling off and on for the last hour or so, and it's starting to come down heavier again. I watch as the dark clouds open up, water pouring from the sky in sheets, soaking through my clothes, leaving the ground below my shoes tacky with fresh mud.

I don't know what to do. I can't go back to the truck—what if the witch follows me? What if I put Jack in danger? But I can't stay in this clearing, either. I'm an easy target here.

It turns out I don't actually have to make that decision because, when I turn back to the cabin, the witch is standing between me and the door, blocking my way back, her face still hidden behind that hideous mask. She's watching me with her head cocked, amused. She holds the bow loosely in one hand, the quiver of arrows still strapped to her back.

I stumble backward. My shoe slips in the mud and then I'm down, scrambling to regain my balance.

She doesn't come toward me. Instead, she calmly removes an arrow from the quiver.

No no no.

I grasp around, desperate and shaky, fear blotting out every other thought in my brain.

The witch slides the arrow into the bow, taking her time to

make sure everything's lined up right. She lifts the bow in front of her, one arm pulling back—

My fingers brush up against something hard and wet: a rock. I grab it and cock my arm back, knowing I don't have enough time to aim or think. I just throw—

The rock connects with the witch's wrist. She swears and drops the bow.

Thank God.

I pull my legs beneath me and run for the trees.

The rain's coming down hard, pounding against my back and shoulders, making it impossible to go very fast without risking another fall. I won't be able to outrun her, not in the mud like this. I need to find someplace to hide.

I break into the trees, my eyes skating over tall grass, overgrown bushes, branches—and then landing on an old footbridge. It can't be more than three or four feet across, just long enough to arc over a rocky creek. No one would think to look for me under there.

I don't dare glance behind me to see if she's still coming—there's no time. I trudge through the mud as quickly as I can, gasping for breath.

The bridge looks like it's been out of commission for a while. It's half-collapsed, one entire side leaning into the creek. I don't have time to worry about whether it's dangerous. I drop to my belly in the mud and slither underneath. Rocks poke through my shirt, digging into my skin. The muddy creek water quickly soaks my clothes, so cold it makes my teeth chatter. I grit my jaw. And wait.

The rain falls harder, making the creek rise. Water laps against my throat, my cheeks. It's soaked through all my clothes. My skin has gone numb. I press my lips together to control my breathing. Tears gather in the corners of my eyes. My chest quakes with sobs I'm trying desperately to hold back.

Please . . . please . . .

I don't know how long I've been hiding when I hear a footstep. It's quiet, the sound of a shoe brushing the dirt path.

I lift a hand from out of the water and press it to my mouth to muffle my breathing. My heartbeat is picking back up again, pounding like a drum in my throat, making it impossible to focus on anything happening outside my body.

Then, a snapping twig, the sound of an exhale. Someone steps into the creek, their foot causing water to splash onto my face. I bite back a scream as a shadow falls over me. The figure kneels to peer beneath the bridge, dark eyes zeroing in on mine.

I shriek, the sound strangled and loud and desperate, softened by my hand.

It's not the witch; it's the girl with the curly brown hair and freckly skin. She's crouching, her head tilted, examining me like something doesn't quite add up.

"Don't get me wrong, I'm very curious about why you're under the bridge," she says. "But mostly, I want to know why you're pretending to be Olivia."

"You," I erupt, gasping. Relief pours through my body like icy water. "Oh my God, it's just you." I crawl out from beneath the bridge on my stomach, cringing as more icy water and mud make their way into my shirt and jeans. The rain has stopped, but the sky is still gray and low, and the clouds look like they could open back up again at any moment. Thunder rumbles somewhere in the distance.

When I'm most of the way out, the girl grabs hold of my hand and pulls me to my feet. She opens her mouth to say something, but I press my hand to her lips, stopping her.

The witch was *just* here. I want to believe she circled back to the cabins or disappeared deeper into the woods when she couldn't find me, but she could still be close. Waiting behind a tree. Ducked down in the shadows. Watching for me to come out of hiding.

The girl blinks at me but says nothing. Her breath is soft and warm against my fingers. I lower my hand, and she stays perfectly still as I scan the trees around us for movement.

A long minute passes. I watch the wind blow through the branches, shaking the leaves, the sound a cold shiver. Those heavy clouds completely block out the sun. It feels like night, even though I think it's still the early evening.

I squint into the darkness, but nothing moves. I know that doesn't mean the witch is gone, but if she was still hiding, wouldn't she have shot at us by now?

"Okay," I say. My voice is low, practically a whisper. "I think she's gone . . ."

I trail off, realizing I still have no idea what this girl's name is.

"Hazel," the girl says, speaking just as quietly as I am. "I'm the real Olivia's best friend. Are you going to tell me who you are and why you're pretending to be her?"

I don't have time to explain my actions to some girl I barely know, not with the witch still lurking close by. I turn, willing my legs to move.

"Hey!" the girl calls in a loud whisper. "Where are you going?"

She hurries after me, but her legs are much shorter than mine, and she has to jog a little to keep up.

"Away," I tell her.

"You can't just *walk away* from me."

"There's a killer out here, in case you've forgotten. I'm not going to hang around here, thanks."

"Then let's go back to the cabin."

I glance at her. "I just left the cabin. Why would I go back?"

"Because it's safer, it's smarter, there are people there, and people can protect you—"

"Yeah? And you know that for sure?"

This seems to throw her. She frowns, searching around for a response for a moment before sputtering, "*Yes!*"

"As convincing as that was, I'm going to stick with my original plan."

She makes a face. "That sarcasm thing you're doing right now? That was my first clue that you aren't the real Olivia. Olivia isn't so—"

A sharp crack cuts her off.

A branch snaps.

We both go silent.

Lightning flashes behind the heavy clouds, the sight oddly eerie. My breath is ragged in my throat. I picture the murderer watching us, aiming an arrow, preparing to take her shot.

Hazel's beside me, not moving, and I know I shouldn't move, either, but I can't help it. I need to feel connected to another human being. I don't want to be alone when I die. I reach for her hand and squeeze. I can feel her heartbeat flickering in her palm, hummingbird fast.

She weaves her fingers through mine, squeezing back.

We stay like that for several long seconds, silently holding hands, waiting. And then a bird leaps from a tree directly above us. The wind must've been pretty strong because, as soon as the bird leaves the tree, the branch it had been perched on tumbles through the brush, to the ground.

I watch the branch crash to the ground, and slowly, slowly, my breath returns to normal.

It was just a bird and a broken tree branch. That's what we heard. Not the witch.

I'm still holding Hazel's hand. It feels strange now that I know we're not about to die, too intimate. I wait for her to pull away. She doesn't. Instead, she looks at me, head tilted, like I'm a puzzle she can't quite figure out.

I jerk my hand out of hers and hug my arms around myself, nerves creeping all over my skin.

Hazel exhales, and, in a much quieter voice, she says, "Where's Olivia?"

I press my lips together, not saying anything. I don't want to tell this girl that I left her friend alone in the woods with a killer. But I can't lie to her, either.

After a moment, I say, "Olivia and I split up when the killer started chasing us. Last I saw her, she was running through the woods." I nod back toward the lodge. "She went that way."

"Okay," Hazel says, releasing a breath through her teeth. "Okay, so we need to go back to the cabin right now and wait for Andie to come back. She'll want to know her sister's still out here. She'll know what to do."

I shake my head. "I can't go back there. I left a friend back in my truck. He doesn't know about the . . ."

I trail off. Hazel is adjusting her glasses, and there's a smear of something on her wrist. I blink, studying it. It's a brownish, reddish streak. If I didn't know any better, I'd say it looks like . . .

Blood.

My entire body goes cold.

Hazel has blood on her wrist.

The events of the last hour spin around in my head. I remember finding a rock, throwing it at the witch, hitting her on the wrist.

Could the witch have been *Hazel*?

Now that I think about it, it's kind of a giant leap to assume there's another person in the world who looks exactly like your best friend. So how did she know? How could she have guessed that I wasn't who I said I was?

She could've seen us together. If Hazel saw me and the real Olivia standing next to each other, she'd obviously know there were two of us, that there was a possibility I was lying about my identity. But there are only two people in the entire world who've *ever* seen me and Olivia together. One of them is dead.

The other one's the witch.

I'm still staring at the smear of blood on Hazel's wrist. Suddenly, all I care about is getting away from her, getting away from this place.

I turn and run, my sneakers kicking up mud, my arms pumping wildly, wanting to put as much space as possible between me and this girl.

I take three steps, four, and the next time my foot hits the earth, a sound like metal scraping against metal fills my ears. Something snaps.

I feel the pain in every part of my body at the same time.

My vision blinks out. I forget to breathe. There's nothing but pain. Thick, nauseating pain that wraps around my ankle like a vise and won't let go. Pain that I feel in every nerve of my body, traveling through my skin and down to my bones, racing up my veins, making my stomach churn. I sway on my feet.

My eyesight comes back, but my vision is still blurry. I blink a few times, then look down.

The first thing I see is blood. So much blood. It's slashed up my leg and glistening over the glinting metal teeth that have clamped down around my ankle. A bear trap.

I've stepped into a bear trap.

The Night of the Murders

Now that Gia knew what she knew, she couldn't just sit around and do nothing about it. Not for a story this big. This was the sort of story that would really put her on the map, gossip-wise. Everyone in school would be talking about it over the next few weeks, whether she was the person who broke it or not. And she really wanted to be the person who broke it.

But in order to do that, she needed something more concrete than the clues and hunches she already had. She needed solid evidence. Preferably on tape.

Which was why she was staking out Matthew's house.

Gia slouched low in her seat, hoping it was dark enough that no one would notice her car. She'd parked on the other side of the street and down the block, but not *too* far down the block because, much to her dismay, she did not currently own a pair of binoculars. She worried that, if she parked any farther away, she might mistake Jacob for Matthew and follow the wrong Knight. She was wearing all black, down to the black stocking hat she'd stolen from her dad, and she was drinking coffee, even though she hated coffee, just in case she had to stay up all night. She'd even thought ahead, making up a story about staying over at a friend's house so her parents wouldn't be wondering where she was.

She didn't think she'd get lucky enough to see something happen tonight. That was fine. She was in this for the long haul. She was planning to follow Matthew around for the next few days, next few weeks, even. She would stake out his house every night, for as long as it took to catch something on film. She wasn't totally sure how she was going to get this past her parents, but she would figure something out.

Luckily for her, it only took about an hour and a half.

Matthew didn't even sneak out his window like she'd expected him to. He walked right out the front door, climbed into his dad's Jeep, and turned on the engine.

Gia's breath caught. She waited until his car was at the bottom of the street. Then she turned her engine on and followed him.

For the first ten minutes that she trailed him, Gia expected Matthew to go somewhere boring, like the Lost Lake Diner or one of his friend's houses or the movie theater down in Auburn. It wasn't until he turned off the main highway and onto the little dirt road that led to the campgrounds that her heart started beating a little faster.

There was absolutely no good reason for Matthew to be going to the campgrounds at this hour. He'd never been a counselor like she had been, and even if he had, camp didn't officially open for another two weeks. No one would even be there.

"Maybe he's picking up one of his parents," Gia whispered out loud to the otherwise empty car. It was just after seven, not too late, and Matthew's parents both worked at camp. Lori as Mrs. D'Angeli's assistant and Jacob as the archery instructor. Unlike the counselors, they'd all started working at the camp already, to get things set up for the summer. It was plausible that Matthew was just swinging by to pick one of them up.

But Matthew didn't drive over to the main office or the archery range. Instead, he cut down a side road that skirted the edge of the camp and drove right up to the old lighthouse.

Gia's heart beat faster. The lighthouse was off-limits even to campers and staff. It was incredibly dangerous. The stairs leading to the top were all old, rotten, and a few of the windows were broken. No one was supposed to go up there.

Matthew had parked his car right under the lighthouse and climbed out. Gia watched him duck into the lighthouse door, and then she looked up, to the little glass-enclosed room at the very top of the tower, catching her breath when she saw a shadow move beyond the windows.

Someone was already up there, waiting for him.

This was it—the story Gia had been waiting for. She pulled out her camera and pressed RECORD.

She didn't know then, but it would be the last video she ever made.

11

Olivia

I spot the glint of metal nestled in the long grass a fraction of a
second before Reagan's foot hits the ground. I open my mouth to
scream, to warn her—

I'm too late. The jaws snap around Reagan's ankle with a sick-
ening *crack*. I'm looking right at her when it happens, so I see the
exact moment the pain hits. Her pupils dilate fast and the blood
drains from her lips, her face going blank and distant.

I can practically feel the metal driving into my own skin, my
ankle bones crunching, the metal teeth ripping through muscle.

Oh God.

Reagan begins to howl. It's a horrifying sound, the scream of
an animal, not a person. Tears spring to my eyes.

I have to help her. I scramble across the clearing and drop to
my knees.

"Oh my God," I mutter, examining the bear trap. It's horrifying. The metal is thicker than my fingers, with teeth that remind
me of vicious animals I've seen on nature documentaries, a wolf,
maybe, or a shark. "Can you move?"

Reagan looks at me like I've just asked her if she knows how to say "Where is the bathroom?" in Russian. The bear trap is closed tight around her ankle. If she hadn't been wearing a pair of thick Doc Marten boots, I think it might've snapped right through her bone.

I lift a hand to my mouth. I can taste vomit at the back of my throat, and it takes all my willpower to swallow it back down. The long, metal teeth of the trap are slick with blood, but at least her foot looks like it's still intact.

Reagan stops howling for the length of one inhale. "*Help*," she gasps, desperate. "Please . . . *help*."

My heart lurches. I wedge my fingers into the trap, being careful to avoid the massive, sharp teeth, and grit my jaw together and *pull*. I feel the exertion all through my arms, vibrating in my muscles, tightening my shoulders. It's the most strength I've ever used on anything in my life, and yet the teeth don't budge.

Dimly, I realize Hazel's here, hovering over us, saying something I can't focus on. Where did she even come from? And is she offering to help? I'm not sure what she thinks she'll be able to do in this situation. I pull harder, *harder*, and then I let go, gasping. "I'm sorry, I don't think I'm strong enough."

Reagan releases a sharp breath. There are tears in her eyes. Empathy worms through me. I have the urge to hug this girl, or hold her hand, anything to make her feel slightly less afraid.

"I'm going to die," Reagan chokes out, her voice so like my voice that it makes me shiver. "I'm going to—"

"You're *not* going to die," I say, cutting her off. "We're going to get you out of here. Just hold on, let me try again."

I've just managed to wedge my fingers between the metal for the second time when I hear a crash in the trees behind us, the sound of someone moving through the woods, fast.

It's the witch, this was a trap—

I tense as the strange, hot guy from the barn stumbles out of the trees. He sees me and Reagan together and does a double take that might've been funny in any other situation.

"Holy shit! *Reagan?*" He's still staring at my face, but at least he doesn't waste time asking for an explanation. Instead, he drops to the ground beside us. "Here, let me."

He leans past me, wedging his own fingers into the bear trap. I'm about to tell him that it's impossible, that the damn thing absolutely will not move, when—

Oh.

The muscles along his shoulders and neck visibly tense beneath his shirt, arms bulging beneath rolled-up sleeves as he grunts, *pulls.* I stare at him. Okay, *gawk* might be a more accurate word. I can't help it. This is very . . . manly.

Sweat beads along his forehead. His sleeves strain against his arms. I'm not kidding, they actually *strain*, as in the fabric gets all tight around his muscles, and the thread in the seams goes taut in a way I've never seen happen outside of a movie starring, like, the Rock.

I glance back down at the teeth, watching them inch apart, just a sliver at first, and then wider. I have no idea how he's doing this, how strong he must be to force that bear trap open. When I tried, all I accomplished was a pulled muscle in my shoulder. How is he real?

Finally, there's a gap of space big enough for Reagan's foot. She twists her body free, and the guy lets the bear trap crash closed again.

The sound of metal on metal snaps me back to my body. I look away from the strange guy, suddenly remembering the events of the last hour. The witch. The pitchfork. Lori Knight.

I push myself to my feet, grasping for Hazel's arm. "We have to get away from them!"

Reagan looks at me like I've lost my mind. *"What?"* Her eyes move from me to Hazel and she points. *"She's* the one who had blood on her arm."

Frowning, Hazel studies her arm. There *is* a faint streak of blood on her wrist.

"I swatted a mosquito," she explains.

"He ran out of the trees right after the murderer chased me into a barn," I say, gesturing toward the guy as he rips a length of fabric off the bottom of his T-shirt, revealing a strip of sweaty torso. It takes me a second longer than it should to avert my eyes. "Right after I found another body," I say. Turning to Hazel, I add, "Eric."

"Oh my God," she mutters, pressing a hand to her mouth.

I keep going. "And *he* was right there, being suspicious and . . . and weird."

"I'm sorry, *I* was being weird?" the guy says.

"Jack's my best friend in the world," Reagan explains. "He didn't kill anyone."

I round on Reagan. "And how am I supposed to trust *you*? He told me the Witch of Lost Lake is your *mom.*"

"Now you think *I'm* the killer? Really?" Regan gestures to the bear trap. "You think I did this to myself?"

She winces, and I stop arguing for long enough to see that the guy—Jack—is knotting the strip of fabric he tore off his shirt around her ankle. His movements are fast and confident, like bandaging someone's ankle after she accidentally stepped into a bear trap is something he's had to do more than once in his life. It's pretty suspicious, if you ask me. But, to be fair, also hot.

I swallow and tear my eyes away from him, feeling my cheeks burn. *Focus, Olivia.* "Hazel's *my* best friend in the world, and *she* didn't kill anyone, either."

"You expect me to just take your word for it?" Reagan asks.

"No, but if you looked at her for two seconds you might realize that the bow we saw the witch using is bigger than she is."

"Guys," Jack says, interrupting us. "This argument is super interesting and all, but Reagan's ankle is in bad shape. She needs medical attention. We need to find a phone and call the cops."

We're all quiet for a moment, understanding that he's right. The only thing that matters right now is getting Reagan help.

"The lighthouse," I start, but Hazel's already shaking her head.

"The lighthouse is all the way across camp, and there's only service at the very top." She looks at Reagan. "Can you even walk?"

"I-I don't know." Regan's face has gone pale and green, and there's a thin sheen of sweat clinging to her skin. Whatever Jack did with that bandage seems to have helped because her injured foot no longer looks like an empty sock. She tries to maneuver her legs underneath her body, cringing.

I can tell, immediately, that it's not going to work. Her face closes down, and she releases another terrible, strangled cry. "No, I-I don't think I can."

"We shouldn't move her, anyway," I say. "You aren't supposed to move someone who's been injured."

Reagan scowls at me. "According to what?"

"Every single first-aid class ever."

"Yeah? Was there a section on running from a killer in these classes?"

I frown. "No—"

"You should listen to her," Hazel says. "She used to babysit back in junior high, and I'm pretty sure she took that online Red Cross training course like four times."

Reagan, still grimacing in pain, says, "So, are you like a real-life Kristy Thomas?"

"I don't know who that is," I say.

"From The Baby-Sitters Club," Jack adds.

All three of us look at him.

"What?" He shrugs.

"Guys," Hazel says, cutting him off. "Focus. We need to get to a phone."

Jack pulls his cell out of his pocket and frowns down at the screen. "We have service back home. It's around the other side of the mountain, but Reagan's truck is just through the trees. We can drive—"

"I'm not making it back to the truck like this," Reagan says. "Maybe you can go and come back for me?"

Jack shakes his head. "There's no way I'm leaving you alone in the woods with a murderer—"

"The old nurse's cabin!" I blurt, recalling the map in our bathroom back home. Everyone turns to me, matching looks of confusion on their faces.

"Sorry, I just remembered. There's an old nurse's cabin right through there." I nod toward the trees. "It's close, and I bet there's still bandages, antiseptic, maybe even some crutches she can borrow."

"I don't know." Jack looks skeptical. "I think it's smarter to find a phone."

Phone. I nearly slap my head with my palm. I can't believe I didn't think of this before. "My sister said the internet guys were supposed to come this morning," I explain. "Since the service out here is so spotty, she got one of those phone and internet package deals. They used to have landlines in some of these old buildings. If the nurse's cabin is anything like the lodge or my mom's old office, there's probably still one there."

"Landline," Hazel says, with a groan. "Right, didn't Andie send Eric out to find one? Because the witch cut the landline in the office sixteen years ago?"

Reagan looks skeptical. "You don't think she would've thought to cut the line in the nurse's cabin?"

"I don't know, but I still think it's the best plan. If it works, we can call the cops and, if it doesn't, we can get Reagan bandaged up and find your car and get the hell out of here." I shiver. It's started to sprinkle again. Thunder makes the ground vibrate, feeling much closer than it was a few minutes ago, and cold rain hits the back of my neck. If we stay here longer, we'll never get dry. "What do you think?"

One by one, Jack, Reagan, and Hazel all nod.

"I still don't think Regan should move her leg," I say. Turning back to Jack, I add, "Can you . . . do you think you can carry her?"

Jack lifts Reagan off the ground like she weighs nothing, like she's a baby or a doll or a really small dog. If I was the kind of girl who got off on fairy-tale princesses being saved from danger by rugged woodsmen types, this would really be doing it for me right now. It's still kind of doing it for me, to be honest. For a moment I can't speak.

"Lead the way," Jack says.

12

Reagan

I barely notice the squat, two-room building when it appears between the trees. It's so overgrown with weeds and vines that it looks like part of the woods. And the pain in my ankle is all-consuming. I don't think I've broken anything, but there's a goose egg forming below my skin.

I squeeze my eyes shut and take long, deep breaths through my mouth. It's taking everything I have not to throw up.

"Are you okay?" Jack asks.

"Yeah . . ." I manage. "It just *hurts*."

"Hopefully we can find some painkillers in this nurse's cabin."

I nod as Olivia hurries ahead of us to try the door. "Oh no," she says, her face falling. "It's locked."

For a second, the only thing I hear in my head is the slightly muted sound of screaming. *Of course* it's locked. Why wouldn't it be locked? It would be too easy otherwise.

I swallow and try to get a handle on my growing panic. The truth is, I was just putting on a brave face for Jack. I'm not okay. The pain in my ankle is like nothing I've ever felt before. I swear, it's like those metal teeth are still digging through my boot, piercing my skin, only now it feels like they're made of fire. I was really counting on this nurse's cabin having painkillers.

"Sawyer had the keys," Olivia is saying when I start to listen again. She looks seriously stressed, probably embarrassed that her big plan is already falling apart. "Maybe I can go back to the lodge and see if they're in his pocket? Or maybe . . ."

She trails off as Jack lowers me onto the top step, being extra careful not to knock my bad ankle. Before she can utter another word, he steps past her and slams his shoulder into the door like a freaking battering ram.

It snaps inward, swinging on its hinges.

Jack shakes out his shoulders, grimacing slightly. Then he picks me up again and takes me inside.

I catch sight of Olivia's face over his shoulder as he carries me past. Her mouth is hanging open, a blush rising in her cheeks. It's funny, I've never thought of myself as a particularly perceptive person before, but I can read Olivia's emotions as easily as if they were my own. She looks like she's undressing Jack in her head.

As Jack carries me past her, I motion to my bottom lip. "Hey, Olivia, you have a little drool, right here," I say.

Olivia snaps her mouth closed, blushing deeper. I can tell, instantly, that she's mortified.

The cabin smells damp and dusty. There's an exam table in the middle of the room, shelves lining the walls filled with old medical equipment, gauze, and jars of aspirin and EpiPens, everything covered in sixteen years' worth of cobwebs. I find myself shivering a little at the sight of it. In the dim light, it all looks sinister.

Jack deposits me on the exam table.

"Thanks," I murmur.

"Any time," he says. Then, turning back to Olivia, he says, "Okay, where would we look for this phone?"

"Through there, probably," she says, nodding to an adjacent room. It's dark inside, but I'm guessing it's some sort of office. I see the edges of chairs, and something long and flat that might be a desk.

Jack and Olivia head inside. Hazel's already on the other side of the room, shuffling around in some cupboards for bandages and antiseptic.

I can't wait any longer. "Are there any painkillers?" I ask. Then, in the hopes that my desperation will make her work faster, I add, "*Please.*"

Hazel turns. Her arms are already full of thick wads of bandages and multiple tubes of things with faded labels. Antiseptic ointments, I'm guessing. But she shifts the supplies to one hand and—oh, thank God—I see that she's also holding a little orange pill bottle.

"You'll have to swallow them dry," she says, handing it to me.

"I'll manage." I pop off the lid, shake two chalky white pills into my palm, and toss them back like candy. They're too big to swallow dry, and I feel them all the way down my throat, but I don't care. Just a few more minutes and the pain in my ankle will stop burning. I close my eyes and lean my head back against the wall, willing time to move faster.

". . . to keep your ankle from getting infected," Hazel is saying, when I start listening again. I open my eyes and see that she's waving a yellowing *Seventeen* magazine at me.

"What?" I ask, taking it from her.

"I said, I'm going to need to change the bandage and apply some antiseptic to keep your ankle from getting infected. And it might hurt, so you should try to distract yourself." She nods at the magazine. "There's a quiz to figure out your flirting style on page twenty-seven."

My fingers move on their own, flipping to page twenty-seven without consulting my brain about it first. But my attention wanders as I stare down at the faded magazine page, not onto anything specific, but jumping from thought to thought, too freaked to settle. I hear the soft tap of rain on the roof, wind pushing tree branches against the windows. There's a low creak of wood, but it's just the sound of the old cabin settling, not someone moving.

"Do you think whoever's doing this to us is the same person who killed Jacob and Gia and Matthew?" Hazel asks suddenly, her voice low.

I look up from the magazine. "I don't know."

Hazel swallows. "I heard that guy, Jack or whatever—he said Lori Knight's your mom. You don't think she—"

My jaw clenches. "Watch what you say about my—"

Hazel's hands come up, defensive. "I'm not saying anything, I swear. But if Lori Knight didn't kill those people, then that means the real murderer was never caught. Whoever it is could still be out there."

I swallow, calming down. "Yeah. That's basically why I'm here."

"But . . . why do you think the killer would come back now?

It's been sixteen years; why risk it?" Hazel looks a little hesitant as she adds, "You don't think it's true, do you? The urban legend? The Witch of Lost Lake came back because she doesn't want us here?"

"No," I say, quickly. "I guess . . . whoever it is, she didn't show up until after we found Gia's camera. Maybe she's worried about someone finding evidence against her, having her secret finally come out, something like that."

Hazel pauses for a moment, thinking. "In that case, we should really watch whatever's on that camera."

"Again, basically why I'm here."

Hazel keeps going. "And it would narrow the suspects down to whoever was at camp when the camera was found," she points out. "No one else even knows about it."

"But the only people here are our age," I point out. "They would've been too young to be the killer sixteen years ago."

"Well, except for Andie," Hazel says. "But she wasn't here the night of the murders. She was down in the city. Maybe the killer's covering for someone else. A parent, maybe? Or an older sibling? It's a small town, everyone here knows someone who was affected by the murders. I mean, Gia North was my dad's cousin." Hazel carefully unwinds Jack's sodden T-shirt from my ankle, her fingers barely brushing against my skin. Then, she gets to work on my boot, slowly loosening the laces. "Is that why you were asking all those questions about Olivia's mom? You think it's her? Because I don't see Mrs. D'Angeli killing anyone."

I still have her photograph in my pocket. M. Edwards, the person I'd suspected for the better part of a year. "She went into labor that night, right?"

I want Hazel to tell me I'm mistaken, that Miranda wasn't in labor after all, that the official story is wrong and she still could be the murderer, somehow.

But Hazel just shrugs and says, "Yeah, that's true."

She pulls my boot from my foot, making sure not to jostle my ankle. Then she uncaps the antiseptic and applies it to my ankle, her touch gentle. Jack and Olivia are talking in the other room, their voices audible but too muffled by the wall for me to make out words.

"That's a very sexy shirt you're wearing," Hazel says out of nowhere, breaking the quiet.

I stare at her, wondering if she's having a stroke. "What?"

"Gross, right?" She wrinkles her nose and points to the magazine lying open on my lap. "That settles it, I'm definitely not a seductive flirt. But I don't fit any of these other categories, either. Like, where's the entry for a flirt who's only interested in having intellectual debates with air signs and also likes tacos?"

I bite back a smile. I want to be annoyed. And not just about the sudden change of topic from murderers to flirting, but by *her*. I don't like cutesy, happy people or astrology—or tacos, actually. But Hazel's kind of obnoxiously charming. And it's sweet how she's trying so hard to be gentle with my ankle. I let my eyes linger on her face for a beat, just long enough to take in her deep brown eyes, her long lashes. She smells good, like lavender or something. It makes me think of clean laundry and fancy candle stores and spring.

Her eyebrows go up a little and I quickly look away, something strange twisting through my stomach.

"Uh . . . playful," I tell her.

She frowns, which makes her nose scrunch up. "Huh?"

"Astrology and tacos and that thing you're doing with your nose. You're a playful flirt. See"—I point to the entry for "playful flirt" and read out—"'A playful flirt uses her fun-loving personality to disarm her crush.' That's you."

She's been maneuvering the bandage around my leg while I speak, intentionally weaving it in a complicated looking pattern that takes some of the pressure off.

She pauses and tilts her head, studying me. "What are your thoughts on bread?"

I blink at her. "What?"

"Never mind. Let's go back to the part where you think I'm disarming."

I can feel my cheeks heat up. "I mean, I never actually said—"

At that moment, she pulls the bandage tight, causing a sharp crack of pain to shoot up my leg. I stop talking, and tears spring to my eyes.

Holy—

"Sorry!" Hazel says. To her credit she does sound very sorry. "I was worried that might hurt, it just has to be tight if we want to stop the blood flow. But I'm all done now. See? That wasn't so bad."

I'd argue with her, but I'm still trying to catch my breath.

13

Olivia

Jack and I don't have to look far to find the landline. There's a phone sitting on the nurse's old desk. I hold my breath as I cross the room and lift it to my ear.

There's a beat of silence that lasts a million years. And then—

A dull hum. It's working.

Relief floods through me. I feel tears in my eyes as I dial 911, my heart lodged in my throat. When the operator answers, I shakily explain what's happened and give her the camp's address.

"We'll have an officer dispatched immediately," she tells me. "But I'm showing that the nearest cruiser is a twenty-minute drive away. Would you like me to stay on the line with you until it arrives?"

"No, that's okay," I tell the operator. I'm pretty sure staying on the phone with her would just make me more anxious. "Just please hurry."

"You've got some scratches on your forehead," Jack says, after I've hung up the phone. "Did you fall or something?"

I touch my forehead. "Oh, uh, no. There were some branches and stuff when I was running. They must have hit me."

"Here, let me take a look at them." He leans in close, right into my personal space. My breath dries up in my throat.

Here's a thing not enough people talk about: thinking you might die doesn't actually make you less horny. You'd think it would. I mean, someone just chased me through the freaking woods. I watched that person kill another kid with an arrow, and just a few minutes ago I was seriously afraid for my life.

And yet when a guy who looks like Jack leans toward me, oh so carefully examining the scratches crisscrossing my forehead, my entire body lights up. It's embarrassing. The timing could not be worse.

He smells like campfires and marshmallows, I notice, and he touches me so gently, like I'm something precious that might break if he presses too hard. There's logic and then there's biology, and when a guy who looks like *this* touches you, it does things to you, physically and . . . chemically, that you have absolutely no control over.

That must be why I have little shivers racing all through my skin. It's why, for several long moments, I forget to breathe, a *very* confusing mix of fear and desire mingling inside of me. Is this why people go on dates to scary movies? Because fear is kind of . . . hot?

Jack has a little bit of stubble on his chin, and I find myself staring at that stubble, wondering if it'd be all prickly or if it'd be soft or . . .

Oh God, and now I'm wondering what it would be like to kiss him. His lips are full, and they're the kind of plummy red that makes him look like he's wearing some sort of really delicious fruity lip balm. I bet he tastes like cherries. I find myself licking my own lips without intentionally making the decision to do so, and then—too late—I realize what I just did and feel heat blaze in my cheeks. I was just staring at his lips and licking my own lips and . . . crap, what's wrong with me?

I look up, and he's watching me right back, one eyebrow arched, almost like he's asking me a question.

I really and truly can't breathe now. My chest feels like it's about to explode. The corners of my eyes twitch. I should move away, but I don't. I'm too lost in my own thoughts, imagining those soft, warm lips pressed to mine, his campfire scent filling my head, that twisting feeling moving through my stomach, lower.

"Sorry," Jack says, pulling away from me. His voice is lower than it was a moment ago. Deeper and kind of . . . rumbly. It hits me low in my gut, that rumble.

Then he says, "I just can't get over how much you look like Reagan."

A spark moves through my body, waking me up. *Reagan.* Of course. That's why he was looking at me like that. Because I remind him of Reagan.

Does that mean they're . . . together? It would make sense. The way he was touching me didn't feel like a friend touch. It felt like a *something more* touch. But that would mean he thought she was hot, which would mean that, by extension, he thinks *I'm* hot. And that's completely impossible, right? I am not hot.

Unless . . . maybe Reagan's cool? Maybe she's dangerous and funny? That would explain why they're together. I have the second highest GPA in the junior class. I am not cool. I'm the class treasurer.

"Yeah," I say, swallowing. "Reagan."

"Speaking of Reagan, we should probably talk about the bear trap," Jack says.

I close my eyes, suppressing a shudder. I would be perfectly happy if I never had to think about that bear trap ever again. It's already going to haunt my nightmares. "What about it?"

"When I was trying to pull it open, I thought . . . well, it didn't look old. I mean, it was old, but not like the rest of the stuff around here. Not *sixteen years* old."

"Do you think the witch left it for us? As a trap?"

Jack frowns. "The witch is supposed to kill with a bow and arrows, right? At least, that's how the story goes."

I feel something cold move through me. "Do you think someone *else* left it?"

"No," Jack says slowly. Then he kind of shakes his head, like it's a thought he doesn't want to acknowledge. "I mean . . . I don't know. My family lives on the other side of those trees, not far from here, and there've been rumors about these woods for as long as I've been alive."

I cross my arms over my chest, trying to ignore the fear working up my spine. I think of the stuff I found in the archery field, the lantern and the sleeping bag and the coffee cup. "After the murders—"

"No, it's not just the murders, this isn't some urban legend about the Witch of Lost Lake. My dad's a serious camper, and he says people easily go missing around here, that you shouldn't go into the trees after dark, stuff like that." Jack rubs his eyes. "I don't know . . . maybe I'm just being paranoid. I mean, that bear trap really freaked me out. I feel like we're being hunted. And this cabin . . . it's basically a bull's-eye."

He looks at me like he's expecting me to argue. And as much as I don't want to go back out into the woods, even I have to admit that we can't just stick around here waiting for the witch—or whoever else might be out there—to find us.

"Can you carry Reagan back to camp?" I ask.

He shakes his head. "It's too far. And it'd slow me down. It'd be faster for me to run ahead for the truck and drive back to pick up the three of you."

I can't believe what I'm hearing. "You want to split up? Are you serious?"

"The truck is a five-minute walk away. Three if I run."

But I'm already shaking my head. "Jack, no way. We stay together, that's the safest thing to do. The cops will be here soon, and then this whole nightmare will be over."

"Twenty minutes is a long time. What are we supposed to do if the killer finds us here? Reagan can't exactly run on that leg."

His eyes lock on mine, and I feel a jolt go through me as I stare back at him. He's got a point. If the killer finds us here, Reagan's a goner. And I'm guessing it would mean Jack would be a goner, too, because I can tell there's no way he's leaving her behind. I feel a sharp pang at the thought. It surprises me. I mean, I barely know Jack and Reagan, but the thought of them being in danger, of being alone and scared, unsettles me.

"You know I'm right," he says in a soft voice.

My shoulders slump. I do know. We can't just wait here to see whether the cops or the killer find us first, not when Reagan's life depends on it.

"Okay," I say, exhaling. "But you have to explain it to your girl-friend. I have a feeling she isn't going to like this plan."

Jack eyes me steadily. There's a twist to his mouth that wasn't there a moment ago, halfway between a smile and a smirk. Something I said must've struck him as funny.

"I just realized I don't know your name," he says.

"Oh." I feel my cheeks heat up, which makes absolutely no sense. He asked me to tell him my name, not have his babies. "It's—"

"I think I'm going to call you Mickey," he says before I can answer.

"Mickey?" My eyebrows go up. "You mean, like the mouse?"

"No, like Mickey Joseph, the fastest QB the Cornhuskers have ever had. I'm pretty sure you beat his record when you tried to run away from me earlier." He smiles at me and, for a second, I think he's going to say something else, but he just shakes his head and walks back into the other room.

My stomach twists. *Mickey.*

I was right, Reagan really doesn't like this plan.

"Are you an *idiot*?" she hisses when Jack tells her what he's going to do. "You can't go out there alone!"

He glances at her freshly bandaged ankle. "You can't exactly come with me."

"Then take someone else." She gestures toward me and Hazel. "Take one of them!"

"I'll be faster if I go alone."

"You'll be *deader* if you go alone!"

I tense and glance at the windows. Reagan's not speaking as

quietly as I'd like her to. "Let's just try to stay calm, okay? Jack, you said it would take three minutes to get to the truck, right? So, you'll be gone what? Six minutes?"

"Less than that." Jack grunts. Quietly, thank God. "Getting back here with the car will be faster."

"Okay, then . . ." I glance at Reagan. Despite how pissed she sounds, I can tell that the idea of Jack wandering off alone really freaks her out. It's obvious. The fear is practically radiating off of her.

I take a breath, worried I'm about to make everything worse. "Then maybe just . . . go."

Jack's eyes lock on mine. Not Hazel's, not Regan's, *mine*. I feel a jolt go through me as I stare back at him, thinking of that strange, charged moment back in the office. But that moment had been meant for Reagan, not me. There's nothing between us, I'm just the girl who looks like his much cooler, more badass girlfriend. I'm no one.

"What?" Reagan whispers. Her eyes widen. "Jack, *no*."

A muscle in Jack's jaw tightens. He's still looking at me, his gaze so intense that I feel like I'm about to catch fire. "Promise me you'll keep her safe, Mickey?"

Maybe it's the way he keeps calling me "Mickey," but I would've agreed to anything he asked just then. "We won't leave her alone," I promise him. "No matter what happens."

Jack stares at me for a beat longer. I can tell he's considering it.

"What are you talking about?" Reagan hisses. "Who's Mickey? You're the one who won't be safe. *Jack*." Reagan grabs for his arm, but he's too far away, just outside her reach. Her voice low and dangerous, she adds, "Jack, don't you dare leave me here, don't—"

But it's too late. He's already out the door, his footsteps banging on the wooden steps. Gone.

Reagan releases a string of very inventive language, but at least she's keeping her voice low, so I ignore it. I must be staring after Jack because Hazel comes up next to me and says, under her breath. "So, I know I'm not a very good judge of these things . . . but that guy's, like, insanely hot, right?"

"Hazel," I warn.

"The muscles and the . . . what do you call it . . . the thing where he's risking his life to save us. You straight girls really go for that kind of thing, right?"

"They're together, in case you haven't noticed."

Hazel smirks knowingly and says, "They're not."

"How could you possibly know that?"

"Just trust me on this. They're not together. No way."

I shoot her a look and she shrugs.

Behind us, Reagan has run out of foul language. When we turn, we find her collapsed back onto the exam table, her eyes glistening like she might cry. She sniffs, loudly, and says, in a low voice seemingly aimed at no one in particular, "Idiot."

I hug my arms around myself. I can't help thinking about what Jack said when we were alone in the nurse's office. *I feel like we're being hunted.* Six minutes seems like forever all of a sudden. Every nerve in my body is on edge.

There's a second of silence, none of us saying a word. Then, almost like she can't take it anymore, Hazel blurts, "Should we . . . talk about this?"

Reagan moves her eyes to Hazel but doesn't sit up. "Talk about what?"

I glance at Reagan. Her expression is blank. She's working hard to make it seem like she doesn't know what Hazel's referring to, but I can tell she does. It's practically printed across her face. She's just as curious as I am.

"She means you and me," I say pointedly. "How we look the same."

"Like, exactly the same," Hazel adds. "Identical. You could be carbon copies of each other."

"Sorry," Reagan says, deadpan. "I don't see it."

"You don't?" I ask, lifting an eyebrow, thinking, *Bullshit*.

Reagan tilts her head, lips pursed like she's studying me. "Your forehead is a lot longer than mine. Like, *a lot*. And your eyes are closer together, and your nose . . ." she makes a face like *yikes*. And then she adds, "I mean, there are doctors who could probably fix that for you if you want."

I take a step toward her, scowling. I don't know what I'm planning to do, exactly. Hit her? I'm not a hitting person, but this girl apparently brings out violent tendencies I didn't even know I had.

Luckily, Hazel grabs my arm, holding me back. "Olivia, chill, she's obviously messing with you."

I know that, of course, but I still don't want to let her get away with it. Reagan snickers, and I feel a flare of annoyance. It figures that my doppelgänger would be kind of an ass.

Hazel looks from my face to Reagan's and shivers. "You have to be related. It's too freaky otherwise."

"Maybe," Reagan says. Her eyes linger on me for a moment, brows dipping low. It's bizarre. Like staring into a mirror, only to have your own reflection frown at you.

"Anyway, we have more important things to discuss," Reagan says, groaning a little as she sits up. She reaches into her pocket and pulls something out. "Like how are we going to find a cord that fits this thing?"

It's Gia's camera.

The same camera that was just in *my* pocket.

I reach into my pocket even though I can see with my own eyes that the camera's not there, that Reagan's holding it. "Hey! You stole that from me."

Reagan presses a hand over her lips, all fake shocked. "Whoops."

"What's *wrong* with you?" I whisper-shout at her. I'm pissed, but the witch could still be close, so I keep my voice quiet. "You can't just go *taking* things out of people's pockets."

Reagan's jaw tightens. "You took it from me first."

"I took it from a *table*."

"I'm going to check the nurse's old desk," Hazel says. "I bet she has a charger. Back in the aughts they only ever used one size of charger for things, right?"

"Are you mad because I took it?" Reagan asks, her voice quiet and raspy. "Or are you mad because you were so busy staring at Jack that you didn't even notice that I took it?"

My cheeks flare. "I . . . was *not* staring at him!"

"*Please.* I bet he has second-degree burns on his cheeks from where your eyes were lasering into his face."

"That is . . . not true!" Embarrassingly, this is the best I can come up with. We're both still whispering, but my heart's beating as hard as if we were having a screaming match.

"Guys!" Hazel says, holding something up. "I—"

Reagan keeps going, "I mean, for all you know, he's my boyfriend, and you were still openly drooling all over him, like a dog in heat."

"Guys!" Hazel hisses, her voice low but sharp. "Charger, Gia's camera . . . am I the only one who wants to know what she possibly could've filmed that was worth killing for?"

I hesitate for a moment, then nod. Of course I want to know.

"Yeah, same," Reagan murmurs, handing over the camera. "Let's see what's on this thing."

Hazel plugs it in, then flips the little screen out to the side.

It takes forever for the ancient camera to power on, and then a tiny hourglass appears, slowly turning up and down, up and down. For several long moments we all just stare. I'm about to say something about how I don't think is going to work after all when the home screen blinks to life.

"Whoa," Hazel says.

"How do we watch the footage?" I ask, but Reagan's already working on it. She touches the tiny PLAY button on the screen, quickly navigating to the most recent video.

The image is fuzzy, the video clearly very old. The screen is practically black—inside a dark room, perhaps? The date stamp in the corner reads JUNE 13, 2008.

I swallow and glance at Hazel. That's the night Matthew, Jacob, and Gia were murdered.

The camera feels suddenly hot between us, burning. I have the sudden urge to rip it out of Reagan's hands, throw it. Maybe we aren't supposed to see whatever it is Gia filmed. Maybe seeing it is what cursed her sixteen years ago.

Even as this thought enters my head, I let the video play, my curiosity winning out over my fear. I need to know. The need is gnawing, like hunger.

The screen is still dark, but now Gia North is leaning close to the camera. I've seen photos of Gia, but she still looks younger than I was expecting, her face round and babyish, her eyes magnified in the camera's fish-eye lens.

"Holy shit," she says, her voice a low, tense whisper. The image bounces as she talks. She must be running. "I . . . I can't . . . I can't . . . she *killed* him. I just *watched* her kill him. I have to get out of here. I have to—"

Someone appears in the frame behind her. At first, it's hard to see who it is because their face is blurry, half in shadow. Then, they step forward and the camera focuses:

Andie.

"Shut that off, Gia," Andie says. She's panting, out of breath. "Now."

Her voice startles Gia, who didn't seem to realize she'd come up behind her. The image stays focused on her face as she spins around. "Andie! What—"

Andie reaches past Gia and tries to grab her camera. "I'm serious, Gia. Don't make me hurt you."

Andie grabs for the camera again, and this time she knocks it to the ground. It stays on its side still recording. There's a shuffling sound. We see feet moving. Then, Andie screams.

"Oh my God!" Gia says. *"Oh my God!"*

A hand fumbles with the camera—it's covered in blood.

And then everything goes black.

• • •

POLICE REPORT

Ulster County Police Department

Case No: 000524-27B-2008

Date: 06/14/2008

Reporting Officer: Angel Lopez

Incident: Double Homicide

Detail of Event: On Wednesday, June 13, 2008, at approximately 2000 hours, Officer Karly Knight responded to a report of a disturbance at 163 Lost Lake Lane, Lost Lake, New York, 13031. Upon arrival, she found Miranda D'Angeli in a state of visible distress. Mrs. D'Angeli was out of breath, bleeding, and holding a newborn. Mrs. D'Angeli indicated that she'd seen her assistant, Lori Knight, at the scene, covered in blood, and that she'd gone into labor due to shock. Officer Knight immediately radioed for assistance and pursued the suspect on foot but was unable to locate her. Tire tracks in the woods indicate that she had a car waiting.

Officer Knight called for backup, and I, Officer Angel Lopez, arrived at the location at approximately 2020 hours. While searching the scene, Officer Knight and I discovered the body of a seventeen-year-old Caucasian female suffering an arrow wound through the chest. Female was identified as Gia North, a camp counselor. Officer Knight and I then searched the grounds, where we found the body of a thirty-five-year-old Caucasian male suffering an arrow wound through the throat.

Officer Knight immediately identified the body as Jacob Knight, her brother. Jacob Knight has worked at Camp Lost Lake as an archery instructor for the last ten years. After identifying the body, Officer Knight became despondent and excused herself from the case, indicating that she could not investigate the murder of her own brother. It is at that time that I took over as reporting officer.

An abandoned bow and arrow were found upon searching the grounds. Markings on the bow indicate that it belonged to Jacob Knight. It has been sent to the lab for DNA testing. Eyewitnesses report that the murderer was wearing a witch's Halloween mask, but no such mask has been found.

Medical examiners arrived on the scene at 2100 hours. Initial impression was that Gia and Jacob died around the same time. The time could not yet be determined, although the pair appeared to have been dead for somewhere between two and four hours, which places the window between 1800 and 2000 hours.

Addendum June 15, 2008: At approximately 0900 hours on the morning of June 15, 2008, Officer Knight alerted officers that her seventeen-year-old nephew, Matthew Knight, had been missing for over forty-eight hours. No body has been found, but signs of struggle were discovered at the top of the lighthouse overlooking the camp. This includes broken boards near one of the windows and blood smears on the floor. The blood has been sent to the lab for testing. Officers are suspicious of a fall, as well as drowning. Plans to drag the lake for a body are currently underway.

Primary suspect is still at large and should be considered very dangerous.

14

Reagan

For a long moment, the only thing I hear is my heartbeat pounding in my ears—the slow, steady *thwump thwump thwump* that tells me that, even though my entire world has cracked open, my body is still moving, still working, still keeping me alive. I keep staring at the little camera screen, willing Gia and Andie to reappear and explain what the hell just happened. But they don't. I'm going to have to make sense of it myself.

I squeeze my eyes shut, blocking everything else out so I can think. *I watched her kill him*, Gia said. And then Andie attacked her.

I inhale, and there's another sound, this one a raspy scrape inside my throat. There must've been some accident . . . Andie killed either Jacob or Matthew, and Gia saw her.

Then Andie went after Gia. She attacked Gia, *killed* Gia. And then . . .

I blink as it all slots into place. This video is proof that my mom wasn't the one who killed her family. It could completely exonerate her. I actually did it.

When I open my eyes again, I see that all the color has drained from Olivia's face, leaving her already pale skin practically sickly. She's brought her hand to her mouth and she's blinking very fast.

Behind us, Hazel says, in a low voice, "Oh man . . ."

Her words seem to snap Olivia back to life. She drops her hands and looks at me, brow furrowed like we're already in the middle of an argument. She swallows and says, "We don't know what any of this means."

"We don't?" The words drop from my mouth like stones. I should've known that when it came down to it, Olivia would protect her family over me.

Besides, she's delusional. We know exactly what this means.

Andie is the Witch of Lost Lake. Andie killed those people years ago. We still don't know why, but maybe that's on the camera, too. Maybe she dressed up like a witch and came after us today because she realized how close we were to learning the truth.

Something pops into my head all of a sudden. It's a phrase I must've read somewhere on one of the police documents, something that got lost in my brain until this moment.

I have a nineteen-year-old daughter, Andie. Full name: Miranda.

I go completely still. Did I really read that? "Is Andie short for Miranda?" I ask Olivia.

Olivia is staring daggers at me. "Why would that matter?"

Which is as good as saying yes. Miranda and her eldest daughter had the same name, M. Edwards. The camp key card belonged to *Andie*, not her mother.

"This doesn't mean anything," Olivia says, her voice firm. Her jaw tightens. "All it proves is that horrible Gia girl saw something weird, and my sister confronted her. That's all. The camera cut out before we could see what happened next."

"You can't be serious," I say. I've never been good at containing my anger. I can feel it building inside of me like a storm, tightening my muscles, turning all the logic inside my head into white noise. "What about the blood? Or the fact that Andie knocked Gia's camera to the ground?"

"Hey," Hazel says. She's looking back and forth between the two of us, anxiously. "Why don't we all just take a breath and—"

"Who cares that she knocked a *camera* to the ground?" Olivia interrupts her. "All that proves is that there's a lot more to the story than we thought there was."

"You don't get to decide what it does or doesn't prove. It's *evidence*."

Olivia rounds on me, something in her eyes flashing. "You just want to clear your mom's name. You don't care if my sister gets hurt instead."

"Stop," Hazel says.

I ignore her. "I don't know why we're arguing about this. That camera needs to go to the cops. It's the *law*. You know it's the right thing to do."

Olivia crosses her arms over her chest. "No, I don't know that."

"Why? Because it's your family instead of mine this time?"

Olivia looks like she's going to say something, but she closes her mouth and swallows instead. The muscles in her jaw pull tight.

Watching her, I feel like I know exactly what's going through her mind. I think she's realizing, for maybe the first time in her life, that doing the right thing doesn't protect everyone equally. That, if the evidence looks bad enough, the truth doesn't actually matter.

Well, tough, I want to tell her. I don't believe Andie is innocent, but even if she is, these videos show she knew a lot more about what happened than she claimed. I remember every single witness statement from that night. *Andie wasn't there, Andie was at her internship, Andie didn't know anything.* Bullshit. She could have exonerated my mom sixteen years ago. She didn't.

"My sister's a good person," Olivia says finally. "Maybe that doesn't mean anything to you, but it's the truth."

"She still lied and hurt people—"

"I'm sure she had a reason. You don't know Andie, but she *always* does the right thing. There has to be a really good reason she didn't tell anyone she was there that night."

"Do you have any idea how messed up that sounds?"

"I—"

"My mom is a good person too," I say, cutting her off. "Even if your sister's innocent, even if this was all some big misunderstanding, she was still there the night of the murders, she saw Gia right before she was killed, and she didn't come forward, she didn't tell anyone. God, Olivia . . . did it occur to you that she might've had evidence that could have gotten my mom off sixteen years ago?"

"No," Olivia says, shaking her head. "No, Andie wouldn't have hidden evidence, not if she could've helped someone. There has to be another explanation."

A short, unamused laugh spills from my lips. "What's the plan, then? We're just hiding evidence until Andie can get her alibi straight?"

Olivia's face hardens again. "This isn't the only evidence from that night. Your mom was seen running from the scene of the crime covered in *blood*! How do you explain that?"

"I don't have to explain that. Andie's at camp now, and my

mom isn't!" I snap. "Who do you think is dressing up like a witch and chasing us through the woods, Olivia? Because my money's on the girl who was caught on tape attacking a murder victim!"

"No," Olivia says again, shaking her head. "You're wrong."

I open my mouth. I'm not entirely sure what I'm going to say, whether I'm going to keep trying to convince Olivia that she's wrong about her sister or whether I'm going to tell her to shove it. Turns out I'm saved the effort.

There's a snap right outside the window. It's a firm, clean break, like someone stepping on a twig.

The three of us are immediately on high alert. We stare at each other, not moving, not even breathing. And we wait.

Several long moments pass without another sound, but that doesn't stop my head from spinning, coming up with horror movie scenarios. Maybe Andie's outside the cabin right now, peering in through the dirty glass windows. Watching us.

Hunting us.

The thought sends fear squirming through my stomach. We can't stay here, I realize. We're easy targets. Three fish waiting in a barrel.

But then I glance down at my injured foot. The painkillers have kicked in and the pain is no longer all I can think about. It's a dull throb now, but blood has begun to seep through the bandage, staining the white gauze a dark, rusty brown. I'm in no state to be running through the woods from a murderer.

Hazel's hovering near the window, squinting to see past all the dirt. She studies the woods outside for a long moment and then, sighing, turns back to us. "I don't see anyone out there," she says. "I think it must've been an animal."

I exhale, relieved. I'm thinking a little more clearly now. There's no longer anger roaring through me. I have to make Olivia see reason, understand that our best bet is to turn this evidence over to the cops and let them sort it out.

She might be my sister, too. And maybe we don't really know each other, but that connection can't mean nothing to her. Maybe I can get her listen to me.

"Olivia," I say, turning to back her, "Listen—"

The words die on my tongue. Olivia's holding Gia's camera. *Why* is she holding Gia's camera?

"I'm sorry," she says. "But I can't let you take this. Not before I talk to my sister."

"Olivia, stop," Hazel says.

But Olivia shoves the camera into her pocket and bolts for the door.

"Stop her!" I shout. Without thinking, I throw my legs over the side of the nurse's cot, and slam onto my feet.

Pain shoots through me. It feels like fire ants burrowing into my calf muscles, like flames wrapping around my bones. My mouth falls open and I release a weak, jagged yelp.

"Oh my God," Hazel says, hurrying over to help me. I want to tell her to help me run after Olivia, I want to tell her that we can't let her get away.

But it's too late. Olivia's already disappeared into the woods, along with the only piece of evidence that my mother might not be a murderer after all.

15

Olivia

I can barely see where I'm going. There's snot running down my face and my eyes are thick with tears I keep trying to blink away. The world around me is all watercolor greens and browns, the dirt trail rocky and uneven beneath my sneakers.

This might be the stupidest thing I've ever done. I don't care. I know Andie can't be the witch. My sister would never hurt me, and whoever's been chasing after us through the woods all day has been shooting to kill. There's another explanation. I just have to get to Andie before the cops arrive and Reagan can tell them what we saw.

But another thought circles my head, even as I tell myself this: How well do I *really* know my sister? There's always been distance between us. So much of her life is a mystery to me. Could she be hiding more than I ever realized?

I'd be an easy target if the real witch found me now. I'm slow and clumsy, my eyes blurry with tears, my heart pounding so hard I wouldn't even hear her approach. I'm probably making so much noise, crashing through the trees like a wild animal. All this should send me racing back to the nurse's cabin, but it doesn't. My head's too full of everything I just learned.

Andie was here the night of the murders, not in New York like everyone thought she was. She knocked Gia's camera to the ground moments after Gia saw someone get killed.

And there's the ultrasound. Everyone knows my mother was there the night of the murders, but the ultrasound proves that she wasn't there for the reason they all think she was. She lied about her pregnancy, about giving birth. Why would she do that unless she was hiding something especially bad?

Like the fact that she framed Lori for a crime Andie committed, that she might have even kidnapped one of Lori's babies.

A lump forms in my throat. I push the thoughts out of my head and force myself to run faster, blood and adrenaline pumping through my limbs, urging me forward even as the muscles in my legs scream at me to stop.

The trees open in a few yards, the ground flattened into a wider clearing. I can see the cabins right ahead, little spots of warmth and familiarity nestled in the trees. Now that I'm almost out of the woods I can feel how tight my chest is, how sore my legs have become. I drop my pace through the trees from a run to a quick walk—

A hand clamps over my mouth, thick arms wrapping around my chest. My stomach knots, my sudden fear blotting out everything else.

No.

I'm so close. The cabins are just yards away. I can see the shadows of people moving behind the windows.

Help! I try to shout, the hand pressed against my lips muffling my voice. I flail wildly, but the arms wrapped around me pin my elbows to my torso, making it impossible for me to move anything except for my head and my legs. I kick as whoever's holding me lifts me into the air so my feet don't even touch the ground. Tears spring to my eyes.

Come on, think, think.

My head. It's the only weapon I have left. I drop it forward, chin to chest, and I'm about to jerk it back where it'll hopefully collide with this asshole's nose, when—

"Stop moving," a quiet voice says directly in my ear. *Jack's* voice. I exhale, relief flooding through me. *Thank God.*

I nod into his palm, and he removes his hand from my mouth, using it to point dead ahead.

At first, I don't see what he's pointing at. There's just trees and shadows. They've turned on the lights in the cabin and I can see people moving on the other side of the windows.

And then, just below those windows, a shadow moves.

My breath catches in my throat. My eyes are glued to the shadow beneath the window, the one that moved, and I'm trying to make sense of the blurry shape, but it's gone still again, making it impossible to see from where I'm standing. Is it an animal?

No, not an animal: a person. My muscles tense. My eyesight adjusts, and the scene I'm looking at shifts: the shadows beneath the cabin's window aren't shadows at all, but someone dressed in a black trench coat, a witch's mask hiding their face.

The witch straightens, and I can see that she's looking over her shoulder, toward the woods.

Toward *us*.

In an instant, I know exactly what happened.

If Jack hadn't grabbed me and pulled me back into the trees, I'd be dead right now. He gave up his hiding spot to save me.

I look back at him. His eyes are wide with fear, and unblinking. He presses a single finger to his lips, and motions for me to duck back behind the tree with him. We're in the shade, and far enough away that it's possible the witch hasn't spotted the movement. I move as slowly as I'm physically capable of moving, holding my breath, all the while praying, *Don't see us, please don't see us.*

Jack speaks directly into my ear, his voice all breath. "She's been there for about fifteen minutes."

I nod, staring at the figure. Something thick and sour forms in my throat.

I know that's not my sister. I *know* it. And yet I can't help studying the shape of the body hidden beneath the trench coat, trying to figure out her height, her approximate size, to see if there's any chance it matches up with Andie's. But the trench is too oversized and bulky. It could be Andie. It could be anyone.

The witch is still facing the woods. I can't tell whether she's looking at us or not, thanks to the mask. She seems to know there was someone running through the trees, but not exactly where the sound was coming from. I look from her mask to her hand and my insides clamp up in terror: she's still holding that bow.

Andie knows how to use a bow, I think. Mom taught her when she was a little girl, and Andie, being Andie, practiced until she became a perfect shot. Our closets back home are filled with ribbons from competitions Andie entered when she was my age.

The witch takes a step toward the trees, her boots silent on the dirt. Each breath I take scrapes my throat, sounding loud enough to my own ears that I don't see how she doesn't hear it.

I watch as she takes another step toward us.

And then another.

I've forgotten that Jack's arms are wrapped around my shoulders until they tighten protectively. I can feel his heart beating fast and hard against my back, his breath warming my neck.

The witch is only a few feet away now. She's scanning the trees, head tilted, listening. She's close enough that I can see the arrow nocked in her bow, aimed at the ground. I can't stop staring at it, imagining what it would feel like for the sharp point of the arrowhead to rip through my skin.

I clench my eyes shut, thinking, *Andie would never hurt me. If Reagan's right, if she is the witch, then I'm perfectly safe.*

There's a rustle of movement a few inches away from me. I freeze, convinced the sound came from *me*, that my foot accidentally brushed against a loose rock.

The witch is alert, bow and arrow up, searching for whatever—whoever—made that sound.

As slowly and carefully as I can, I look around.

There's a squirrel perched on a tree trunk a few feet away. I watch, horrified, as the squirrel scurries down the tree and onto the ground, the rustling sound of its movement so soft I have to strain to hear it.

"Shit," Jack breathes into my ear. I swallow. I don't have to ask why he's so freaked out. I already know. If the squirrel comes any closer to our hiding spot, it won't matter how quiet we are, how still. The witch will find us all the same. The squirrel will lead her right here.

Jack seems to tense behind me, the muscles in his arms going very, very still. I stop breathing, stop blinking. My entire world is that squirrel.

It scampers along the dirt path, then stops to pick up a nut. It's three feet away from us now, just on the other side of our tree, and it must catch our scent in the wind because it looks up all of a sudden, nose twitching.

Wood splinters just above my head. I flinch, and Jack's arms tighten around me, holding me still. I press both hands to my mouth to keep myself from crying out in fear.

The arrow just misses the squirrel, instead burrowing deep into the tree trunk I'm hiding behind.

There are tears in my eyes, and I'm shaking all over. *This is it. The witch is going to find us. She's going to look behind the tree, I know she is.*

She stops on the path directly ahead of us. The trunk is big enough that I can't see her on the other side, but I can hear her heavy breathing, muffled by the mask she's still wearing, and I can hear her boots rustling through the underbrush as she turns toward the tree we're hiding behind.

I close my eyes. I can't watch. I don't want to see that arrow flying toward my face. I don't want to know it's coming. Jack holds me closer, tucking me just below his chin. I turn toward him and knot my hands into his shirt. I still have enough functioning brain cells to be grateful that he's here, that I'm not going to die alone.

Please just do it already, let it be over, please, please, please.

For a long time, nothing happens. Then: another splintery wood sound as the witch removes the arrow from the tree trunk. A shuffle of footsteps.

The next time I lift my head, she's just a shadow in the trees, walking away.

"I think she's gone," Jack says directly into my ear. His voice is quiet enough that I don't think it's possible for anyone else to have heard him, but I still tense, my eyes scanning the trees for movement.

What if she's still close? What if she comes back? What if—

Jack starts to move away from me, but I grab his arm, holding him in place. I'm not ready to give up our hiding spot yet. I want to stay here, where I know it's safe, for just a little while longer. Maybe more than a little while longer. Maybe forever.

Jack must realize I'm still completely freaked out because he relaxes against me, his arm sinking heavily onto my shoulders, a comforting weight. Like a weighted blanket or one of those vests they make dogs wear during thunderstorms. I can feel my heartbeat steadying.

"She didn't see us," Jack says. Again, he speaks softly and directly into my ear.

"You can't know that for sure."

"Yeah, but I'm pretty sure."

"*Pretty sure* doesn't mean anything. *Pretty* doesn't have a numerical value."

"Okay, then I'm . . . eighty-eight percent sure."

I look up at his face because he can't be serious right now. "Eighty-eight percent is a *B*."

"It's a B-*plus*," Jack clarifies. "B-plus is good."

"If I got a B on an assignment, I'd be humiliated. I'll start moving again when you're ninety-four percent sure."

"Mickey," Jack says, in a gentler voice. "If she'd seen us, she'd be chasing us right now."

Yes, I think, *yes, that makes sense.*

Unless the witch is Andie. Unless she's just pretending she didn't see us, because she doesn't want to hurt me.

My arms, my legs, everything is frozen in place. I watch the tree line. A minute passes, and then another, and no one appears. Jack's right. The witch is gone.

It's time for me to start moving now. But I feel a strange churning in my stomach, and all of the frustration and fear and stress of what's been happening seems to bubble up my chest.

This is too much. I can't take it anymore. I just want it all to stop.

I try to hold it back, I really do, but I guess I'm not that strong. My eyes flood, and my shoulders start to shake and then it's all over and I'm crying, openly crying in front of some strange guy in the middle of the woods, while a killer probably watches from a few dozen feet away with a freaking *arrow* aimed at my face. At least I manage to throw a hand over my mouth to quiet the sobs.

Jack stiffens behind me, clearly taken aback by my sudden display of intense emotion. I bet *Reagan* doesn't burst into hysterical sobs when she should be running. I bet Reagan is always cool and pulled together and never overly emotional at inappropriate times. She seems like that kind of girl, and I feel a little twist of jealousy, wishing I could be strong.

I expect Jack to say something logical and cool-headed, to tell me to pull myself together, maybe, or to remind me that we're in a lot of danger and we need to get out of here, fast. Both true statements. But he doesn't do that. Instead, he tightens his grip around my shoulders, pulling me into his chest so that his chin rests on top of my head. He doesn't tell me to calm down or lie and say it's all going to be okay. He just holds me.

"I'm . . . I'm sorry," I choke out when the sobs have subsided some.

"Don't be sorry," Jack says. After a moment, he clears his throat and adds, in a lower voice, "My mom gets these panic attacks sometimes. They used to really freak me out. She was always this larger-than-life superhero when I was a kid, you know? So seeing her crouching on the ground, struggling to breathe, I'm not going to lie, it was really hard to watch. Then this one time I asked her why it happened. You know what she told me?"

I shake my head.

"She said that even strong people need to fall apart. And if you go too long without letting yourself do that, your body's going to do it for you. We're not made of stone."

I blink the fresh tears from my eyes and lean away from him, so I can see his face. "She sounds like a badass."

"She really is," Jack says. "You'd like her."

"My dad says something like that, too," I tell him, only hesitating for a second on the word *dad*. "He likes to say that you have to feel your feelings, even the unpleasant ones."

"Smart guy."

"Yeah." I wipe my eyes with the back of my arm. "Thanks."

"Anytime," Jack says. Weirdly, it sounds like he means it. He's looking at me now. Really looking at me, in a way that feels different than how he's looked at me before. It takes me a second to realize what's changed: for the first time since I've met him, it feels like he's looking at *me* instead of at Reagan.

I look away first, feeling heat rise in my cheeks. For a moment neither of us speaks. Then, as though he's only just realized he's still holding me, Jack pulls away and scrubs a hand over his jaw, still staring down the dirt road where the witch just disappeared.

"I wish we knew who she was," he says.

I hear Reagan's voice shouting in my head, *Who do you think is dressing up like a witch and chasing us through the woods, Olivia? Because my money's on the girl who was caught on tape attacking a murder victim!*

And then I'm picturing the Andie I saw on Gia's video: the fury in her face, the blood on her hands. She'd certainly *looked* like a murderer.

But that doesn't mean she is one, I tell myself, forcing the image away. I know how it looked, but there's another explanation. There has to be. Andie and I might not be the closest sisters in the world, but I *know* her.

Don't I?

"We should move," Jack says. "Before she comes back."

I look down the path, feeling uneasy. It's late, nearly sunset, and long, creeping shadows have crawled across the ground. Thunder rumbles overhead.

"That's the path I just came down," I realize.

A muscle tightens in Jack's jaw. "The nurse's cabin. It's down that way."

"She'll find them for sure."

"The truck is parked right through there." Jack nods to the trees on the other side of the cabins. "I can grab it and circle back for Hazel and Reagan."

We meet each other's eyes and I know, without asking, that we're thinking the same thing: Can he get there before the killer does? Or is he already too late?

"Go now," I tell him. "Hurry."

Jack hesitates just a second, a question on his face. He wants to know why I'm not coming with him. It's probably just now occurring to him to wonder why I followed him in the first place. But there's no time to explain.

"You'll be faster without me," I say. I don't know whether he accepts this or if he's just aware of the ticking clock, but he nods and dashes into the trees.

As soon as he's gone, I reach into my pocket, and tighten my fingers around the stolen video camera.

Time to get some answers.

WITNESS STATEMENT
Investigating Officer(s): Angel Lopez
Incident No: 000524-27B-2008
Description: Miranda D'Angeli's official statement
Date: 06/14/2008

MIRANDA D'ANGELI

1. I swear to the following, to the best of my recollection, under penalty of perjury.

2. My name is Miranda Michelle D'Angeli.

3. I am thirty-five years old and competent to testify in a court of law.

4. I currently reside in New York State.

5. I grew up in Ulster County and have been working as the director of Camp Lost Lake for three years.

6. I have a nineteen-year-old daughter, Andie. Full name: Miranda.

7. Andie was out of town at the time of the murders, at an internship in New York City.

8. While director at Camp Lost Lake, I knew the victims, Gia North and Jacob Knight, as well as the accused, Lori Knight.

9. Gia was a camp counselor last year and had plans to work as a camp counselor again this summer. Lori has been my assistant for three years. Jacob has worked as the archery director at camp for the past ten years.

10. On June 13, 2008, I was working late at camp. Camp staff traditionally starts work two weeks before the first day of camp, so they can help clean out the cabins and get everything set up before the kids arrive. Jacob and Lori had worked until approximately 7 p.m. that day. I was under the impression that they had gone home after that.

11. Gia was not working at camp that day, however I saw her briefly that morning. She told me she needed to speak with me. I was in the process of running an errand and told her to wait in my office until I returned. She was not there when I got back.

12. To my knowledge, the only other person on the campgrounds was Henry Roberts, our groundskeeper.

13. I left my office at approximately 7:30 p.m. I heard a noise and turned around. Moments later, Lori Knight ran out of

the trees behind the lighthouse. She was covered in blood and carrying something I assume was a weapon.

14. Lori told me to run. She then headed back into the woods. A few minutes later I believe I heard a car starting. At that time, I went into labor.

15. I did not see Matthew Knight on the grounds that evening, nor have I seen him since.

16. I have retained counsel in New York City, Jeremy Rosenberg, and I respectfully ask that any attempts to contact me be made through him.

17. I have reviewed this affidavit with my attorney.

Witness: *Miranda D'Angeli, 6/14/2008*
Investigating Officer: *Officer Angel Lopez, 6/14/2008*

EXCERPT FROM THE INTERVIEW OF MIRANDA D'ANGELI

Date: 07/10/2008

Officer Lopez: Okay, Miranda, first I want to thank you sincerely for talking with us. I know you have a newborn at home.

Miranda D'Angeli: Anything I can do to help.

Officer Lopez: What did you and Johnny end up calling her?

Miranda D'Angeli: Olivia, after my mother.

Officer Lopez: That's a beautiful name, Miranda. Just beautiful. Okay, if you're ready to begin, can we start? You were good enough to provide a statement immediately following the incident.

Miranda D'Angeli: Yes, I did.

Officer Lopez: That statement was very helpful, thank you. Before we get to my questions, I want to make sure you still stand by everything you wrote.

Miranda D'Angeli: I'm sorry, I don't know if I follow your question.

Officer Lopez: I'm wondering if there was anything you wanted to change or amend about the statement you provided.

Miranda D'Angeli: Are you asking if I lied?

Jeremy Rosenberg: Mrs. D'Angeli and I have been over that statement several times. I assure you that it's accurate.

Officer Lopez: Of course. I'm sorry, Mrs. D'Angeli, that question was not intended in the least to sound like we are accusing you of anything. Let's move along. One victim's son, Matthew Knight, has been missing since the night of the murders.

Miranda D'Angeli: I heard that.

Officer Lopez: I was hoping you might help me get in touch with your daughter, to see whether she's heard from him at all.

Miranda D'Angeli: My daughter? Why do you think Andie would know anything about Matthew Knight?

Officer Lopez: Correct me if I'm wrong, but your daughter was . . . uh, involved with Matthew Knight, was she not?

Miranda D'Angeli: I'm not sure who told you that, but no, that's not correct. Andie barely knows Matthew.

Officer Lopez: Is that right? I heard differently.

Miranda D'Angeli: You might be confused because Matthew's father, Jacob, and I dated for a short time back in high school. I'm happy to provide you with Andie's phone number, if necessary, but I'm certain she won't be able to tell you anything. Andie wasn't even here the night of the murders.

Jeremy Rosenberg: Mrs. D'Angeli has answered the question. Shall we move on?

Officer Lopez: Thank you, Mrs. D'Angeli. That's all we need for the moment.

16

Reagan

"Want a turn?" Hazel holds out her phone. Her winning game is still on the screen, decks of cards and confetti exploding outward while the sound of cheering echoes from the speakers. We've been passing the time waiting for Jack to come back by playing solitaire on her phone. Without Wi-Fi, it's the only game that still works.

I take the phone, barely paying attention to the virtual cards on the screen. Instead, my eyes are on the countdown clock in the corner. It's been eight minutes and twelve seconds since we started playing. Jack should be back by now.

After a minute, Hazel says, "I can't stop keep thinking about how messed up that girl was."

I look up from her phone. "You mean Andie?"

"No," Hazel says, frowning. "Gia."

I feel my jaw clench. "*Gia* didn't kill anyone."

"Okay, no, but people say she posted all sorts of stuff online, people's college rejections and homework and who was hooking up with who. I don't know, I think that's pretty shitty. Can you imagine what it would have felt like to go to school with someone like that? To always be worried that your deepest, darkest secret might get completely taken out of context, misunderstood, and then put up on the internet for everyone to see." Hazel shudders. "It's like . . . psychological warfare."

I want to argue, tell her that doesn't make what Andie did okay, but then I think of the podcast about the Camp Lost Lake murders, how easy it was for my entire life to be taken away from me, all because of what someone else put online, and I decide to keep my mouth shut. Hazel's right. It is easy for someone to completely misunderstand something and ruin everything.

"I'm pretty sure my brain will turn into oatmeal if I play any more solitaire," I tell her, handing the phone back.

Hazel smiles. "Mmm. Oatmeal brain."

Something about the way she says this annoys me. It's like she's not taking my complaint seriously, which is crappy of her considering *I'm* the one sitting on an exam table, unable to move because my foot's about to fall off. I feel like I deserve some serious pity here.

"Not good oatmeal," I tell her. "Overcooked oatmeal. *Cold* overcooked oatmeal."

"What sort of toppings does it have?"

I frown. "What?"

"I don't mind cold, overcooked oatmeal if the toppings are good. Are we talking peanut butter and banana? Apple, cinnamon, and walnut?"

God, she's weird. "I don't know. It was metaphorical oatmeal. I haven't gotten as far as the toppings."

"Have you ever tried just throwing anything you could find in your cupboard into your oatmeal? Like dried cherries and coconut and pecans and peanut butter?"

"Uh . . . *ew.*"

"No, it's awesome. You'd think those flavors wouldn't go together but they actually taste totally amazing. I call it kitchen sink oatmeal."

I stare at her. I sort of can't believe she's talking to me about oatmeal so soon after my entire world just imploded. "Why would you call it that?"

"Come on, you know the phrase 'everything but the kitchen sink'? That's what this is, you throw everything but the kitchen sink in it."

"I'll have to take your word for it." Oatmeal makes me think of homey, comfortable things. My mom and me in the kitchen before school, Mom making me breakfast, kissing me on the cheek, and telling me I was her whole world. Things I used to have, before everything got ruined. A lump forms in my throat.

"I bet I can change your mind," Hazel is saying now. "I'm pretty good with food."

I swallow the lump. "What does that mean? Are you, like, a chef?"

Hazel laughs softly. "Not professionally or anything." She shifts so she's sitting a little closer to me. "I do cooking tutorials on TikTok, though. I'm going to be a food influencer someday, like Sophia Roe. My one on oatmeal got a ton of views. You should let me make it for you sometime."

"I won't be sticking around here that long, but thanks."

"Come on, you won't be here long enough for one measly meal?" Hazel frowns suddenly, like something just occurred to her. "Or, I'm sorry, have you tried it before? Do you already know you're not into oatmeal? Because you can just tell me, I won't be offended or anything."

Wait, what? I stare at her, pretty sure we're not talking about oatmeal anymore. Were we ever talking about oatmeal?

As though realizing I'm going to need a little help, Hazel reaches out and touches the backs of my knuckles. It's the lightest possible pressure of her fingers against my skin, barely a touch at all, more like an accidental brush except that she looks at me when she does it, as though to say, *Is this okay?*

Heat bursts into my cheeks. "Oh!" I say. Finally getting it.

Hazel smiles. "Yeah."

"I didn't . . . I didn't realize that's what you were talking about."

"No shit."

"To be fair, oatmeal is the grossest metaphor for that maybe ever."

Hazel makes a face. "You know, I'm getting that. I just couldn't think of another way to ask what you were into."

"Right." I drop my gaze from Hazel's eyes to her lips. They look soft and a little shiny, like she's wearing lip gloss, maybe. My skin hums, surprising me a little. If everything weren't so messed up right now, I might actually want to kiss her.

I swallow hard and look down at my hands. It's a feeling I don't have with Jack. The fireworks in my belly, like all my nerve endings are flaring at the same time. I first realized it when I saw Olivia staring at him, practically drooling. As much as I love Jack, I've never felt that way about him.

"Knew it," Hazel says softly.

I look up at her, frowning. "What does that mean?"

Hazel must've realized she's said something wrong because she tries to backtrack. "No, it's nothing. Just that when I was talking to Olivia earlier, she said—"

"You and Olivia were talking about me?" Heat floods my

cheeks. It really pisses me off that they might've been discussing my sexuality behind my back. "You can't be serious."

To her credit, Hazel looks horrified. "Reagan, no, that's not what we were doing—"

But the damage is already done. I pull my hand away from her, feeling suddenly gross where she was touching me. I bet she didn't mean anything she just said to me. She was just trying to get a reaction, so she could go back to Olivia and talk about me some more. God, how could I be so stupid? Was I going to have to learn this lesson over and over for the rest of my life? Other people and me don't mix. "Did Olivia put you up to this because she's all into Jack?"

"Of course not—"

"Were you just flirting with me to figure out if I was queer?"

Hazel reels away from me, like I slapped her. "I was flirting with you because you're hot, and I—"

Outside, there's a shuffle of movement in the grass that quickly goes still. Hazel and I immediately fall silent.

I hear a buzzing in my head. *No.* It can't be her; she couldn't have found us. It was an animal or the wind or a leaf falling. Not Andie. Not the witch.

I look back up at Hazel. Her lower lip is quivering. She looks catatonic, too scared to move or breathe or think.

I'm about to grab her shoulders and shake when her eyes swivel up to mine and she mouths, *Hide.*

17

Olivia

I'm halfway across the clearing when the cabin door swings open.

"Olivia? Is that you?"

Andie's voice. I stop walking, emotion swirling inside me. Andie's framed in the doorway, light spilling out of the cabin behind her. She's all in shadow, her expression just the barest suggestion in the darkness.

She takes a step away from the cabin, and in the light I see that my sister looks like she always looks: the same pale, heart-shaped face as mine, the same long, blond hair, the beginnings of wrinkles just starting to crawl away from the corners of her eyes.

I think of that video: Gia, terrified, whispering into the camera. *I watched her kill him.* Andie's furious face appearing only moments later.

My nerves prick and again I think, *How well do I know my sister?* Beyond the nice exterior and the perfect persona, who *is* Andie? My whole life, she's always been on the other side of the country, climbing the tech ladder, running the world. I'd always thought of her as a role model, the kind of person who goes after what she wants no matter what stands in her way. But she's always kept me at a distance.

I think of how ugly her voice sounded on that video clip. *Don't make me hurt you.* Andie goes after what she wants, all right. She's been keeping secrets from me and everyone else for sixteen years. Her entire identity is built on secrets.

What's she going to do now that it looks like those secrets are going to get out?

I swallow, but I don't say anything

"Olivia?" Andie's still staring at me, frowning slightly. "What are you doing out here? Did you go off to look for Eric?"

I feel suddenly sick to my stomach. *Poor Eric.*

"Did you find him?" Andie asks in an undertone. "Did he get through to the cops?"

I frown at her. For a second, I was sure I heard something in her voice. Fear, maybe. Is she afraid that Eric *did* get through to the cops? That they're on their way here, now?

"Andie . . ." I say quietly. "Eric's dead."

Andie's face seems to visibly pale. She lifts a hand to her mouth, staying quiet for a long moment. I study her expression, looking for cracks. Is this the reaction of a vicious killer? Is this how someone would act if they'd just murdered a boy in cold blood?

"The killer must have cut him off in the woods," I tell her. "I found his body."

Andie nods, then licks her lips. "Okay . . . we need to get inside. Hurry."

She's still frowning as she ushers me into the cabin. Everyone else must've shoved into cars and taken off because we seem to be the only two people left.

"I let Amir take my car to drive the rest of the kids into town, but he should be back soon to pick us up," Andie says, reading my mind. She squeezes my shoulder. "This is almost over."

"I called the cops," I blurt, shrugging her off. I don't want to be touched right now, not by her. "There was a landline back at the nurse's cabin. A cruiser's on its way."

"Oh, good." Andie's voice is completely devoid of emotion. She doesn't sound like she thinks the cops coming is a good thing. She sounds distracted, like she's thinking of something else completely. She glances behind her and then leans a little closer to me, adding, "Do you know where Sawyer put Gia's camera?"

Without thinking about what I'm doing, I reach into my pocket, fingers lightly brushing the camera's plastic case. "Why?"

"I asked the others before they left, and they said he put it in the lodge, but I was just over there, and I couldn't find it. Do you know if he might've taken it somewhere else?"

I feel something uneasy settle in my stomach. *The lodge.* Andie was just over at the lodge.

I think of the figure all in black creeping through the woods. I look down at Andie's feet and see that she's wearing black boots, the soles crusted in mud.

Just like whoever I saw creeping around outside in a witch's mask.

My voice shrivels in my throat. It takes a lot of effort for me to squeak out, "When did you go there?"

Andie frowns. Something flashes across her eyes. *Suspicion?*

"I just got back a few minutes ago," she admits.

I try to keep my expression impassive even as the uneasy feeling spreads through me. There are tons of twisty little side paths veering off the main dirt path through the woods. One of them circles through the trees for a few hundred feet before dumping you out directly behind the cabins. Andie could've made her way down the path and ended up right back at the cabins before I'd even crossed the clearing. Which means she could've been that figure stalking through the woods while Jack and I hid in terror. She could've been the one who shot at that squirrel.

For a second, it feels like I'm still hiding behind that tree with Jack, trying to keep my breath as quiet as possible as the witch creeps closer and closer, flinching at the splitting wood sound when she ripped the arrow out of the tree.

My chest twists. I can't do this anymore.

"*I* have the camera, Andie," I tell her carefully. "I took it from the lodge after Sawyer died."

Andie stares at me, her lips slightly parted. "Did you . . . watch it?"

When I don't answer, Andie reaches out to grab me, adding in a fierce whisper, "Olivia . . . I know it looks bad, but I—"

Thunder booms right outside the window, making me jump. There's a flash of lighting.

And then the electricity goes out.

MURDER WEAPON

Incident No: 000524-27B-2008

Item Description: 44 in. adult male recurve bow with letters "JK" etched into the side and four 28 in. arrows.

Admitted into evidence JUNE 14, 2008, by Investigating Officer Angel Lopez.

FINGERPRINT ANALYSIS

Investigating Officer(s): Karly Knight

Incident No: 000524-27B-2008

Case Description: Double homicide of Gia North and Jacob Knight

Test Request:

Test fingerprint sample of accused against sample found on weapon discovered near the scene of the crime.

Evidence Items:

000332-53: Adult recurve bow

000332-43: Hairbrush, Lori Knight

Test Results:

Positive. Fingerprints found on bow are a match for Lori Knight.

18

Reagan

Hazel presses a finger to my lips. *Quiet*, she mouths silently.

I nod and she lowers her finger, her eyes still locked on mine.

Neither of us moves.

Wind rustles the leaves on a tree right outside the cabin window, sending shadows through the dirty glass. Thunder booms, so close to the walls of the cabin that I jump. The skin along the back of my neck tingles as I wait and wait . . .

Nothing. No footsteps. No breathing. No voices. Hazel blinks and looks away from me, the small movement like a spell breaking.

My chest heaves as I suck down a breath. "What the—"

The shuffle of a footstep against the dirt, followed by the soft scattering of rocks, both sounds so quiet they're barely perceptible. I snap my mouth closed and whip my head around to look at the window. There's the barest twitch of movement, a shadow sliding behind a tree.

I look back at Hazel.

Hide, she mouths to me. I grope for her shoulder at the same moment that she slides an arm around my waist, helping me climb down from the table without banging my ankle up too badly.

There aren't many places in the small cabin to hide: a few pieces of furniture, none of them large enough to conceal us, and a door that I'm guessing leads to a closet or a bathroom.

We head for the door. Hazel gets there first and swings it open. I follow her, hopping on one leg. She ushers me inside, then pulls the door closed behind us.

The closet is small and cramped. Hazel's knee ends up near my chin. With nowhere to put my arms or hands, I lean forward, letting them rest on her jeans. We're so close that our faces almost touch, and even though I try to stay calm, every breath I take is ragged, scared. Hazel presses a hand over my mouth, raising a finger to her own lips.

A door clicks open. The wood groans as someone steps into the cabin.

Hazel's shaking. I can feel her fingers trembling against my lips. It's too dark to see anything, so I keep my eyes trained on the thin strip of silvery light below the door.

Whoever just came inside doesn't turn on any more lights. They take a few steps in one direction and then another, the sound of their footsteps echoing off the walls.

I stop breathing. I can't take this. It's bad enough knowing they're on the other side of the door and infinitely worse not being able to see what they're doing. I imagine them looking around the small room, searching for signs that we were there. They'll for sure see the medical supplies Hazel grabbed from the shelves and, oh God, did I leave blood on the floor? My heart crashes against my rib cage as I imagine a dotted red trail pointing out exactly where we're hiding.

Please, I think, curling my fingers around Hazel's knees. *Please just go. Don't find us, please.*

I watch the shadow move below the door and listen to the sound of their footsteps, the groan of wood, the long, slow sound of breathing. They're not rushed or nervous. They know they have time to look over every inch of this space. I mentally catalog every place they could think to look for us, under the desk and behind a cabinet. It's only a matter of time before they open this door.

They cross the cabin, seeming to stop directly in front of the closet where Hazel and I are hidden.

I look straight ahead, somehow finding Hazel's eyes in the darkness, twin glints of reflective light in the pitch black. I stare straight into them, hoping that she too feels some comfort in the fact that at least we're not alone. A second later, I feel her hands on my hands, her fingers wrapping around my fingers. Something warm shoots through me, followed immediately by a sick twist of disappointment.

It's not fair. None of this is fair.

There's a beat of silence. My muscles tense as I wait for the closet door to swing open, for whoever's on the other side to find us at last. There's a rustling sound, a low sigh. And then, the footsteps turn and walk in the opposite direction.

There's the click of a door, and they're gone.

I'm not sure how long Hazel and I stay hidden in that closet waiting for them to come back and find us. It could be ten minutes or an hour. It really doesn't matter. Neither of us makes any move to open the door or reveal our hiding spot—just in case they're waiting on the other side. Toying with us.

An eternity later, I hear Hazel's voice. "We can't stay here forever."

"I know," I whisper back.

"If they knew we were in here, they would've opened the door."

I nod, even though I'm sure she can't see me in the darkness. *Yes. This is true. If the witch knew we were here, she would've opened the door. She would've discovered us and killed us. That's what killers do.* I've been going over and over this line of reasoning, and yet I still can't get over the part of my brain that keeps telling me that it could be a trick, that the witch could be waiting on the other side of the door to surprise us.

"I'm going to get up now," Hazel tells me.

I make no move to stop her as she stands and eases the door open. A creak of hinges, a gust of slightly cooler, fresher air, and then we're peering into the cabin.

The *empty* cabin.

Relief floods through me. I push myself to my feet, carefully easing my weight onto my injured ankle. Pain shoots up my leg, but I'm able to breathe through it.

"Look," Hazel says. She holds up a crutch.

A *crutch*.

"Yes," I say, reaching for it. There only appears to be one crutch in the closet, but that's completely fine with me. I only need to make it as far as my truck, and I can do that with one crutch.

I wedge it into my armpit and take a few practice laps of the cabin. So far, so good. My ankle still kills, but it's not so bad that I'm going to collapse. I look at Hazel. "Okay, so . . . I guess I'm out of here."

Hazel looks completely taken off guard. "Wait, *what*?"

"I was stuck here because of my leg, remember?" I shake the crutch at her. "Now, I'm not so stuck."

"But . . . Reagan, no. Jack could be back any second!"

"Jack's been gone for at least twenty minutes," I say, speaking as calmly as I can manage. I stop my mind before it can spiral off into the million and one horrible things that could've happened to him. "There's no reason it should've taken him this long to get the truck. Something must've . . . happened." *And he needs me*, I think. I close my eyes. He's out in the woods somewhere, alone, and possibly hurt. I can't just stay here praying he'll find his way back. I have to find him. Help him. Besides my mom, he's all I have. Olivia's made that perfectly clear.

I hobble for the door.

"Reagan, stop," Hazel says. "It's dangerous out there and . . . and the sun's about to set. Think about what you're doing."

"You can keep waiting if you want, but the only thing I want to do is get the hell out of these woods."

"So, what? You're just going to wander around by yourself?"

"No, I'm going back to my truck." Whatever happened to Jack happened between here and the truck. If I can find him, I can help him. And if I can't . . .

I don't want to think about that part.

"Okay," Hazel says, "Then I'll come with you."

I hesitate for a second. Staying together is the right thing to do. It's what Olivia would do. But I can't help thinking about the way

Hazel looked at me, the way her fingers brushed the back of my hand, so softly.

And then, seconds later, how it all went to shit when I realized she hadn't actually *meant* any of it. That she was playing me, that she's probably going to tell Olivia everything I did and said the second she's out of here.

The twist of pain I feel hurts just as bad as it did the first time. "Sticking together" is only smart for people like Olivia, people who have friends and family they can trust. But I'm not one of those people. Not anymore, at least.

"Thanks, but no," I tell Hazel, shoving the cabin door open. "I'm better on my own. Maybe you should go back to the cabins, catch up with Olivia. If she's confronting that sister of hers, she's the one who needs help right now, not me."

I cringe as I awkwardly hobble down the two concrete stairs. The crutch is harder to maneuver than I want it to be, a touch too tall for my five-foot-four frame and wedged painfully into my armpit. I have to hold on to it with both hands as I step onto the dirt path leading through the woods.

"Don't be an *idiot*, Reagan," Hazel says, following me. She's lowered her voice now that we're in the woods, and this comes out in a harsh whisper. "We need to stick together."

"I'm not being an idiot," I snap back, matching her lower voice. "And this isn't a movie. I don't need your help."

"Everyone needs help from other people sometimes. Even you."

"My problem has never been needing help, my problem has been finding people willing to offer it."

"I'm offering it right now!"

I whirl back around to face her, anger rising in my cheeks. "How do I put this in a way you'll understand?" I snap. "I don't *trust* you."

Hazel freezes, looking stricken. I feel a momentary pang of guilt, but the guilt dissipates the moment I duck into the trees.

It's better this way. Some people can't rely on anyone else. Friends only ever disappoint you, in the end.

The woods are dark. A little darker than I was expecting, to be honest. The sun has begun its descent beyond the distant hills, and the feeble golden light sends shadows creeping through the storm clouds.

I feel like I'm going to pee my pants. Strange movements keep moving behind trees and bushes, going still the second I turn to look at them.

Was that twig snapping a footstep? I wonder. *Was that shadow large enough to be the witch?*

Walking with this stupid crutch is a lot harder than I expected. I thought I'd get the hang of it after a few minutes, but somewhat paradoxically the too-tall crutch gets harder to maneuver the longer I use it. It sinks into the ground, gets stuck in the mud, and keeps catching on little rocks embedded in the path, sending me flailing, desperate to right myself before I lose my balance and fall. I'm able to put a little weight on my ankle, but every step I take is agony.

And there's this annoying, nagging voice at the back of my head muttering that maybe I *should've* accepted Hazel's offer to come with me. I've been tempting fate every time I've stepped into the woods alone. I'm not a total idiot, I know it's a lot smarter to stay with other people in situations like this. I know that, even if I keep ignoring it.

My stomach has twisted itself into a hard knot by the time I reach my truck, and each breath I take is a little trembly. It doesn't matter how many times I tell myself I'm fine, that I'm not scared. My body knows the truth. I feel it in my sweaty palms and my shaking knees. I'm terrified.

My truck looks different in the fading light, almost as if it belongs to someone else. A fresh wave of fear moves through me. I stagger up to it, and I'm about to throw myself inside and hit the gas when I remember an urban legend I heard once: a girl is driving alone at night, but she doesn't realize a killer has climbed into her back seat when she stopped for gas.

Swallowing, I hobble around to the back, flinching every time the bottom of my crutch hits the mud. The forest is so quiet that each sound is like a gunshot, making me flinch. If Andie is in the back of the truck, she'll hear me for sure. She'll know I'm coming.

My palms aren't just sweating now, they're *shaking*. I feel tremors of fear shooting up and down my legs, and I grip my crutch with both hands to keep from falling.

Please don't be there, I think.

Please.

The sides of the truck bed are taller than I am, so I can't see inside as I make my way past. I listen hard, trying to catch the sound of someone breathing, moving, but it's impossible to hear anything over my own pounding heart. I hesitate, nerves making my chest tight. Then, I lower the back and force myself to look.

The bed is empty.

I half collapse against the side of the truck, relief leaving me weak. My exhale hitches, already halfway to a sob.

It's okay, I tell myself. *There's no one in my truck. It's going to be okay . . .*

I turn for the driver's side door. And that's when my gaze drops to the front tire.

The *flat* front tire.

"No," I murmur. The tire has been completely drained of air. I picture Andie walking past, jabbing it with an arrow, and the back of my neck crawls. I feel, suddenly, as though there is someone behind me, creeping up on me, reaching for my throat, and I wheel around, holding tight to my crutch.

The trees are still, quiet. I draw a long, hitching breath as I search the shadows beyond. If Andie's here, she's well hidden.

I swallow hard. I need to move. She could be back any second.

I hobble back to the truck bed, moving as quickly as I can on my crutch. My spare is right where it always is, covered in an old tarp in the back of the bed. I rest my crutch against the side of the truck and climb into the bed on hands and knees. It's easier to move like this, without putting any weight on my ankle. I crawl to the back of the truck bed and wrestle the tire out from beneath the tarp, my hands sweaty and shaking. It seems to take me forever to get it free and push it out.

It bounces when it hits the dirt path and rolls for a couple of feet, before toppling onto its side.

I try to hurry, but the act of climbing into the trunk and removing the tire was hard enough. My ankle throbs like another heart, the blood below my bandage seeming to pulse. Despite the painkillers I took at the nurse's cabin, the pain is so bad I can hardly breathe.

My chest starts to heave, panic threatening to take over. I didn't think this through. How am I supposed to *change a tire* before the witch finds me? And, even if I do, can I even drive with my foot like this?

Tears gather in my eyes and I collapse against the cool metal side of the truck bed, breathing hard, trying to calm down.

I can do this, I tell myself. *I have to do this. Come on, get up, keep moving, you're so close now . . .*

Something moves in the trees. I jerk my head up.

No, no, not now, I can't handle anything else now . . .

My eyes water as I stare into the darkness, refusing to blink, just in case I miss something important. Lightning flashes, but the branches are still, the woods looking deceptively innocent. I won't be fooled. I know how much that darkness hides, and I know what I heard. The sound of footsteps moving in the leaves.

I swallow and wait. After a few moments, my shoulders begin to drop away from my ears, my breath returning to normal. *Now it's time to get up, Reagan. Come on, you can do it, just move your legs.*

And then, I hear it again. This time, it's not the faint rustle of someone hiding in the trees, watching without being observed. No, these footsteps are purposeful. I hear them cut a path through the trees, the steady *thump, thump, thump* against the dirt telling me that whoever's coming has no interest in keeping quiet. My chest seizes. I look around for anything to help protect myself, and my eyes fall on the tire iron sitting in the back of the truck.

Desperate, I crawl over to it, my fingers trembling as I work them around the cool metal.

I raise the tire iron over my shoulder, ducking down low on the flat bed to avoid arrows. I peer over the edge of the truck.

And I wait.

A moment later, Hazel appears from within the trees, a few fallen leaves in her dark curls.

"Hey, so it turns out that I didn't really want to be alone," she says, sounding a little anxious. Her eyes flick up to my tire iron and she gives me a thumbs-up. "Cool, that'll keep the witch away."

I exhale and collapse against the side of the truck, letting the tire iron drop to the bed with a clunk. I'm so relieved to see Hazel instead of the murderer that I don't even bother giving her crap for her bad joke. I just release a single, relieved sob.

Something in her face softens. "Hey, it's okay."

"I thought you were her," I say. "I thought I was all alone out here, and I-I can't move very fast and—"

"It's okay, it's just me. And look, no arrows." She seems to realize for the first time that I'm in the back of a freaking truck. "Need some help getting down?"

I nod and grab for her hand, but I lose my balance when I try to get down, and sort of fall into her arms instead. Like this is a bad romantic comedy and I'm the clumsy lead.

"Nice," she says, her voice breathy. "Very smooth."

"I'm sorry," I tell her.

She shakes her head. "Don't be sorry."

She's warm beneath my arms, her chest rising and falling against mine. Her skin is soft. When I pull away from her, I see that she's watching me, her gaze steady and unblinking. Like she's asking me a question.

Something inside of me cracks. No, that's not the right metaphor. It's like something that was already cracked fits back into place, two puzzle pieces coming together to finally become whole. I had no idea how much I needed someone to come after me, to prove that I was worth following into the dark, to catch me when I fell. And yeah, I know how cheesy that all sounds, but there's a reason it's a cliché. It's because it's true. Everyone needs someone. Even me.

I don't think. I don't have to. The kiss just happens, like nature, like fate. One second, we're holding each other, staring at each other, and the next our lips are pressed together, and then parting, and my hands are in Hazel's hair and hers are around my waist, and I can feel her heart beating against my chest, so fast, like a little bird's.

She's just as soft as I thought she'd be. Her lips taste like cherries and vanilla, and it's unbelievable how I never realized before how those are my favorite flavors. I can't get enough. I want this kiss, this moment, to last forever.

When I finally pull away, I see someone's staring at us. It's Jack, standing at the edge of the trees.

I don't think I've ever seen him look so completely gutted before. His eyebrows are furrowed, his lips parted, and there's an expression of mingled confusion and devastation on his face. My stomach drops.

"You . . ." His eyes move from me to Hazel. He shakes his head.

I search my brain, trying to come up with something to say that might make me seem like less of an asshole. But there's nothing.

I wet my lips. "Jack, I . . . I didn't mean to . . ."

"Stop." Jack lifts a hand. "This isn't even about that. I came out and *asked* you. All you had to do was be honest and you couldn't even do that."

There's a sound like a thin whistle, like wind in the trees, followed by a wet *thwunk*. Jack's expression goes blank. His mouth drops open, like he's trying to say something but can't find the words.

I don't know what's happening until I lower my gaze from Jack's face and see the arrow protruding from his shoulder.

19

Olivia

Andie is suddenly beside me, her fingers gripping my arm so tightly they pinch my skin. "Come check the breaker with me," she says. Her voice sounds normal enough, but I know Andie and I hear something else threaded through her words. Something low and simmering.

Anger, I think. My sister's voice is dripping with rage.

I stare at her. In the sudden darkness, she doesn't look like the sister I've known all my life at all. There are new shadows under her eyes and in the hollows of her cheekbones. Her expression is distant and impossible to read. She looks strange, *other*. Like someone I never really knew.

I don't want to go with her to check the breaker, I realize. I don't want to be alone with her, *period*. I want to go back to before I ran out of the nurse's cabin, before I saw what was on that video, and before I accidentally knocked the damn camera loose in the first place. I want to start today over. I want my biggest problem to be knowing that my dad isn't really my dad.

Andie steers me into the hall. It doesn't even occur to me to fight her, to do anything. Not until we're already on our way to the basement.

"Andie—" I start. My heart is beating so loudly I wonder if she can hear it. "Andie, listen—"

But Andie just pulls a door open and shoves me through it, pushing me toward a stairway.

Oh God, she really is taking me down to the basement.

I hesitate at the top of the stairs, breathing hard, and Andie gives me a little poke in the back. "What are you waiting for? The breaker's down there. *Go*."

She's behind me, hemming me in. There's nowhere else for me to go, not unless I want to barrel my way through her, and there's still a part of me that's hoping I got it wrong somehow—that this is all a big misunderstanding, that the next words out of her mouth are going to be a perfectly logical explanation.

I've never been afraid of Andie before. Not *ever*.

But now . . .

My legs feel numb. There's no way I'm running right now, not when it takes every ounce of my concentration just to put them one in front of the other, down one stair, then two, then three. The basement reaches up to grab me, the air heavy with the smell of dust and mold, the scent of the long neglected. It's colder down here than it was upstairs—a deep, bone-chilling cold. I wrap my arms around my chest and try not to shiver.

Then I'm moving my boot from the bottom stair to the dirty, concrete floor. If Andie is planning to hurt me, this is exactly the right place to do it. It practically screams *murder basement*. The ceiling is low, not even a full foot above our heads, with bare wooden beams and a tangled spiderweb of old wires leading no-where. Otherwise, it's empty except for a wooden folding chair and a pile of old cardboard boxes tied together with a string. The only light comes from a high, narrow window, but the setting sun does very little to illuminate the space.

Then, a bright light flashes on, shocking me so much I flinch backward, my hands flying up over my face. It's a long moment before I manage to squint past the assaulting glow, realizing the light's coming from Andie's phone.

She aims the beam at the far wall. "Breaker's over there."

She moves past me, and there's an ancient creak of metal as she throws the door to the breaker open. I glance over my shoulder. She's left the path to the stairs clear. I could make a run for it now. I could be up those stairs before she even turns around. I could probably lock her down here. I doubt the door itself has a lock, but there are chairs and stuff upstairs. I could wedge one of them under the doorknob, trap her. Andie's fast, but her boots have chunkier heels than mine do. I could outrun her for sure.

But something stops me. Loyalty? Maybe.

More than that, I think I just really want to know the truth.

There's an old crowbar leaning against the wall, the only thing down here that could potentially be used as a weapon. I reach for it, moving as slowly and silently as I possibly can, hoping my sister doesn't notice.

The metal is cold beneath my fingers, and dusty.

I don't think Andie sees that I've grabbed it. She's facing away from me, using her phone to illuminate an electrical panel. I think she actually is trying to fix it because she's quiet for a long moment, fumbling with the wires and breakers. I hear the sharp crack of plastic as she flips them on and off, one by one.

"The video," she says after a very long moment. "I haven't seen it, but it must look . . . bad."

I swallow, but I don't say anything. My fingers tighten around the crowbar, and I shift a little, so it's hidden behind my leg.

"I've been afraid of someone finding that stupid camera for years," she continues, closing her eyes. "Gia had no idea what she was . . . I *knew* that if anyone saw that video, they would totally misinterpret things. But Gia never really cared about getting things right."

Andie stops fumbling for a second and glances over her shoulder at me. "I wanted to destroy it, but Gia hid it really well. I've been trying to find it since that night." Andie gave a little shrug. "I guess, after a while, I let myself hope it was lost forever."

"Is . . . is that why you hurt her?" I ask.

"*Hurt* her?" Andie frowns at me in the dark. Her phone illuminates the bottom half of her face, sending long shadows over the rest of her features. It reminds me of being twelve and listening to her scary stories, one of the few times the two of us spent time together, just us. We'd cuddle up in my twin-size bed, and she'd use her phone as a flashlight and hold it under her chin, just like this.

I feel a sick twist, nostalgia and fear curling inside of me at the same time. I tighten my grip on the crowbar, trying to mentally prepare myself to hear my sister's confession.

But when Andie speaks again, her voice is disappointed. "Olivia . . . do you think *I* killed Gia?"

"Andie . . . come on, what am I supposed to think? She said she saw you kill someone. And you and Mom lied and told everyone you were in New York the night of the murders when you were actually here. You threatened and attacked Gia and . . . and when Gia went to turn off her camera, her hands were covered in-in *blood*." My voice shakes as I force those last words from my mouth. My stomach gives a sick twist.

Andie pinches the bridge of her nose with the hand that isn't holding her phone. "I *know*," she says, punctuating the words with a sharp nod. "I know it looks bad, really. But, Olivia, you have to believe me when I tell you that I had *nothing* to do with murdering those people that night! I-I couldn't have—"

"What does that mean, you *couldn't* have?" I snap back at her. "You've been lying to me my whole life. I'm supposed to just believe you're too moral or—"

"No, Olivia, I mean that . . . *physically*, I couldn't have." Andie lifts her gaze to meet mine and, even in the dark, I can tell there's something complicated happening behind her eyes.

I go still, my skin buzzing.

Andie inhales and says, carefully, "I couldn't have killed anyone the night of the murders because I was too busy giving birth."

The Night of
the Murders

Andie stood at the top of the lighthouse. She swayed on her feet, a wave of dizziness overcoming her.

What am I doing here? What just happened? Her hands went automatically to her belly, and she blinked a few times, waiting for the vertigo to fade, for the world to slam back into her. It had been like this for the last few hours that she'd been having contractions. After they were over, it seemed to take her forever to remember where she was, what she was doing. Really, it was only ever a couple of seconds.

Darkness pressed against the floor-to-ceiling windows surrounding her, but it didn't quite hide the spinning, vertigo-inducing sensation of being up very, very high. Andie could feel how far away the ground below her was, even if she couldn't see it.

She heard the telltale creak of feet stepping onto the lighthouse stairs and jerked her head around, suddenly alert.

There was *Gia*, ducking into the stairwell, bent over that camera, *whispering*.

Andie lurched toward the stairs, anger rising inside of her. She remembered now. She'd been planning to meet Matthew up here, and then . . . then *Gia* had appeared, with that stupid camera. And now, she'd caught Andie's biggest mistake on tape.

"Shut that off," Andie choked out, stumbling after her. The stairwell surrounded her, a narrow concrete spiral, its stone walls covered in layers of graffiti. She braced a hand against the wall as she struggled to make her way down the stairs. *"Now . . ."*

The word had only just left her mouth when another contraction began to build in her lower back. She keeled over in the middle of the staircase, breathing hard, both hands pressed to her stomach.

Gia whirled around, eyes wide. "Andie! What—"

Andie didn't bother answering. All she could think about was that damn camera, getting it away from Gia, and turning it *off*. Who knows what Gia already had on that thing? If Gia captured her labor on film, she wouldn't think twice about putting it online. And then everyone would know, everyone would see what she'd spent the last six months hiding.

That there hadn't really been any internship in the city. She'd made it up. She'd been hooking up with Matthew Knight all last year and, when she got pregnant, she left school to keep everyone from finding out. She'd been lying to everyone, including her parents, for months.

Down in New York City she'd found an adoption agency that agreed to set her up with a place to live and doctor's visits and everything she needed to get through her pregnancy, as long as she agreed to give the babies up for adoption.

Only, when the time came, she couldn't do it. She couldn't imagine just . . . giving them away.

So she'd come back here. And now she was having second

thoughts, again. She just wasn't ready for people to find out. Not like this.

"I'm serious, Gia." Andie groaned. "Don't . . . make me hurt you!" It was a somewhat ridiculous threat, considering how big she was, how hard it was for her to move. She reached for the camera, but Gia pulled away and she wound up only groping at air.

Gia's eyes dropped to Andie's midsection and widened. "I was right," she whispered. "The ultrasound *was* yours."

Andie glanced at the camera, wondering if Gia's voice had been loud enough to get picked up on the tape. She'd spoken quietly, it's possible the camera didn't get it. Andie inhaled and swung. This time her fingers made contact with the smooth, plastic casing. The camera slammed to the stairs—

Pain rose so suddenly it blotted out everything else. Andie's exhale was a sob. She couldn't remember how to stand. The idea was impossible. She opened her mouth to tell Gia that something was wrong, that she needed help, but she couldn't make words form.

Instead, she screamed.

Gia was hovering behind her. "Oh my God! *Oh my God!*"

"Shut *up*," Andie hissed, and then doubled over, gasping. The muscles around her spine constricted so suddenly that, for long moments, she couldn't breathe.

When it felt like the worst had passed, she inhaled slow, hoping it was all okay, that it was over—for a few seconds, at least. She fumbled for the camera again, just to make sure it wasn't still recording. It wasn't. She exhaled, her eyes closing.

Gia was still watching her. She was blabbering now, releasing a steady stream of words, like she wanted to make sure Andie understood exactly how she'd put the whole story together. "Andie's short for Miranda, I can't believe no one else thought of that, but people forget that you and your mom have the same name. I didn't, though. When I saw that second ultrasound, I knew, and I realized that must've been why you left school early! Everyone knows internships don't start in the middle of the year! And then, when I found out Matthew had your key card, I realized he must be the father, and so I followed him out here and that's when I saw—"

"Gia . . ." Andie gasped. *"Stop."*

She forced her eyes open, and the first thing she saw was the blood. There was so much of it, soaking into the concrete and streaked across her hands and down her legs. She was bleeding.

Did that mean there was something wrong with the babies?

"I need . . . help," she gasped, looking up at Gia. "You have to . . . find my mom . . ."

Her mom already knew everything. Andie had come back to town a few days ago. She'd been hiding out on the campgrounds while she worked up the courage to tell her parents what was going on and figure out what she wanted to do next. Camp Lost Lake wasn't open for the season yet. The only people here were a few members of the staff: her mom, Jacob and Lori Knight, and Henry, the groundskeeper.

Andie had been sleeping in the empty counselor's cabin and using her old key card to get into the cafeteria in the lodge, where there was always frozen food in the industrial-size freezers and cans of beans and fruit in the cupboards. She'd told Matthew first. Then her mom. They were supposed to be coming up with a plan for what to do next. Everything should've worked out.

It *would've* worked out, if tonight hadn't gone so badly wrong.

"Andie," Gia said. She was staring at her, wide-eyed, and Andie could see that her skin had lost all its color. She was terrified, probably in shock. She looked down the stairs and said, "What about Matthew?"

"He's gone," Andie snapped. She could feel another contraction starting. She didn't have time to explain this. "Gia please, I-I need your help. I need you to find my mom. *Please!*"

Gia looked back at the blood splattered ground and said, her voice trembling, "I-I'll go find her, okay? Just-just stay here. Don't move."

Andie nodded. She couldn't do or say anything else. She heard the soles of Gia's shoes slapping against the ground.

And then, nothing. She was alone.

She didn't know how long she stayed hunched on the stairs. Hours? Minutes? The pain rose and fell so quickly that she didn't even have time to count through it, like they told her to do during her birth classes. The second the pain crested, she'd inhale, thinking *one* . . . but before she could get to *two* the pain hit all over again, and everything in her head turned to black. This was all happening much, much too quickly. The babies were coming too fast.

Where was Gia? She should've been back by now.

An eternity later, Andie heard footsteps thudding up the stairs. She could've cried. Someone was here with her. *Thank God.* She forced her eyes open, but it took her a moment to focus.

It wasn't her mom, it was someone else.

"Shhh," the woman said, squeezing Andie's fingers. It was Lori Knight, Andie realized, her eyesight clearing. Matthew's mom.

When Andie last spoke to Matthew, he said he'd told his parents and grandma about the babies last night. So Lori knew.

"My-my mom—" Andie started.

"I don't know where Miranda is, but we need to get you to the hospital, dear," Lori was saying. "Everything's going to be okay. Just breathe . . ."

"I . . . I can't . . ." What Andie wanted to say was that every time she tried to inhale, she got so nauseated she felt like she was going to throw up. But another wave of pain swept over her and the words died in her mouth.

". . . can't wait for an ambulance," she heard Lori saying. "Your contractions are too close together."

I don't want to have my babies here, she wanted to say. But she couldn't say that. She couldn't say anything. The pain was rising inside her, again, higher and higher, until it was all she could think about.

She screamed and screamed—

20

Reagan

I stare in horror as Jack rocks back on his heels. His eyes roll in their sockets, unable to focus, and then his mouth drops open as he gropes for the arrow protruding from his chest. His hands are clumsy, fingers grasping but never quite gripping the shaft.

"Reagan . . ." he gasps, his eyes finding mine for a fraction of a second. *"Run."*

Fresh terror sweeps through me.

"Jack," I croak. I grab for him, to steady him, but I reach out too late and my fingers pass through air. He stumbles backward, and then his knees give, and he's falling.

No no no no no.

He crashes onto his back in the dirt and goes suddenly still. My heart goes still with him. I feel as though everything inside of me has gone numb. This can't be happening. There's some mistake. I want to throw myself to the ground next to him, but something is grabbing me by the arms, holding me back. No, not something, someone.

Hazel, I realize, distantly. At least I think it's her. It's hard to know for sure. The rest of the world seems to blink in and out, like a faulty lightbulb, but I can hear her screaming at me, saying something that doesn't make its way to my brain. All my thoughts are on Jack. Jack, my best friend. My *only* friend. Jack, who looked so betrayed when he saw me and Hazel kissing. Jack's face going blank with pain. The arrow protruding from Jack's chest. Jack falling.

I have to help him. I have to go to him. Jack needs me. Jack's *hurt.*

"*Reagan,*" Hazel says, harshly and directly into my ear. "We have to run."

I turn to her, and it's as though I'm seeing her again for the first time in a very long time. Her eyes are too wide in the growing darkness, staring from bluish, shadowed sockets.

"We have to run," she says again. "The witch—"

Another arrow whizzes past. I feel its heat on my arm and, when I look down, I see that my sleeve has torn, and there's a line of red on my skin. Blood seeps up from inside of me.

"Run, Reagan! We can't help him right now. We have to go!" And then Hazel's pulling me, and the two of us are running—stumbling—toward the trees.

My ankle screams out in protest the second it hits the ground. I don't have my crutch anymore, I don't even know where I dropped it, but it's too late to look for it now. I'm hobbling, hopping after Hazel on one leg, slowing her down.

"You have to go ahead of me!" I tell her, but she just looks at me like I've lost my mind.

And then we're ducking into the darkness of the trees, running harder. Something in my brain short-circuits. How can we run when Jack is lying in the dirt behind us, bleeding? I feel the distance between us and Jack grow with each step we take. We have to go back.

But we can't.

Another arrow whistles through the air, burying itself into a tree inches from my shoulder. I release a jagged cry and force myself to run faster. Every step I take is agony. I feel a hard jerk each time my foot slams into the dirt, the feeling of bones crunching together, pinching nerves and skin. Instinct keeps me going, even as everything inside me screams to slow down.

It's much darker in the woods than it was in the clearing around my truck. The sun has mostly set by now and, with the cloud cover still so heavy, it feels like the dead of night. I can't see where I'm going. Tree branches reach out, snatching at me, slicing my cheeks. I know I should be relieved—darkness means the witch can't see us either, that it'll be harder for her to aim an arrow, but that's not how it feels. It's a million times worse to know she's behind us but not see where she is. To feel, every second, like she could pop out from behind a tree trunk.

I don't know how I'm still running. My ankle is a swollen, hot mess.

Suddenly, my calf explodes with heat and I stumble, falling to my knees in the dirt, a shriek escaping me.

I hear Hazel running ahead, her breathing heavy. She doesn't know that I've been hit. It's too dark to see more than the dim outline of her body, but I hear her feet shuffling against the ground, fast, and there's a part of me that's relieved. By the time she realizes I'm not behind her, it'll be too late. She'll never be able to find me again, not in this dark. She'll have no choice but to keep running. Save herself.

I lie crumpled in the dirt, breathing heavily, unable to move. I need to get up now. I know that. Every second I stay here is another second for the witch to find me.

But the pain in my leg is excruciating. My hand shaking, I reach down and feel the shaft of an arrow protruding from my calf. It's ripped through my jeans and buried itself deep in my muscle. My leg is on fire with pain and my jeans are wet with blood.

My breath grows shallower, shuddering. I'm close to panic. If I don't get up now and move, I'm going to die here.

"Come on, Reagan." I mouth the words, much too terrified to use my voice, in case the witch is close. "Get up. Keep going."

I force myself to my feet, jolt after jolt of pain shooting up my leg. My eyes are watering, and my breath hitches. I sway and have to grab for a tree trunk to steady myself. After a moment I take a step forward—

My leg immediately collapses beneath me, sending me sprawling back into the dirt. Something sharp scrapes straight through my jeans and peels the skin away from my knee. My mouth drops open in a wordless scream, but I'm too scared to make any noise, just in case she's close, listening for me.

Using the last of my strength, I make my way across the forest floor, half pulling, half crawling. Luckily, most of my injuries are on the same leg, so at least I have one strong leg remaining. I wedge it up beneath me, the other dragging behind. I press my lips together, swallowing the pain as I move. I can't run anymore, so I'll have to hide. It's dark, thank God, but I still want to be behind something. I aim for the thicker shadows, eventually tucking myself beneath the spiky leaves of what I think is a tall bush. I pull my legs as close to my body as I can, reasoning that

I need to make myself into as small a target as possible. And I wait.

Fresh tears hit the corners of my eyes. Everything hurts. But I don't think the witch is nearby. The only sounds I hear are my own gasping breaths, the wind, and a distant rumble of thunder. Maybe she doesn't realize she hit me. Or maybe she's looking for me in the wrong place. I can only hope.

Time passes. I'm not sure how much, and I have no way of knowing. After several minutes, I press my hand to my chest and count my heartbeats. There are around sixty to a minute, I think. Maybe more, since I'm agitated. I count two-hundred and fifty beats.

Four hundred.

Seven hundred and twenty. Seven hundred and twenty-one . . .

Lights flicker through the trees.

My entire body seizes up. It's her, the witch. She must be using a flashlight to search for me in the dark. I cower behind a tree, my head hanging forward, waves of dizziness washing over me. I don't have it in me to run, not anymore. It's taking everything I have just to fight off unconsciousness.

Then the lights flash red and blue.

Not the witch.

The police.

Hope blossoms inside of my chest and spreads, fast. I release a long, hitching gasp that almost sounds like a laugh. The police are here; they've come to rescue us, at last.

I'm saved.

I force myself to my knees and then claw my way to my feet, my fingernails pulling little strips of bark off the trees. I hobble forward as fast as I can, ignoring the pain in my leg. Relief spurs me on, and the pain seems to diminish a little.

I glance over my shoulder, hoping to see Hazel behind me, drawn by the lights of the cruiser, toward safety.

But there are only trees and deep, unfathomable darkness.

She kept running, I tell myself. *She got away.* I have to believe that. Otherwise, I could never keep going.

The squad car is parked at the edge of the woods. The cop we drove past earlier is standing beside it, her hand resting on the gun at her hip.

Karly, I remember. That's what Jack called her.

I half walk, half fall the rest of the way out of the woods. She flinches when I appear.

"Oh my God," she says, hurrying to my side. Her eyes go to the arrow protruding from my leg and widen. "What happened? You're hurt."

"She-she's in the woods," I choke out. I know I need to say more. I need to explain that my friends are still back there hiding. I need to tell this cop that Jack is badly hurt and needs medical attention, that Hazel ran but the witch is still looking for her, that she'll kill her if she finds her.

But pain is howling through me and all I can manage is "We have to . . . my friends . . . they . . . *hurt.*"

The officer is already standing and jerking the door to her cruiser open. She grabs the radio handset off the dashboard. "This is Officer Knight," she says to whoever's listening on the other side. "We have a code eight at Camp Lost Lake. I need an ambulance and backup. I repeat, we have a code eight at Camp Lost Lake. Over."

I've stopped listening. All I heard her say is *Officer Knight*.

Officer *Knight*.

I look from her face to the name tag pinned to her uniform: KARLY KNIGHT.

I know the name Karly Knight. Of course I know the name Karly Knight. I've read it about a million times on true crime websites and Camp Lost Lake forums and every single piece of badly photocopied evidence that's found its way online. Officer Karly Knight was the first cop on the scene of the Camp Lost Lake murders sixteen years ago. Her name was on the initial police report, but she excused herself after finding Jacob Knight's body, since he was her brother.

As in, my *dad*, Jacob Knight.

A shiver moves through me. I've seen pictures of him, first in Jack's mom's scrapbook, then online after I started looking into the case. I look like him. I have his nose, and our eyes are the same color, and we make the same thin-lipped, narrow-eyed expression when we're thinking about something deeply. Officer Knight was his sister. Her nose and lips and eyes look a lot like mine. They would. This woman . . . she's my *aunt*.

Turning back to me, Officer Knight says, "Get in the car."

I blink, still struggling to catch my breath. I can't get in the car, not while Jack and Hazel are still in the woods with the witch. "I-I can't," I say. "My friends—"

"We won't find anyone stumbling around the trees in the dark, not with your leg in that shape. We'll circle the woods in the cruiser. If your friends see the lights, they'll come to us."

"But Jack's . . . he's hurt." *Hurt* is such a small word for what happened to him. It doesn't explain the way his eyes went blank, how he fell into the dirt, his body so still.

"An ambulance is on its way," Officer Knight says. "If you tell me where Jack is, I can give the driver his exact location."

I hesitate, still feeling unsure. It doesn't seem right to climb into a police car, to be safe while Jack and Hazel are still fighting for their lives in the woods. I should be with them, helping them. But Officer Knight is right. I'm no help to anyone right now.

Officer Knight seems to understand my dilemma. In a softer voice, she says, "This is the fastest way to help your friends, hon."

She's right. I know she's right.

Swallowing, I climb into the car.

21

Olivia

"Olivia—" Andie starts, but I shake my head. I'm not ready to hear this.

"No . . . *Mom* was pregnant," I say, but even I can hear how hollow my voice sounds. My hand goes to my pocket, and I feel the sonogram inside crinkle. I know Mom wasn't far enough along in her pregnancy to have given birth the night of the murders. Even if I had a reason to think Andie would lie to me, I have proof that she's not.

Tears blur my vision, when they clear, I see that Andie looking at me, her eyes searching my face.

My voice is a croak. "What happened to Mom's baby?"

"Mom miscarried a couple of days before the murders," Andie says. "She hadn't told anyone yet, so it was easy for her to pretend you were hers. She was so small, she started showing right away. Everyone thought she was further along than she was. When she showed up with a baby, they assumed she'd lied about when she first got pregnant because she didn't want people to know it had happened before she and Dad got married."

I barely register any of this. I closed my eyes on the word *miscarried*, finding it impossible to keep listening.

Oh my God.

I don't know what to say. Andie's not my sister. Our mom's not *my* mom.

Nothing's what I thought it was.

"I lied and told Mom and Dad I was in New York for an internship," Andie continues. "I was so worried they'd be disappointed in me when they found out I was pregnant. I wanted to hide it. I never wanted anyone to know the truth."

"I-I don't get it," I blurt out. "If you didn't want anyone to know you'd gotten pregnant, why not just . . ."

I don't want to say the words out loud. It's too weird, when I know I'm talking about myself. Luckily, I don't have to.

"Things were different back then," Andie explains. "Most places wanted you to have your parents' permission, and I didn't want to tell Mom and Dad. I just thought, if I could give the—" She falters here, her eyes flicking up to mine, "If I could give the babies up, then everything would be okay."

Babies. Plural. A shiver moves through me.

"I'm a twin," I say, my voice quiet.

"Olivia, I'm so—" Andie starts, but I lift my hand, stopping her. I don't want apologies right now. Not when there's still so much I don't understand.

"How did we get separated?" I want to know.

A pained look crosses Andie's face. "You came too fast. Your sister, especially . . . She came *so* fast, and she didn't cry, and she-she looked sort of . . . sort of small and sick. Gia had run off to get help, but she never came back. I know, now, that she'd gotten shot before she could find Mom. Lori found me instead. She helped me. If she hadn't come, I . . ." Andie's voice cracks. She closes her eyes, exhales, and after a moment she says, "We needed to get your sister to the hospital. Lori didn't think we could wait for an ambulance to arrive. She thought the baby might not make it. But I was in so much pain from giving birth, and I-I couldn't really move, and you were crying, and everything was so hectic."

"Andie," I breathe, feeling numb. "Oh my God . . ."

Andie rushes on, like she doesn't think she'll be able to start again if she stops. "I told Lori to take the baby and go, get her to a hospital, any hospital, just keep her safe. It seemed like the only thing we could do at the time, the *safest* thing we could do. But then, after she left, I-I heard the screams."

I feel a chill as all this information washes over me. Lori must've been holding my sister when she was mistaken for the Lost Lake Killer. And she was covered in blood, but it was *Andie's* blood. She only ran because she needed to get Reagan to a hospital.

"I know Lori didn't kill anyone," Andie continues. "She was with me, helping me give birth when Gia and Jacob were murdered. But I had no idea how I could exonerate her. You have to understand, the evidence against her was overwhelming. Officer Knight said there was DNA and eyewitnesses, she said Lori's blood was found at the scene, her *fingerprints* were on that stupid bow. Everyone was completely convinced she did it. The only way I could've cleared her name was by telling people I'd been at camp that night, and that would've meant . . ." Andie trails off, her voice cracking.

"Admitting I was your daughter," I say, bitter. I shake my head. "I don't understand. Why *were* you even at camp that night? If you were so intent on hiding us, why come back before we were born?"

"I-I was confused. I started having all these second thoughts.

I thought maybe there was a way Matthew and I could make it work, that we could be your parents. I came back here to tell him I was pregnant, and then I told Mom. I really thought we could be a family. But then he died, and the murders happened, and everything changed. I realized there was no way I could do this on my own."

"So you lied, again. And this time you got Mom to lie with you."

"I didn't know what else to do! I just kept thinking that if there was some way I could still hide it, then everything would be okay."

I'm completely horrified by what she's telling me. I think of Mom handing me her handkerchief, telling me tears made people uncomfortable. All those years learning to bury my emotions, hide what I'm feeling, look and act and *be* perfect. No wonder Andie thought this was a solution. But that doesn't make it okay.

Reagan was right, Andie *did* know the truth, and she hid it. "You let Lori take the fall for those murders even though you knew she didn't do it?"

Andie closes her eyes, tears leaking onto her cheeks. "I was a teenager, Olivia. I was so young. At first, when I lied about the internship and left town, all I could think about was how everyone around here thought I was so perfect, such a good daughter and student . . . I just couldn't let go of that image they had of me . . . God, that *I* had of myself. I thought it would be the end of everything, all the dreams I had for college and my future.

"Then, just when I finally started thinking that maybe I could do it, that maybe telling the truth about the pregnancy wouldn't be the worst thing in the world, Matthew *died*." Andie swipes the tears from her eyes. "How was I supposed to tell the truth about the pregnancy when everyone was mourning? How was I supposed to take care of two babies all alone? At the time it really did seem like admitting I'd gotten pregnant would be the end of the world."

"Those are all really thin excuses for letting someone take the fall for murdering their family."

"I know," Andie agrees. "I was young, and I was selfish, and I thought of myself instead of her. I'll never forgive myself for that." Her eyelids flicker. "A couple of days after the murders, I started to realize what I'd done, how awful it was to let Lori take the blame for something so horrible. And I couldn't stop thinking about my other baby, your sister. I was desperate to know what happened to her, to know she was okay. Mom had already lied for me the night you were born, but I told her that I thought we should come clean. We were even talking to a lawyer, trying to figure out a way to get the truth to the police, but then I got this postcard, and I knew it was from Lori. It said that she and the baby were starting over, that she didn't want me looking for her, that it wasn't safe for her to come back. After that, I wondered if maybe she knew who the real murderer was. She could've seen something, or . . . I don't know, if maybe the killer saw her and she was worried they'd retaliate." Andie lifts her eyes to mine. "You can blame me for not telling everyone the truth about what happened that night, but *that's* why Lori stayed gone. More than anything, I think she wanted to protect you and your sister."

I think of the postcard I found in Andie's things. *I'm sorry. Don't try to fix this and don't try to find me. It isn't safe. We're starting over.*

But this doesn't make sense. Lori saw the killer and was afraid for her safety, so she ran away? Why not tell someone who it was?

Why would she think it'd be safer to spend the rest of her life in hiding?

"Are you saying Lori *kidnapped* my sister?" I ask.

"I don't know. I-I didn't see it that way." Andie's talking too fast, almost like she's trying to convince herself as much as me. "Is it really kidnapping if she was her grandmother? And I'd been planning on placing you for adoption . . . It was better that your sister end up with Lori, that Lori was going to have another chance at having a family, after what happened to hers."

Something about the way she says that—*after what happened to hers*—makes my stomach tense. I look at her and she stares back for one beat, two, giving away nothing. I've almost convinced myself I'm imagining things when a muscle near the corner of her eye twitches. She blinks, fast, and looks away.

In the fraction of a moment that she keeps her head turned I realize what I saw: nerves. There's something Andie's still afraid of, something she's hiding.

But then she straightens and meets my eyes, blank-faced. Whatever I saw is already gone, buried under layers of calm.

I'm desperate to know what she's not telling me, but now isn't the time to drag it out of her. The one thing I'm totally sure of is that she isn't the murderer. Which means the real witch is still out there.

"Andie," I say, and my voice shakes as I force the next words from my mouth. "There's something you need to know. Your other baby . . . my twin sister, she's *here*."

Andie brings a trembling hand to her lips. She sways and for a moment I worry that she's about to collapse. "She is?"

I nod. "And I think she might be in a lot of danger."

•   •   •

We check the nurse's cabin first: empty.

"No," I gasp, panting. I collapse in the cabin doorway, breathing hard. Andie and I ran all the way here, neither of us wanting to spend any more time in the woods than necessary. Now I look back at her, desperate and scared. "Jack was supposed to get the truck so he could pick them up, but I don't know if he got here or where they would've gone . . ."

Andie chews her lower lip as she looks around the small, one-room cabin, and I notice that her eyes linger on the blood smeared across the floor. She shudders and turns away. It looks like it's taking everything she has not to cry. "We have to find them."

I swallow. *Find them?* After sunset, in the pitch-black woods, on the night of the Witch of Lost Lake's return? There aren't words in the English language to adequately explain how terrified I am to do that.

The smart thing to do is leave. I know it in my bones. We're not going to help anyone by wandering around the woods with a killer on the loose. Andie and I are small, and we don't have any way to defend ourselves. We're useless. We need to find a way out, come back with the cops.

But I can't make myself say the words *we have to leave* out loud. I can't make my body move away from the woods. I don't care that what we're doing isn't smart. Maybe Reagan was right all along, maybe there isn't any way to know what's right and what's wrong. Maybe you just have to follow your gut.

All I know is that I have to find them. I have to go back into the woods. I won't be able to live with myself if I don't.

• • •

I don't know how long the two of us wander around the woods before we find an old red truck with a slashed tire. It looks like whoever was changing the tire gave up in the middle of the job. *Is it Reagan's truck?* I wonder. There's no way to know for sure, but looking at it makes my skin crawl. I don't want to think about what would make her abandon her truck this close to getting the tire changed. Andie and I check the clearing for blood or any sign of a struggle, but we find nothing.

Fear creeps over me like mold. I feel in in my lungs. I feel it coating my throat. I don't look at Andie because I know that if I do, I'll see the same fear reflected on her face, and then I don't know how I'll be able to keep looking.

"We have to think," Andie says, pinching the bridge of her nose with two fingers. "Maybe there's a reason they had to abandon the truck. Maybe they couldn't finish changing the tire because they didn't have the right tools or-or something?" I finally look over at Andie as she looks up at me, her eyes so hopeful it makes something inside of me ache. "Where would they go if that happened?"

"I don't . . ." I stop talking. The wind has risen in the trees, rustling the leaves overhead, but I could've sworn I heard something else. A muffled groan.

I squint against the dark, my skin tingling. I'm too afraid to call out just in case the sound I heard was her. The witch.

I'm scanning the woods when my eyes fall on something lying across the ground just outside the clearing. A shape in the darkness.

It's . . . it's *moving*.

Plucking up my courage, I step into the trees. Now that I'm closer, it's clear that the shape is a body. Someone is lying in the dirt. There's another groan, low and muffled. I take a step closer—

And throw a hand over my mouth. "Oh my God, *Jack*."

Andie glances at me, confused, but I don't have time to explain. I race to Jack's side and drop to my knees, thinking, *Please don't be dead, please don't be dead . . .*

He doesn't look good. There's an arrow in his shoulder. His eyes are closed, there's a trickle of blood coming from his ear, and his lips are parted, just barely.

"He needs an ambulance," I say.

"If we can get the tire changed on the truck, we can drive him to the hospital," Andie says, but I'm not listening, I'm distracted.

There was a sound deep in the trees. A crack.

I stand, nerves pricking up my arms. "Andie . . ."

I trail off as the sound comes again, louder and growing. Now it's a great, roaring sound, a body crashing through low branches, feet kicking through dirt and undergrowth: someone coming at us. *Fast.*

I shrink back against Andie, my bones jackhammering, terror taking over me. We should run. But Jack needs our help; if we don't get him an ambulance he could die. We can't just leave him.

But, if we stay, *we* could die.

I look up at Andie and see the same conflict playing out on her face. Leave or die. Save Jack or save ourselves. I bite down on my cheek until I taste blood.

And then—branches part like swinging doors as Hazel stumbles out from the trees, gasping. "Olivia!" she sobs, throwing herself into my arms.

My body shudders in relief. I grab Hazel and bury my face into her hair, hugging her tight. "You're okay," I say, almost not believing it. "I was so worried."

"Me too." She sniffles and pulls away, still breathing hard. "But something happened to Reagan. I don't know what it was . . . she was right behind me and then suddenly she wasn't anymore. I don't know how it happened. I've been looking everywhere for her." Her eyes drop from me to Jack, still lying on the ground. Her hand comes up to her mouth, trembling. "Oh my God. Is he alive?"

"He is, but he needs an ambulance," Andie says. "He needs to get to the hospital *now*. I think we can change the truck tire and drive him, but someone needs to stay behind and find Reagan."

"I know how to change a tire," Hazel says. "I've done it a ton of times. If you guys can help me get him into the truck, I can drive him."

I exhale. That leaves me and Andie to find Reagan.

"Where did you last see her?" I ask Hazel. But Hazel's not looking at me anymore. She's staring at something in the distance. I turn, following her gaze. There are flashing red and blue lights over by the old lighthouse.

Police lights.

22

Reagan

Dark pavement stretches ahead of Officer Knight's cruiser, intermittent streetlights illuminating the way. I'm jittery in the back seat, knotting and unknotting my hands in my lap, my knee bouncing up and down. I feel, quite literally, out of it, like my brain is hovering somewhere far above us, disconnected from my body. I couldn't hold myself still if I tried.

A bulletproof partition separates me from Officer Knight, the thick plastic muffling the occasional voices emanating from her radio. I'm not looking at her, but I can see her reflection in the rearview mirror in my periphery and I know that every minute or two she glances at the mirror, checking on me. I can't bring myself to look back. My entire brain is focused on the window, on the woods to the side of the road. I can't see anything. Even the soft glow from the streetlights is no match for all that darkness, that perfect, inky black. Unfathomable. But I keep watching, desperate for some sign of movement. Hazel running toward the street, the witch lifting her bow to aim another arrow, but there's nothing. From here, the trees could almost be peaceful.

We're halfway around the woods when Officer Knight says, "You know my brother died here? Jacob Knight. He used to work at this camp, years and years ago."

The nerves in the backs of my arms light up. Jacob Knight. She's talking about my dad right now, the family I never got the chance to know.

"I've been thinking about Jacob a lot lately," Officer Knight continues, glancing at me in the rearview mirror. "Our mom died last week. We just had the funeral and everything. He should've been there. God, it was weird going through that without him."

Something about the way she's telling me this doesn't feel right. It's not so much what she's saying—I've met plenty of people who feel the need to unload their entire life story the second we meet—it's something else.

What is it?

She keeps going. "We just had the reading of the will and, the whole time, I was thinking how hard it was to do it alone. It's like I was telling Olivia's sister, Andie, this morning: I'm still a bit of a wreck."

Olivia's sister. Not *your* sister.

A cold pit of fear opens inside me.

"How did you know I'm not Olivia?" I ask.

Officer Knight glances at me but doesn't answer the question. "You know, I put my whole life on hold to take care of our mother," she says instead. Her voice doesn't change, it's still conversational, almost casual. But there's something in the way she's gripping the steering wheel, her fingers holding so tightly that I can see the veins standing out against her knuckles.

I reach for the door handle, try to open it—

But, of course, it doesn't work. This is a police car. I'm trapped back here.

"Jacob, he got to go to college, got to fall in love and start a family," Officer Knight continues, "while I stayed here, taking care of her. In the years since Jacob passed, I tried to tell myself I didn't mind. Our mom wasn't going to last forever, you know, and she always said she didn't want to split up her estate, that the idea of dividing up money and possessions gave her a headache. Her plan was to leave everything to one person and let them deal with it after she was gone. Well, I was the only one left, wasn't I? And I'd taken care of her, handled her money, the house. It made sense that I'd be the one to inherit everything." She finds my eyes in the rearview mirror. "Police work doesn't pay much, but our family's always had money. It would have been a significant inheritance. Once she was gone, I figured I could travel, live somewhere warm, maybe. Seems like a fitting payment for all the work I've done over the years, don't you think?"

She pulls off the gravel road and onto the highway that leads back toward town. Dark pavement stretches ahead of us, streetlights illuminating the way. For a second, I feel something like relief. This is a safe, normal, well-lit road. Bad things don't happen on roads like these. There must be some misunderstanding.

And then Officer Knight cuts the wheel left, pulling off the main, well-lit road—and toward the lighthouse.

I feel a sick churning in my gut.

"Only I found out at the will reading that my mother never meant to leave her money to me. She'd left it all—her entire estate—to her grandson, Matthew's, twin daughters." Silence falls over the car. Officer Knight isn't even watching the road anymore. Her eyes are glued to the rearview mirror.

She says, simply, "To you."

I stare back at her, startled by the feeling of something rising in my chest, something that might be a laugh or a sob. *Matthew's* twin girls. Not Jacob's, Matthew's.

I was wrong about absolutely everything.

"Gia's camera—" I start.

"I don't care about the camera," Officer Knight says, cutting me off. "I saw you this morning, remember? Waved to you from the side of the road. You look just like Olivia D'Angeli. Identical, actually. I thought you *were* Olivia, but then I saw her a few minutes later, in a completely different car. I figured it out when I saw the two of you back-to-back like that."

Her eyes flick to me. "There's only been one set of twins born in this town since I've lived here. So I did the math in my head, realized Olivia was born right around when Matthew's twins mysteriously disappeared." Officer Knight shakes her head, a disgusted look on her face. "God, you even *look* like Matthew." Officer Knight's lips twist. "He told his parents about the babies the night before he was murdered, and Jacob told me and Mom, wanted us to help out.

"I didn't see how Matthew's babies had anything to do with me, but Mom was desperate to find them, to help, like she promised Jacob she would. God, she could be such a bleeding heart. She wanted to make sure you and your sister were taken care of, probably had her will changed the very day she found out about you. She still had some lucid days back then," Officer Knight explains, at my confused look. "She used them to make sure you and your sister got every last cent of her money.

"It was a bit of a nasty surprise when I found out that she'd changed her will. I thought all that nonsense about Matthew's babies was in the past. You have to imagine how I felt. I mean, I had my bags practically packed. I was looking at property in Florida and Hawaii, and it turns out I'm broke. I'm not going anywhere, not unless I can find a way to dispute the will. And then, to make everything so much worse, I saw *you* this morning. All of a sudden everything clicked. All these years I thought Lori had taken off with both Matthew's babies. But she didn't; she only took one, and the other was right here, right in front of my nose for sixteen years. When I realized what Miranda must've done, how she'd lied to protect you . . . I guess I lost track of things a little."

The shadow of the lighthouse falls over the squad car. I peel my eyes away from the rearview mirror for long enough to glance out the windshield, my throat tightening at the sight of the rounded brick walls and circular windows.

There are pictures of Lost Lake Lighthouse all over the internet. I have the structure practically memorized, but that doesn't prepare me for how it feels to see it in person, how it seems heavier than the things around it, the gravity of the place pulling you toward it.

Matthew died in that lighthouse, I think, my stomach tightening. Then, the thought changes:

I *might die in that lighthouse.*

I don't even notice that the car has stopped or that Officer Knight's climbed out, not until she yanks my door open and shoves a gun in my face.

"Get out," she says.

• • •

Officer Knight doesn't speak as we ascend to the top of the light-house. I don't either. I grip the stairwell with both hands and try to hobble up the stairs, but I can't put any weight on my ankle without howling in pain and, eventually, Officer Knight has to wrap an arm around my waist to help haul me up. She makes sure to keep her gun aimed at the side of my head as an incentive to keep me moving.

After several long moments, I can't take it anymore. "Are you going to kill me?" I blurt. My voice is low and choked, close to tears. I struggle up another step, and then another, listening to Officer Knight steadily inhale and exhale, waiting for her to answer. She's quiet for so long that I'm sure she won't.

Coward, I think.

And then, like she can hear my thoughts, she takes a ragged breath and says, "It's not personal. It's just that with you and your sister out of the picture, there's no one else left to inherit my mom's money. It's my last chance of getting out of this place."

Her voice hasn't changed since we were in the cruiser together. But there's something in the way she's working her mouth, jaw moving like she's chewing something over. I can see the veins standing out on her neck.

I can't keep climbing. The pain in my ankle is searing, blinding. But I suddenly feel the barrel of the gun pressed into my cheek. It's cold and hard against my skin.

"We're almost there," she says. "Move."

I swallow, letting my eyes travel up the curved lighthouse walls as we climb so I don't have to think about the perfectly round barrel tapping against my skin, the bullet waiting just a few inches away. The bullet that will almost certainly find its way into my body, a tiny piece of metal ripping through my clothes and skin and internal organs, ending my life. The thought makes me feel like my legs are about to collapse beneath me, and it's already hard enough to ignore the pain each time I have to put even the slightest bit of weight on my ankle.

I look at the walls, instead, the names that have been scrawled onto the brick over the decades. *Julia Anderson* and *Crystal Thomas* and *Rachel Hart* and—

My breath catches in my throat. There they are, in black Sharpie against the whitewashed bricks:

Matthew Knight

Gia North

Their handwriting doesn't look anything alike. Gia's is wide and bubbly. She dots her *i* with a tiny smiley face. Matthew's handwriting is cramped and spiky, like it's angry at the world. But there's something about it, a teenage quality that I can't quite put my finger on.

I feel the gun press against my face again. This time, it doesn't freak me out—it pisses me off. Matthew and Gia were so young when they died. They were just teenagers, *my* age. They barely even had a chance to live or make mistakes or become people.

And now this monster is going to kill me, too. I'm going to die, just like they did.

I pull my eyes away from the names on the wall and keep climbing, anger pumping through me like blood. I don't want to die. It's too soon. I'm not ready.

The staircase opens into a small, circular room made entirely of windows. The sun has long set, and all I can see is miles of black, a distant moon reflected in the wide, still waters of the lake below. As far as last images go, you could do a lot worse. The thought makes me want to scream, to sob.

I'm not ready.

I step off the last stair, gingerly easing my injured foot onto the scarred wooden floor. Most of the floor-to ceiling windows are still intact, I notice, but there's one that's been boarded over. Staring at it, I feel a chill creep up over my skin.

Will I fall after she shoots me?

I turn around, that thought still blazing through my head, when I notice that Officer Knight has lowered her gun. I feel an instant hit of relief. Maybe I was wrong. Maybe she's not going to kill me. Maybe she just wants to scare me or threaten me or—

She crosses the small space and picks up two now familiar items.

"Gotta make this look right," she says. "Everyone knows the Witch of Lost Lake uses a bow and arrow."

The Witch of Lost Lake

Karly Knight can tell you when exactly everything went to hell. She knows the exact moment, the exact second. Sometimes, when she feels guilty, she plays it all back, wondering if she would do anything differently, if she would change anything. She still doesn't know.

The date is June 13, 2008. It's just after 7:00 p.m., and the sky has gotten all dusky as the sun begins to set beyond the distant hills.

In just one week she'll be boarding a plane to Key West and leaving this place forever. She can feel her excitement humming through her skin, pumping in her blood like adrenaline. Just seven more days until sun and sand and margaritas . . .

She's come to the campgrounds to talk to her brother about the final details. She's been trying to call, but he never picks up the phone and she's tired of leaving voicemails. If they're going to stay on schedule, they need to discuss when to move their mother over to his house, not to mention all the details of her care. There are lots. Karly's been making notes for the past few weeks, making sure to jot down exactly when to give their mother her medication, when she needs to eat and walk and go to bed. So far, she has three whole pages in her notebook. She's getting a little nervous, worried there won't be enough time to teach Jacob everything he needs to know.

But no. She's being silly. It's just a few pages of notes. He'll figure it out.

Jacob is out in the archery field when she gets to the campgrounds, unpacking archery equipment, getting ready for summer. His bow is leaning against the wall of the shelter, the wood gleaming in the dim light. As Karly approaches, he's setting up the straw-filled targets in the field, hauling them out of the equipment shed one by one. They must be heavy because he's panting hard, a sheen of sweat on his face. The target he's moving still has an arrow sticking out of the bull's-eye, a leftover remnant of the previous summer.

"Hey, Karly," he calls out to her, his voice a grunt. She instantly feels her body go still and tight. He's using that low, serious tone he only ever uses when he's preparing to disappoint her. She knows that voice well.

All of a sudden, she's nervous. She can feel what's coming, and she already knows she's really not going to like it. The only thing she can think to do is prolong this moment, keep him from saying whatever he's about to say. She looks around for something to change the topic, to keep him from talking.

There's an open box of assorted camp things next to the nearest target. It looks like a mix of whatever Jacob had to pack up at the end of last summer: some lost-and-found items, a camper's missing flip-flop, an iPod, a rubber witch's mask. Campers and counselors bring these masks every year, use them to scare the younger kids after dark. They're a staple of Camp Lost Lake.

Karly plucks the mask out of the box, holds it up. "You planning on terrifying some little kids?"

Jacob gives her a weak smile that doesn't reach his eyes. She doesn't blame him. It wasn't a particularly good joke.

He swallows and shifts his gaze to the ground. He's working his mouth like he's chewing on something and Karly knows, instantly, what he's about to say. Her mouth goes dry and, in that moment, the only thing she can think is how badly she wants to stop him from speaking.

So she pulls on the witch's mask and turns to Jacob like she's trying to scare him. "Better get back into your cabin," she says in a low, cackly voice. She even curls her fingers toward her palms. It's all she can do to keep from shouting *Boo!*

This time he laughs, but it's a low, pitying sound. He feels sorry for her. Karly drops her hands, anger bubbling inside of her. *Screw you, Jacob*, she thinks.

He rubs a hand over his chin and takes a breath. When he speaks, it's in a rush, just trying to get the words out. "Look, Karly . . . there's no easy way to say this, but . . . we're not going to be able to take Mom next week, after all. Matthew . . . uh, well, Matthew came to us last night and confided that he's gotten himself into some trouble. He, uh, well, he got someone pregnant, is the thing. Twins, if you can believe it. We all talked about it, and we agreed that the right thing to do is to take this girl and her babies in, help them out for a few years, just until Matthew graduates and finds a job so he can take care of his family himself." Then, as if it makes up for anything, he adds, "I told Mom already. She's disappointed, of course, but I think she's excited to meet the babies."

"Where is this girl's family?" Karly sputters. "Why is it up to you to take care of her?"

"Don't be that way," Jacob says, frowning. "The kids are young, and twins are a lot of responsibility; they're going to need all the help they can get—not just time, but money, too—and taking care of Mom on top of it all . . . it's just too much for us right now. You understand, right?"

He doesn't say it like he's asking a question, he doesn't ask, "Do you understand?" It's a statement. *You understand.*

As in, you *have to understand* because I'm not offering an alternative. *We all talked about it, and we agreed,* he said. But that isn't true. Karly didn't talk about it. Karly didn't agree.

Karly feels like the entire world has gone quiet and still and dark. She *doesn't* understand, not at all. She's already put her entire life on hold to take care of their mother. For *fourteen years* she's put her life on hold. Jacob got to go to college, got to fall in love and start a family. And the whole time Karly's been *here,* stuck in a town she despises, playing nurse, taking a job at the police force because it was the only thing she could train for locally. And they *talked* about this! They agreed it was Jacob's turn, that Karly deserved a chance at having a real life.

What's happening now is selfishness, pure and simple.

Karly does the math in her head. Four years until Matthew gets out of college. And then, what? It's not like he'll instantly be on his feet, able to take care of a new family. He'll need time to find a job, earn a living, save up for rent on an apartment. And what if they have *another* kid? What if this girl wants to go to school, too? What happens then? Karly can already see it, how four more years will turn into eight, then twelve.

All around, the sky seems to simmer, the stars pulsing like distant heartbeats. Karly doesn't even remember grabbing the arrow from the target. She doesn't hear her brother ask her what she's doing or tell her to put the arrow down. She can't think, can't see past the blood thumping in her temples.

She stares at Jacob, watching his eyes go wide, watching the way he trembles as he starts to back up, his hands lifting in front of his chest, like he's warding off a wild animal. She doesn't breathe. She just stares, the sound of her own heartbeat like cannon fire in her ears.

You deserve this, she thinks. Her anger is hot and all-consuming. She can't think past it. The past and the future don't exist. There is just this moment, him and her.

She lunges forward and stabs her brother through the throat.

Karly and Jacob used to go hunting with their dad when they were kids. Karly remembers shooting a deer once. It was her very first kill; she was only nine years old. She got the deer in the shoulder, took it down but didn't kill it. She remembers walking up to the dying animal, her heart lodged in her throat. Its eyes were wide and scared, and it couldn't stop shaking, trying to get back up, to run away. It released the most terrible sound, a low, keening wail. Karly will never forget it.

"You have to put it out of its misery," her dad had told her, putting a heavy hand on her shoulder. Karly had been scared, but she'd lifted the bow and arrow—she and her dad and brother always used to hunt with bows and arrows—and she shot that deer in the head, killing it instantly.

Before this moment, that had been her most visceral experience with death. That deer in the woods, the sound it made right before it died. If she'd stopped to think about it, she might have thought that killing a man would be like that, that it would be hard and horrifying.

It's not. Killing a man, it turns out, is quick.

Jacob's mouth falls open after the arrow enters his throat. His eyes go wide, but he doesn't seem able to focus them anymore. They roll around in their sockets for a few seconds, before landing on some point above him. His body jerks, and then he falls to his knees, blood pouring down his chest. Seconds later, he's still. It's that fast.

What did she do? Oh God, what did she do?

She's still wearing that stupid mask. Her breath is hot and sour against the rubber. The smell of it fills her nostrils, making it feel like she can't breathe. She thinks she might start hyperventilating. She grabs for the bottom of the mask and tries to pull it off, but her hands are shaking too badly, she can't peel it away from her skin—

She hears a sound behind her. A creak of wood, a gasp of a scream. She whirls around and there's a girl standing on the porch outside the camp director's office, watching her. The girl's mouth hangs open, and she doesn't blink. It's clear to Karly that she just saw everything.

Karly doesn't think. There's no time for that. She just snatches her brother's bow and arrow from the ground, aims—

And shoots.

23

Olivia

The first thing we see when we get to the lighthouse is Officer Knight's cop car parked at a reckless angle.

Andie swallows hard. "We should hurry," she says. "Just in case . . ."

She doesn't have to finish her sentence because my brain fills in the blanks. I hope we're not too late.

We make our way around the car, toward the lighthouse. My skin itches as we get closer. The two of us look up in unison, cold fear spreading through us.

"I guess we have to go up," I say.

"The stairs," Andie says.

"What? They're dangerous, right?" I glance at them, thinking that they look pretty sturdy to me, but I guess that's the problem with rotten stairs—they look fine until you put your foot on one.

Andie shakes her head. "No, they're just . . . *loud*. You can't walk up them without alerting whoever's at the top that you're coming. If the killer's up there, they're going to hear us."

I carefully place my foot onto the lowest stair, staying as close to the edge of the wall as possible. It's the same thing I did earlier in the day when I was sneaking up to Mom's office.

The stair is silent as I shift my weight onto it.

Andie looks at me, amazed. "When did you get so good at sneaking around?"

"It's a gift I didn't realize I had," I tell her, quietly climbing up another step. "Follow me and stay as close to the wall as possible."

Andie nods.

Silently, we begin to climb.

24

Reagan

"That's why you murdered all those people?" I say, once Officer Knight has finished telling me her story.

She twitches when I say the word *murdered*. I can tell she doesn't like that. Maybe she doesn't want to believe she's a murderer. "Weren't you listening? Jacob expected me to just put my life on hold *forever*. To be our mother's caregiver *forever*."

"So you killed your family," I say, my voice bitter. I'm not really trying to hide what I think of her anymore. Why bother? She's going to kill me no matter how polite I am. "And not just them, but Gia North, too, because you didn't want her telling anyone what she saw."

Officer Knight licks her lips, but she doesn't deny it.

"And now you've come back to kill me and Olivia, just so you can get some money?" I feel sick to my stomach. I'm desperate to sit down, take some of the weight off my ankle, but I'm sure that if I move even the slightest bit she'll take me out. "And not just us, but also Sawyer, because he was in the wrong place at the wrong time."

But Officer Knight is frowning now. "I didn't mean to kill that kid with the purple hair, but he stepped in front of you right after I took my shot. I get that you're going to die thinking I'm a monster, but I never killed when I didn't have to."

"Jack—"

"I shot Jack in the shoulder," Officer Knight explains, cutting me off. "He'll live. In fact, I went out of my way to try to get you on your own. I could've killed you out in the woods, but I didn't want to risk hitting another kid instead."

"Yeah, you're a real humanitarian," I mutter. "What about that bear trap? *Anyone* could've stepped into that."

"I didn't leave a bear trap in the woods." Officer Knight fits the arrow into the bow and raises it to her shoulder. Points it at me. "Any last words?"

I grit my teeth together, thinking, *So unfair.*

I say, "Wait."

Officer Knight doesn't lower the bow and arrow, but she lifts her head slightly. It's the only sign she gives that she's willing to listen to anything I have to say. This is my chance, my last shot. I feel something inside of me harden.

I'm standing at the top of a lighthouse, at a *murder scene*, with a rogue cop. I'm seconds from death. And I'm nowhere closer to clearing my mother's name than I was this morning.

Screw this, I think. I'm done. I tried to do the right thing. And now?

Now, I just want to live.

Steeling myself, I say, "Maybe I can help you."

Officer Knight stares at me, head cocked. "Why would you want to help me?" she asks, skeptical.

"The only reason I came to this horrible place was to clear my mom's name," I say, my voice shaking in a way that completely undercuts my confidence. It doesn't matter, this is my only chance. I keep going. "I don't actually care who the real killer is. We could help each other."

Officer Knight stares at me, her expression giving away nothing. But she lowers the arrow so it's no longer pointed at my face. "Has it occurred to you that maybe I don't need your help?"

I have absolutely no idea how to respond to that, but I have to come up with something. "You were planning to blame this all on my mom again, right?"

"Worked out pretty well for me last time," Officer Knight says, her tone dead even.

"Maybe, but it's going to be a lot harder this time."

Officer Knight just raises her eyebrows, clearly not believing me.

"She's on her way here now, you know. She's taking the bus, so there's going to be evidence: bus tickets, witnesses, maybe even cameras . . ." I'm thinking on my feet, trying to come up with anything that might convince this cop that her plan won't work, when I look from her face to her hands. Her strong, healthy hands, so different from my mom's gnarled, arthritic ones. Hope leaps in my chest. "And she's older now. She has arthritis all in her hands. Most days she can't even drive our truck or tie her shoes. She'd never be able to shoot that thing." I nod at the bow and arrow. "Any doctor will back me up."

"You're lying," Officer Knight says. But she's working her jaw again, grinding her back teeth together. She looks concerned.

"Look," I try, "you're clearly smart, otherwise you never would've gotten away with this last time. But no one's going to believe my mom killed anyone this time around." I wait, leaving space for Officer Knight to refute this or even offer some part of this plan I haven't yet thought of. But she only frowns slightly. Like she's thinking this over.

"We want the same things," I continue. "And your story is going to be a lot more convincing if you have a witness to back you up."

After a long moment, Officer Knight says, "If I took you up on that . . . what, exactly, would you claim to have witnessed?"

"The way I see it, you and I both need someone else to blame all of this on," I say. "Another killer."

"Got someone in mind?"

I say, "Andie Edwards."

Officer Knight's eyebrows go up.

I force myself to keep going. "No one knows that Andie Edwards was here that night back in 2008, but we found a video proving she was on the grounds *and* that she attacked Gia North. She's the perfect person to take the fall."

"You'd set your own family up for murder?"

I feel something move through me. A jittery, anxious feeling, the feeling I get when I'm about to do something I know I shouldn't do. When I'm about to hurt someone.

When I think of *family*, I don't think of Andie and Olivia. I think of my mom, kissing bumped knees and bruised shoulders, teaching me to ride a bike, telling me that I didn't need to go with her when she went on the run, even though I knew it killed her to imagine letting me go, giving up her whole life to keep me safe.

It takes everything I have inside of me to swallow and push that feeling far, far down.

Out loud, I say, "Olivia and Andie aren't my family. I don't even know them."

25

Olivia

Andie and I are crouched on the stairs outside the landing. We hear everything. I'm watching Andie as Reagan talks, so I see the pain flash across her face when Reagan says, "I don't even know them."

I feel something sick twist through my gut, a pocketknife plunged through my belly button and jerked up a few inches.

"How am I supposed to trust you?" Officer Knight is saying. She hasn't lowered her bow completely, but the arrow threaded through it isn't pointed at Reagan anymore. It's pointed at the floor. If I were thinking clearly, I might've figured out that this was my moment. I might've darted out of the staircase and attacked her while she was still off guard, her attention entirely focused on someone else.

But I'm frozen in place, too shocked and devastated to move.

By the time it occurs to me to try to attack, Reagan's already looking into the stairwell. I feel a jolt go through me as our eyes meet.

"Because Olivia and Andie are hiding on the stairs," she says calmly. "If all I wanted to do was get away, I'd just let them attack you."

Officer Knight reacts immediately, swiveling around with a jerk to aim the arrow directly at me. I inhale sharply, feeling every muscle in my body seize. She's so fast. I was an idiot to think I might've been able to take her down. If I'd tried to attack her, she would've killed me for sure.

Andie's been holding tight to my arm, but the moment Officer Knight aims that arrow at me, I feel her nails dig into my skin.

"Run," she hisses. "I'll make sure you get away. I'll—"

I'm already shaking my head. "I'm not leaving you here!"

"Neither of you are going anywhere," Officer Knight says. "Out here, *now*."

Her voice doesn't leave any room for argument. I feel my body obey, even as my head is screaming at me to *go*. Moving as slowly as I possibly can, I rise from my crouch and put one foot in front of the other, crossing the space to stand beside Reagan. Even moving as slowly as I am, this feels like it happens in an instant. It's like time is glitching, rocketing forward when all I want in the world is for it stop, to slow, to reverse.

"Wait," Andie says from the stairway. She looks at me, her expression ragged, then crosses the room to Officer Knight. "I'll say I did it. I'll admit to all of it, I swear. Just let them go. Please."

I stare at Andie, shocked. I've never heard her like this before. She's always been so composed. But now she sounds utterly destroyed.

Officer Knight studies us for a moment, seeming to consider this before she shakes her head. "I'm sorry, but no. Having this many witnesses is trouble. Eventually one of you will talk."

"We won't," Andie says.

"Shut up," Officer Knight snarls. She turns back to Reagan,

seeming to have made her decision. "Does a double-murder sui-cide work for you?"

I look at Reagan, hating her, and that's when I notice her eyelid twitch. I don't think anyone else noticed it, but I have Reagan's face, and I recognize that twitch because it happens to me, too. My eyelid twitches like that whenever I'm nervous.

Or when I'm lying.

Andie's shoulders have slumped, and she's crying silently. So she doesn't see when Reagan glances at me. It's just a subtle flick of her eyes, and I think I see her chin move a hair to the left, and then a hair to the right. She's shaking her head. It's such a small, nothing movement that my brain immediately starts explaining it away, telling me I imagined it, that it wasn't real. But I know it was. It had to be.

It means: *Don't say a word.*

I nod at her. It's the same subtle movement, just the slightest incline of my chin, but I know that Reagan will see and under-stand what I'm telling her.

You can trust me.

Reagan looks back at Officer Knight. She steps forward and moves to the side, so that she's standing directly in front of her. And then she sticks out her hand. "Shake on it."

Officer Knight looks at her, skeptical, then holds out her hand, too. Their hands clasp—

I figure out Reagan's plan a fraction of a second after she puts it into motion. It's the way she angled herself to be directly in front of Officer Knight. From where I'm standing, I can see that this was intentional, that she's lined up her body—and Officer Knight's body—so that they're right in front of the window.

I think of what Sawyer said this morning when he was telling us all the camp rules.

The most important rule is that you don't go up in the old lighthouse. Some of the windows are broken, and it's easy to fall . . .

I feel a catch in my throat when I figure it out.

Reagan grasps Officer Knight's hand in her own, and then she jerks forward with a grunt, throwing her shoulder directly into her chest, knocking her off-balance.

I see an instant before she does it that it won't work. Officer Knight is too broad, too steady, and Reagan's my size—small and lightweight. She's not going to be able to overpower her, even by taking her off guard. The second this information hits my brain, my body springs into motion. I'm crossing the tower, throwing my weight behind my sister's.

Together, we do what neither one of us would've been able to do on our own: we knock Officer Knight off-balance. She takes a quick step backward, and the safety rail hits her just below the knees. I watch her legs buckle and her arms windmill. The bow and arrow clatter to the floor.

Her eyes go wide when she realizes that she's not going to be able to regain her balance. There's a *slap* as her body slams into the cardboard covering the broken window, and then the cardboard splits open—

And she falls.

26

Reagan

We climb down from the lighthouse together and, the whole time, I'm thinking to myself, *She's not going to be there, her body's going to be gone, she's still alive, she's waiting for us.* Like Officer Knight is a serial killer in a movie and this is the beginning of a franchise. Like I'm going to spend the rest of my life looking over my shoulder, waiting for her to jump out from behind a bush.

But when we step out of the lighthouse and into the cool, woodsy night air, there she is, splayed, spread-eagled across the rocky shore of the lake, water tugging at her legs.

Dead.

I'm so relieved I almost start sobbing. It's over. This nightmare is finally over.

The feeling only lasts a moment, long enough for me to re-member leaving Jack in the woods. A little sob hiccups out of me.

"Jack," I say, turning to Olivia. "He got shot. He . . ."

"We found him," Olivia says quickly. "Hazel, too. They're on their way to the hospital right now."

I'm so relieved I want to scream. It takes everything I have to choke the emotion back down, and when I finally speak, my voice is quiet. "Thank you."

"Of course," Olivia says. Then, like an afterthought, she adds, "Family takes care of each other."

"Right," I say, taking her hand. "I think I always knew that."

We called the police again before Olivia and Andie helped me climb down from the tower. We explained what happened with Officer Knight as best we could and asked them to send an ambulance and more officers. I have one arm around Andie's shoulder and one around Olivia's, still waiting for the cops to arrive when I see movement just past the trees. Not an ambulance or a police cruiser; a car.

Olivia says, "Who is that?"

I follow her gaze. It looks like Jack's dad's car, but the tall, thin figure in the driver's seat doesn't look like Henry. I frown into the darkness just beyond the headlights, trying to make sense of the dark, messy hair, the sharp shoulders . . .

My stomach drops.

"Oh crap," I mutter, hobbling away from Andie and Olivia.

It's my mom.

I feel a jolt go through me. I'm not ready to face her. I'm not ready to hear what she has to say about everything I learned tonight, all the secrets she's been hiding from me for the past sixteen years. But it seems that I don't have a choice because Lori Knight has barely even pulled the truck to a complete stop before she throws the driver's side open and leaps out.

I thought seeing her would feel different, but it doesn't. She's still the mom I've known my whole life, the only mom I've ever known. Tall and thin, her gray hair dyed so dark it's almost black, wearing a soft, threadbare flannel that I already know will smell like burnt gas station coffee and the oranges she eats every morning for breakfast. My mom.

I'm not ready for this.

Lori slams the door closed. The road she drove up twists around the eastern side of the lighthouse, and Officer Knight's body lies to the west, so she doesn't see her, but her eyes sweep warily over Andie and Olivia. I see the moment she recognizes my twin, her sharp inhale, the flickering of her eyelids.

Her gaze moves back to me. "Reagan," she says. There's a breathlessness to her ordinarily soft voice. I start to hobble toward her, but she crosses the clearing and sweeps me into a bone-crushing hug before I can take more than two steps. "You have no idea how worried I was. I'm so glad you're okay."

"Mom," I moan against her flannel.

"I was so worried about you," she says again, squeezing me tighter. I don't remember how many times she's held me like this, crushing me to her like I was the most important thing in her world. A lump forms in my throat.

Then, releasing me, she adds in a low, urgent whisper, "We have to go, it isn't safe—"

"It's okay, Lori," Andie says, coming up to us. Her eyes flick from me to my mom. I go still, watching them watch each other. My mom breathes a soft swear word and closes her eyes, tears already trailing down her cheeks.

When she finally opens them and looks at me, all she says is "Does this mean you know the truth?"

I stare at her, my eyes blurring. I'd been telling myself there had to be another explanation, that my mom never would've kidnapped me. I'm her daughter. I don't know who I am if I'm not her daughter.

But all it takes is one look at her face, the resignation in the lines around her mouth, the way she's looking at me so intently, wanting to make sure I'm okay. It tells me everything. The woman who took care of me, who nurtured me for sixteen years, who raised me, she's not who I thought she was. She's not my mom.

"No—" I say, my voice breaking. I want to unknow this. "Mom, no, it's not true, tell me it's not . . ."

But I can't make any more words come, and I trail off, my voice cracking too badly to continue. *Second chance*, I think. *Fresh start.* Finally, I understand what she was saying, all this time.

"We can't stay here, Reagan," My mom—no, not my mom, my *grandma*—grabs both my shoulders, so I have no choice but to look at her. "I'll tell you everything, we just—"

"I'm not going anywhere until I know the truth," I snap, pulling away from her.

Mom swallows. "I've been trying to find a way to tell you for months now," she says in a low, urgent voice. "Ever since that stupid podcast came out. You deserve to know the truth, and you deserve more than this." She motions around her, as though to indicate the camp, her history, every horrible thing that's happened to us in the last year. "More than a life on the run."

I'm shaking my head, tears falling freely down my cheeks. "I don't understand," I say. My voice is choked, raspy. "Did you just . . . *take* me?"

"I was taking you to the hospital," she explains. "You weren't breathing right when you were born. You didn't cry, and we were worried there was something wrong with your lungs, so I told

Andie I'd take you to the hospital while she waited here with your sister.

"But then, when I got down from the lighthouse, I saw Officer Knight kneeling over Gia's body. I didn't understand what I was looking at. It was surreal and . . . well, I think I must've been in shock. I asked her what happened and—I'll always remember this part exactly—Karly looked at me and said, like she didn't even hear me, 'Lori, what did you do?'"

"That's when I looked down and saw that she was holding Jacob's bow and that horrible mask. And I realized what she'd done, and that she was going to try and make sure I took the blame."

"Mom," I breathe, shocked.

"And then you started crying." Mom smiles a little, remembering. "I don't think Karly realized I was holding a newborn until you started screaming like that. Jacob must've told her about the babies because she seemed to realize right away that you were Matthew's. She stood and sort of reached for her gun and I—" Mom closes her eyes, like the memory is too much for her. "I still have nightmares about that moment, how she reached for her gun like that. That's the most terrified I've ever been in my life. I knew she was going to kill you, just like she killed Gia. All I could think about was getting you away from her. I didn't know what she was capable of. She'd already killed one little girl and . . ." Her grip on my arms tightens, still afraid, even now. "Reagan, I was so scared for you."

Tears pool in the corners of my eyes. I don't want to cry, not until I hear the rest of her story, but my body doesn't listen. I blink, hard, trying to hold myself together. "Did . . . did you take me to the hospital?"

Mom shakes her head. "By the time I got you to the car it was clear that your lungs were fine. And I remember thinking that she'd be able to find you at the hospital, that I needed to hide you, so I took you to Henry's instead. I didn't find out that she'd already killed Jacob and Matthew until much later that night." Her voice cracks, and she closes her eyes, tears leaking down her cheeks. "I knew then that I'd made the right decision. She was a monster. I had to keep you hidden, no matter what."

"Why didn't you tell someone about her?" I want to know. "You could have stopped her."

"I didn't know how," Mom admits. "They found my DNA on Jacob's bow, and they were saying the blood at the top of the light-house was a match for Matthew's. Everything was pointing to me. I realized Karly must've planted it, that she'd twisted all the evidence so it looked like I did it. It felt like I had two choices. I could either stay and fight the charges, or I could take you far away from that woman and protect you." Mom opens her eyes, smiling at me. "And I chose you. I never regretted it for a second. You were my second chance at having a family, my fresh start. I knew I was going to have to tell you everything eventually, but I didn't know how . . . I didn't know how to give you up."

"You don't have to give me up. You're my *mom*." As soon as I say the words, I realize they're true. It doesn't matter what our biology is. She's the only mom I've ever known.

She pulls me close, hugging me tight. "There's so much of him in you, so much of my Matthew. I've always loved you like a daughter. You have to understand that."

I open my mouth, but it takes me a moment to find the right words. Just a few hours ago everything had seemed so simple. But so much is different now. Everything I thought I knew is tumbling around inside my head, arranging and rearranging itself until I don't know what's true anymore.

My mom isn't really my mom. She lied to me my whole life. Matthew wasn't my brother; he was my *father*. There's so much pain and loss in this clearing that it's almost too much to bear.

I came here to learn the truth, but the truth was so much more complicated than I ever thought it could be. Maybe family's like that, too.

I pull back, planning to tell my mom all of this. The lights interrupt me. They're red and blue and flashing: police lights. The cops have come. *Finally.*

My mom swivels toward the trees, fear seeming to completely take over her. "I have to go," she says, swallowing hard. "Before they get here. They can't find me—"

"Lori, no," Andie says, turning to her. "I know I'm sixteen years too late, but I'm going to make this right. I'm prepared to come forward and tell the cops everything I know about what happened the night of the murders."

Mom looks confused. "But Karly—"

"She's dead," I say. I shift to the side, pulling my mom around so that she can finally see Officer Knight's body, still splayed across the rocky shore below the lighthouse. "She fell from the top of the lighthouse. She can't hurt us anymore."

Mom's still staring at Officer Knight, shocked and horrified, when I say the words I've been dreaming of saying for the last year. "We don't have to run anymore. We finally know the truth."

Three
Months
Later . . .

27

Olivia

Reagan stands in front of the mirror hanging from the back of my closet, every item of clothing I own spread in heaps on the floor around her. She stares at a reflection that looks just like my own, and then she adjusts the hem of her shirt so it doesn't bunch around her waist.

My twin sister.

I can't stop thinking those words. Even now, three months after I first learned of her existence, they're still so surreal.

Reagan turns to me, frowning. "What do you think about this?" She motions to her loose-fitting, white tank top and ripped jeans.

I tilt my head, trying to decide how to put this. It's still a little tricky to figure out how to talk to her. We're not completely comfortable around each other yet. We're still feeling each other out, trying to figure out when we need to be tactful and when it's okay to just tell the truth, even if it comes off as mean.

"Well . . . it depends," I say after a moment.

Her eyebrows disappear beneath a swoop of bangs. "On . . . ?"

"On whether or not you're trying to look like a serial killer's daughter who spent the last year living in a truck, or if that's unintentional."

Reagan snatches a flip-flop off the floor and throws it at me, but she's laughing, so I guess I chose right. She must not be trying to hit me because the shoe smacks into the wall behind me, a good two feet from my head.

"I'm pretty sure that joke isn't funny yet," she says, turning back to her reflection. She's wrong; it totally is.

There's cool wind coming in through the open window, carrying the smell of the fireplace, reminding me it's almost autumn. It's a sunny day at the beginning of September, the first day of senior year, a whole summer since the night at Camp Lost Lake when my whole life blew apart and then came back together in a different and, arguably, more interesting way.

Things aren't back to normal, but they're probably as close as they're ever going to get again. Lori's hired a lawyer and is in the process of fighting the Camp Lost Lake murder charges. We're all a little nervous about what's going to happen—the case against her is very strong, and the fact that she ran doesn't look great. But because of the new evidence being submitted, Andie's eyewitness testimony, Gia's camera footage, and Reagan's statement about her encounter with Officer Knight, the lawyer thinks she has a fantastic shot at having the charges dropped

I still don't understand everything that happened that night. I don't think anyone does, not fully. Officer Knight admitted to killing Jacob and Gia and Sawyer but not Matthew or Eric. And she said she didn't leave that bear trap in the woods. Why would she have admitted to part of the crime, but not the rest?

And then there's the timeline. Gia saw someone die before Andie went into labor. We've been over that last video of hers at least a dozen times. *I saw her kill him*, she whispered. But, according to Officer Knight's story, she didn't see Jacob get murdered until after she'd left Andie to go find help. So who was she talking about? Did she see Officer Knight murder Matthew before going after his dad?

We might never know for sure, but I think I can deal with that. The most important thing is that Lori and Reagan are no longer on the run. They've even decided to settle here in Lost Lake, in a little rental house down the street from us. We're all just taking it one day at a time, figuring out how we can fit into each other's lives.

"Should I wear, like, a cardigan?" Reagan asks. She's staring at her reflection again, and she looks like she's just stepped in something gross. She insists she's not nervous about starting school today, but I'm pretty good at reading her. She can't stop pulling at the hem of her shirt and obsessively pushing her hair behind her ear. Which means she's about to pee her pants.

I suppose I should put her out of her misery. I get up and dig through the clothes on the floor, finding a form-fitting, V-neck T-shirt with a little row of buttons down the front. It's my favorite because it makes me look like a sexy college girl, particularly when I pair it with my new, chunky loafers. Really, I should be getting some kind of medal for lending it to Reagan.

"Try this," I tell her, handing her the shirt. "It looks awesome on us, trust me."

She visibly exhales, shoulders slumping, breath rushing out from between her teeth. "Thank you."

"Are we sure 'first day of school outfit' isn't more of a girlfriend job?" I ask, plopping back onto my bed. Reagan and Hazel have been officially dating for about a month and a half now, ever since

Hazel got back from visiting her nana and nani in St. John's, and I can't stop teasing them about it.

"Nope," Reagan says. "It definitely feels like a sister job."

I pretend to fuss with a loose thread on my jeans, trying to hide the fact that the word *sister* has sent a jolt of pain through me. I love having a new sister—a *twin*—but that doesn't make my relationship with the woman I always thought was my sister any easier.

Reagan won't forgive Andie for what she did: for lying, for taking so long to exonerate her mother. She says she'll never want to know or speak to her. I don't think that's true. I think Reagan just needs some time to process everything that's happened. Lori was as much a part of the decision to separate us and lie about who we were as Andie was. She said it herself, she wouldn't have been able to keep Reagan and clear her name at the same time. She made a choice.

And Andie's our mother, whether Reagan wants to admit it or not. Eventually, she's going to want a relationship with her. I think. I hope.

For now, I've been siding with Reagan, but I'm not going to make Andie pay forever. She's really trying to make things better. She's paying for Lori's lawyer and doing everything she can to help the case. It's not perfect, but it's a start.

My relationship with Andie isn't the only thing that's strained. Neither of my parents seem to know how to act around me anymore, so they've settled on being completely weird. Like how Mom didn't punish me when I broke curfew three nights last week, and how Dad keeps brewing me tea. He brings fresh cups to my room every few hours, as an excuse to check on me, see if I want to talk about anything. I'm pretty sure every mug we own is currently in my bedroom.

And then there's the whole new grandmother I never knew about. Would you believe that the woman who's been on the run for the last year is the only one acting semi-normal? I didn't expect this, but she's actually really nice. I can see, now, why Reagan was so desperate to protect her. She borrowed some old photo albums from Jack's mom and spent a few hours showing us pictures of the family we never met. Our dad, Matthew, as a teenage track star with dimples and shiny hair. Our grandfather, Jacob, this total Gen X hipster who was obsessed with the outdoors and brewed his own beer. It was really strange. But also kind of nice.

Reagan changes her tank top for the shirt I handed her, anxiously fussing with the frame as she looks at herself in the mirror.

"Is this really okay?" She turns around, wrinkling her nose like she's still unsure. "I feel like I'm trying too hard."

"Not at all," I tell her. "Trust me, you look perfect."

A car outside honks, just two quick beeps. I glance at the window, my cheeks already feeling warm. That'll be Jack. He insisted on driving Reagan to school today. Well, me and Reagan, technically. Reagan thinks it's because he's got a thing for me. I think Reagan just wants him to have a thing for me because it'll make her feel better about breaking his heart and stealing my best friend.

She looks at me now, eyebrows lifting. "You ready?"

No, I want to say. Or, *Maybe*. Or, *I don't know.* Jack's still the best-looking guy I've ever seen and now that I know him better, I also know that he's funny and athletic and smart. He's completely out of my league, and I can't be in the same space with him without feeling warm and tingly all over my body, like there are fireworks exploding inside of me. And a car's a very small space.

I'm pretty sure he's still not over Reagan. But I think that's okay.

Reagan's with Hazel now, and Jack knows that. He's happy for her. Getting him to realize how amazing I am is the next step.

Reagan is grabbing her wallet, notebooks, an embarrassingly old phone, rambling as she packs up her school bag. "Hazel was telling me I should think about getting a good padlock for my gym locker. Apparently someone stole her tennis shoes last year? Anyway, it's probably a good idea. I should be extra careful after . . ."

I nod along, but I'm not really listening. I'm too distracted by how much Reagan looks like Andie just now. It's all these subtle things, the twist of her mouth when she talks, the way she pushes her hair behind her ear, the slant of her eyes. She'd hate it if I ever told her, but it's the truth. I know I must look like Andie, too, but I haven't spent as much time studying my face while I talk as I have studying Reagan's.

Maybe it's because I was just thinking about how all the details of the murders don't add up, but I feel something spark when I watch Reagan now, a memory. It's from the night Andie told me about her pregnancy, the furtiveness in her eyes, the way she couldn't look right at me but stared at the floor instead. Like she was hiding something. I've thought of that moment dozens of times over the last three months, certain I missed something, that I'll figure out what it was if I just play the memory over again. But whatever it is dissolves whenever I try to examine it more closely.

"C'mon, I don't want to be late!" Reagan says, heading for the door. I shake my head, following her.

It's probably nothing.

Andie has always loved the woods, ever since she was a little girl and her mother would take her on nature walks, pointing out deer tracks and bluebirds, quizzing her on the different shapes of leaves. No matter where she lives, Andie has always thought of the woods in Lost Lake as her real home.

It's fall, the sun setting earlier and earlier each day. The fallen leaves create a carpet under her feet, and the early darkness turns the light beneath the trees a dirty yellow. The air smells of fire and damp wood.

Andie follows the dirt path from the parking lot through the trees and around to the edge of the lake, directly below the light-house. She knows when she's found the right spot, she feels a little hum in her bones as her feet shift into place. *This*, right here. This is exactly where Matthew died.

The moment comes to her as clearly as if it just happened. She remembers being at the top of the lighthouse with Matthew, right before the sun set. They'd always thought of it as their spot. No one else went up there, so it was secretive, even a little roman-tic. She remembers waiting for him, expecting him to tell her that everything was going to be okay, that they'd find a way to raise their babies together.

Instead, Matthew told her that his parents would help her with the babies while he was at school. His *parents*, not him. He seemed to expect her to give up everything she'd worked for while he went away to start his new life. She remembers everything he said, every moment of it.

"Why can't we both go to school?" she'd asked. "We could go somewhere around here, take turns with the babies and classes? Maybe our parents could trade off helping us."

Matthew looked genuinely confused. "But . . . I got into NYU."

"I got into Berkley," Andie had said, but her voice sounded hollow and small. Didn't he understand how important that was for her? How hard she'd worked?

That's when Matthew said, "My parents don't want me to give up my future. They were really serious about that."

"Your future?" Andie had echoed. It was as if her future meant nothing. As if it didn't matter.

Matthew had been standing directly in front of the lighthouse's floor-to-ceiling windows. He'd been backlit by the setting sun, his face all in shadow, his hands out in front of him, like she was a wild animal he was trying to keep still. "Hey," he'd murmured. "Calm down. I don't think stress is good for the babies."

That's what had made her do it. Those words. *Calm down.* She remembered how the rage had flared through her, white hot and so bright she couldn't think of anything else. It was the final straw. How *dare* he tell her to calm down? She felt like she just lost her entire future, everything she'd worked so hard for her whole life.

They *both* had sex. They made these babies together. Why was she the only one who had take any responsibility for it?

She had wanted to hit something, throw something. Before she could think about what she was doing, she pressed her hands to Matthew's chest and *pushed*.

Matthews had been a big, solid guy. At most, Andie figured he'd stumble back a few feet. She was not a particularly strong person, and she was eight months pregnant. There was no way she'd do any real damage.

But Matthew had flown backward fast, arms cartwheeling. His foot had caught on something—a loose piece of floorboard, maybe—and then he was falling, stumbling right into the window. His movements were clumsy, heavy. He'd slammed into the glass with the full force of his body—

And the glass had shattered. In an instant, he was gone.

Tears pool in Andie's eyes as the memory swims in her head. She'd gone to the window immediately after he fell, hoping there was some chance he was okay. She'd prayed she would see him on the shore of the lake, injured maybe, but not dead.

Instead, she'd seen a broken body. She'd watched as he was pulled into the water.

She'd started having contractions almost immediately after he'd disappeared below the water. Even Gia had realized there was no way they could save him, that he was already gone. She'd still blamed Andie for what happened, though. If she'd lived, she would have told the cops. But she hadn't lived.

Andie swipes a sleeve-covered hand over her cheeks to dry her tears. That's the real reason she didn't work harder to exonerate Lori. She just couldn't risk it. If people found out Lori wasn't the murderer, they would have looked a little more closely at the crime itself, and then, maybe, they would've realized that the details didn't add up. Someone would've double-checked Officer Knight's DNA analysis of the blood and realized it was Andie's blood, not Matthew's. She'd long suspected that Officer Knight had falsified that detail to make it seem more likely that Lori was the murderer, just as she'd falsified the fingerprints on the bow. But if Andie had said a single word, if she'd told anyone the real story, they would've known *she* was at the top of the lighthouse moments before Matthew died. Eventually, someone would've figured out what she'd done.

It was selfish. Andie knows that. But Matthew's death was an *accident*, not murder. And she's made sacrifices, too! She let Lori take her daughter and raise her as though she was hers. She'd wanted to go looking for Reagan so many times over the years, but she never did. She owed Lori a child. She hoped it made up for some small part of what she'd taken from her.

Andie sniffs, pushing the maudlin thoughts away. She's holding a bouquet of flowers. Not the tiny, sad-looking ones like they have at the general store—a good bouquet, with peonies and dahlias. She drove all the way out to Auburn to get it. She knows it doesn't mean much, but she wanted to do something to show Matthew, if some part of him was still watching from somewhere, just how sorry she is. Maybe she doesn't deserve to mourn him, but she *did* love him. That love didn't go away just because she hurt him.

She kneels at the edge of the lake and places her bouquet right up next to the water.

"I'm sorry," she says. "I really am."

Water touches the edge of her bouquet, gently nipping at the petals of a dahlia. The air has an icy edge to it. It creeps up Andie's sleeves, makes her shiver.

"Okay," Andie says. She did what she came here to do.

She stands, dusting her hands off on her pants, turns—

Her chest tightens.

There's a man behind her. He's tall and broad-shouldered, his arms thick with the kind of muscles you only get from doing manual labor for many hours a day. His clothes are dirty, old, tattered, and he has a thick chain thrown over his shoulder.

At the bottom of the chain is a bear trap, its teeth slick with blood.

Andie freezes, her mouth going bone-dry.

The man . . . he looks *feral*.

She's certain he's about to attack her. And then her eyes take in details she didn't notice at first. The blond hair, longer than it was sixteen years ago, falling past his shoulders in tangled knots. The dimples in his cheeks. The big, full lips, chapped now, but not so different from the lips she kissed sixteen years ago.

Andie's heart stutters. "M-Matthew?" she croaks. She doesn't know how it's possible that he's alive, but he is. He's standing in front of her.

Matthew tilts his head, considering her. His expression is closed, cold.

Oh God, she thinks. *How can this be real?*

"Matthew?" she says again, hesitantly. "Don't you know who I am?"

She searches his eyes, waiting for that spark of recognition. It doesn't come. She frowns and takes another step closer to him. "Do . . . do you know who *you* are?"

It's possible that he doesn't, she realizes. He would've hit his head really hard when he fell. She'd assumed that he'd drowned after he'd been pulled out into the lake. *Everyone* did.

But what if the cold lake water had shocked him awake? What if he'd swum back to the shore, clawed his way onto land, then wandered into the woods with no idea who he was? It was possible. Almost no one's been to the campgrounds since that night. There would've been food in the fridges, shelter for him to stay in, supplies he could've used when the food ran out.

He could've been out there all this time, just trying to survive.

"Matthew," she gasps, breathless. She needs to tell him who he is. "I-I can't believe it. Do you have any idea how many people have been looking for you?"

"Stop," Matthew says, dropping the chain from his shoulder. His voice is hard, emotionless. He holds the chain between his thick, sun-reddened hands. The bear trap sways above the ground.

Andie stops. Fear flickers to life inside of her. She stares at the bear trap and for the first time, she wonders what Matthew's been doing out in the woods all these years, why he hasn't come forward, found people, asked for help.

She's heard stories of head trauma *changing* people, turning them mean. Is that what happened to him?

She thinks about the things she's heard about these woods. People who get hurt, who go missing, never to be seen again.

"What are you doing?" she asks. Her voice trembles.

"I don't like it when people come out here," Matthew says. "I leave you all alone. Why can't you just leave me be?"

Andie swallows. This isn't the Matthew she remembers.

She starts to back up. "Matthew," she says. "Please . . ."

He doesn't seem to be listening to her. He swings the chain in a lazy circle. It flies off the ground and above his head.

Andie lifts her hands, cowering, as the hard, metal trap rockets toward her face.

Acknowledgments

Two Sides to Every Murder took quite a while to start feeling like a real book. There were many, many, *many* drafts where something wasn't quite right, but I couldn't figure out what it was. To that end, a huge thanks to my editor, Tiara Kittrell, for helping me clean up all the little plot holes, for finding brilliant sensitivity readers, and for helping me (very slowly) find the interesting story beneath all the rest. I couldn't have done it without you!

Hillary Jacobson, as always, thank you for so much. For your faith, your guidance, and your keen eye. For reading absolutely everything I write at least five times. And for always wanting everything—whether it's a draft, a cover, a title, or even a character's name—to be perfect. Also, a huge thanks to Josie Freedman, Sarah Mitchell, and the many, many others over at CAA who helped this book in thousands of ways, both big and small. I'm very grateful to be surrounded by so many talented, passionate people.

Every writer talks about wanting to find a publisher to grow with over their career, a publisher that will support their work as it changes and evolves. The team of booklovers over at Razorbill (now Putnam) has been all of that and more. A huge thank-you to Jen Klonsky; to Felicity, Shannon, and James for your marketing brilliance; to copy editors Krista, Abigail, and Katie for cleaning up my many mistakes; and to Polo for everything he's done to tie up all the loose ends. This amazing cover is courtesy of cover designer Maria Fazio and cover artist Lisa Sheehan, and the only reason you're holding this book at all is because of Natalie, Jayne, and Madison over in managing editorial, who kept us on schedule. Thank you to readers Jiahong Sun and Kaya Binti for your invaluable feedback. And these are only the people I've had the pleasure of working with directly. There are so many more working behind the scenes, whose contributions have made this book what it is. Thank you, thank you, thank you.

Thank you to my beautiful family. To Ron and Harriet, of course. To Sawyer Rollins, to whom this book is dedicated and who was given the honor of being the first victim as part of a babysitting negotiation back in 2022. And to all the others who did not bother to negotiate to get their names written in. Your support has been everything.

I wanted to save my final thanks for someone who's been part of my career since I sold my very first book to Razorbill all the way back in 2013. Any writer lucky enough to have had a long career knows how rare it is to get to work with the same people over any length of time. In the ten years I've been doing this, I've changed agents and editors and publishing houses, I've switched genres and written for different age groups and changed names again (and again), but Casey McIntyre has been a constant. She's been my publicist, my editor, my friend, and my advocate. I want to say something profound about how much she's meant to me, but everything I come up with sounds trite, so let me just say this: My career and my life are infinitely better for having had her in them. I truly don't know how I'm going to keep doing it without her. Thank you, Casey.

About the Author

DANIELLE VALENTINE is a pseudonym for bestselling horror novelist Danielle Vega. Her work includes the Merciless series, *How to Survive Your Murder* and *Delicate Condition*, and has been translated into several languages worldwide. Danielle lives outside New York City with her husband, daughter, and two ornery cats.

YOU CAN VISIT DANIELLE VALENTINE AT
DANIELLEVALENTINEBOOKS.COM